P9-AFL-045

FINDING
DAD

OTHER BOOKS AND AUDIO BOOKS
BY ALMA J. YATES:

Race to Eden

Sammy's Song

A Homemade Christmas

FINDING DAD

A NOVEL

ALMA J. YATES

Covenant Communications, Inc.

Cover image: Truck photo courtesy of our neighbors, background image *Man and Woman Walking on a Country Road* © Alamy Images

Cover design copyrighted 2008 by Covenant Communications, Inc.

Published by Covenant Communications, Inc.
American Fork, Utah

Copyright © 2008 by Alma J. Yates
All rights reserved. No part of this book may be reproduced in any format or in any medium without the written permission of the publisher, Covenant Communications, Inc., P.O. Box 416, American Fork, UT 84003. This work is not an official publication of The Church of Jesus Christ of Latter-day Saints. The views expressed within this work are the sole responsibility of the author and do not necessarily reflect the position of The Church of Jesus Christ of Latter-day Saints, Covenant Communications, Inc., or any other entity.

This is a work of fiction. The characters, names, incidents, places, and dialogue are products of the author's imagination, and are not to be construed as real.

Printed in Canada
First Printing: May 2008

15 14 13 12 11 10 09 08   10 9 8 7 6 5 4 3 2 1

ISBN 10: 1-59811-607-X
ISBN 13: 978-1-59811-607-6

*To my seven talented sons, who, in their own unique ways,
can fix almost anything, even an old '71 Ford truck,
and who have also taught me so much about being a father.*

1

Three miles from the small southern Utah town of Panguitch, Porter Huggins felt an annoying tightening in the pit of his stomach. Shifting uneasily in his seat, he unconsciously lifted up on the accelerator even though he was still in a sixty-five-mile-per-hour zone and his custom was to drive five miles over the posted speed limit.

Porter recognized the slow-moving Sevier River meandering to his right through the flat, green meadows and stands of massive cottonwood trees. Numerous times he had hunted and fished along the banks of that river with his friends Walter Henrie and Calvin Crosby. But that was ages ago, in a different time—part of a lost, idyllic life.

Porter eyed the hill ahead and knew that once he reached the summit, Panguitch would lie below him, along with a past that he had spent the last several years trying to evade, or at least forget. Anxiously, he glanced in the rearview mirror to make sure he still looked presentable. He was relieved to see that the wind hadn't mussed his hair too much. His thick, dark hair was trimmed short and had a straight, precise part down the right side. A few gray hairs intruded about his temples, but at thirty-eight he was still handsome and maintained a young appearance. He noticed he did look a bit tired around his eyes, which were an intriguing shade of blue, contrasting with his dark brows and slightly tanned face. He knew he shouldn't care how he looked for this visit, but he wanted to look as responsible as he was trying to act.

The last time Porter had driven into Panguitch was three and a half years earlier, when his life had still been in turmoil. During his short, three-hour visit, a pervasive, almost tangible tension had hung in the air. He had almost come to blows with Walter Henrie, his ex-brother-in-law and ex-best friend. Fortunately, he had managed to make a quick exit before any fighting actually developed, and he'd vowed never to return. But here he was again.

Even though the windows in his black 2000 Mercedes were up and the air conditioning was on, tiny beads of sweat dotted Porter's brow. By contrast, his mouth was dry. He picked up the water bottle from the console cup holder and took a long, slow drink. It bothered him that he was nervous. He prided himself on always being in control of his emotions, which made the slight flutter in his gut that much more aggravating.

Returning to Panguitch was unnerving for Porter. Specifically, he dreaded looking into people's faces. But at the same time, he was determined not to avoid their eyes, convinced that looking away was a sign of weakness and guilt. Long ago he had concluded in a logical, rational manner that brooding over his untouchable and irreversible past was senseless. After all, over the past three years he had changed considerably; nevertheless, he figured that trying to convince the common folk in Panguitch of that change was probably futile.

In another life, one so distant and detached from his present circumstances, Panguitch had been Porter Huggins's home. Some of his best memories of his growing up years had their roots in Panguitch. At one time he'd been something of a celebrity—a sports hero, one of Panguitch's golden boys, destined to leave his mark. The mark he'd left, however, was not the one that he—or anyone else in the town—had anticipated back in 1985, the year he had graduated from Panguitch High with thirty-seven other ambitious and confident seniors.

Porter had considered asking Walter to meet him in Kanab, a small town sixty miles south of Panguitch. He was sure Walter would have accommodated him; however, Porter also knew that such a request would appear cowardly. He chided himself for his fears and determined to boldly face whatever might lurk in Panguitch. Most people in town wouldn't recognize him, he told himself. After all, it had been over fifteen years since he'd spent any serious time there. And it was unlikely that anyone, besides Walter and his family, knew he was coming today.

By the time Porter had almost reached the top of the hill over-looking the town, he had already slowed to fifty miles per hour, and yet the first Reduced Speed Ahead sign was still a mile away. He took another long drink from his water bottle, keeping the last gulp in his mouth and swishing it around momentarily before swallowing.

Suddenly, the long, green valley stretched before him with the town of Panguitch nestled neatly in the southwest corner at the foot of low-rolling, juniper- and pine-covered hills. There were fewer than twelve hundred inhabitants in the town, and most of the houses and businesses were hidden among the trees that flourished within the town proper.

To the right of the highway, just outside of Panguitch, was a blue pond sparkling in the afternoon sun. Also to the right was a thick stand of tall trees that crowded the banks of the Sevier River, which zigzagged haphazardly across the valley floor. The Sevier wasn't a river in the traditional sense—in actuality it was little more than a mean-dering brook. But 150 years earlier, the first pioneers had declared that tiny ribbon of water a river. They knew that after a wet winter and spring the tiny brook would swell dangerously beyond its banks and tumble in a rolling torrent across the valley, and at those times the Sevier would evolve into a bona fide river.

North beyond the town, the valley was surrounded by low hills, dark with juniper trees, and a few intermittent patches of green fields and brown-and-gray flats covered with sage and dry grass. Immediately beyond the low juniper hills to the west rose the moun-tains. Green meadows and pastures dotted with hundreds of horses and cattle surrounded the town and stretched the entire length of the valley. There were also squares of alfalfa fields bordered by sagging barbed-wire fences and lorded over by men on slow-moving tractors that were cutting lush, green alfalfa and laying it in precise furrows, which would soon be gobbled by balers.

Porter was struck by the pastoral scene before him. While growing up there he had never thought of Panguitch as a beautiful place, but he was impressed by its beauty and tranquility on this early June afternoon.

Porter drove past the redbrick town sign located in a neatly trimmed patch of green lawn and surrounded by decorative lamp posts. The sign bore the town's name, its 1864 founding date, and the elevation, which was over six thousand feet. Porter slowed the Mercedes to a mere crawl. He told himself that his slowing down was not caused by apprehension; he just wanted to see the town and perhaps reminisce.

As Porter inched down the main road, he was grateful for the Mercedes' dark, tinted windows. He would make only one quick stop in town, just long enough to book a room at a motel. He had already concluded that having a room in advance was good insurance, because he didn't anticipate any hospitality from Walter or his wife, Toni.

Porter passed the old, two-story high school where he had spent so much of his teenage years. It was now a museum. The new redbrick high school, which had been finished the year Porter graduated, was a couple blocks away. At the intersection of State Road 89 and Main Street, Porter turned right and passed through the downtown business district, a short block made up of shops, offices, and eating spots that catered mostly to tourists and people just passing through.

On Main Street, Porter spotted the Blue Pine Motel and immediately decided that he would spend the night there. There were other motels, perhaps even better ones, but he was just interested in finding the quickest place to drop off his things before confronting the Henries.

Porter pulled into the parking lot of the Blue Pine and, from behind the security of his tinted windows, glanced toward the tiny motel office. The desk clerk there looked young, probably not more than sixteen. Porter did the mental math and concluded that there was no possible way she would know who he was.

Putting on a disarming smile, Porter stepped through the glass door into the office and greeted the young clerk. "Looks like another booming day in the big city of Panguitch. Is the place booked?" He chuckled and winked at the girl as he tucked the back of his white knit shirt back into his cream-colored khaki slacks.

The girl was pretty and smiled shyly as she tucked a strand of long brown hair behind her ear with a quick hand movement. "It'll be really tough finding you a room on a Tuesday," she answered pleasantly, reaching for a registration card. She pretended to think, pressing her lips together and cocking her head to one side. "But I figure I can find you something." She brightened and added with a laugh, "There are twenty-one units in the whole place. So far only three are booked for tonight. You have your pick of the rest." She shrugged, continuing to laugh. "Of course, they're all exactly the same, so it doesn't really matter which one you choose."

Porter grinned. "All I need is a bed and a shower." He filled out the registration card and pushed it and his Visa across the counter.

The girl scribbled a note on the registration and swiped the credit card in the machine. "Huggins," she muttered, studying the card.

Porter looked out the glass door toward the street, silently willing the girl to hurry.

"There's a Huggins family in Panguitch," she mused and then quickly reconsidered her statement. "At least there was. Mrs. Huggins was killed about a month ago." A shadow descended over the girl. "Now there's only her son, a boy my age. He lives with his uncle now. It was really sad about his mom." She pushed the credit card across the counter, and Porter returned it to his wallet. "You'll be in number six," she announced, snatching a key. "It's just out the door to your left."

Porter picked up the key and turned for the door. "By chance, are you related to Allyson Huggins?" the girl inquired.

He hesitated, trying to decide how to answer.

"She was the greatest," the girl went on, seemingly anxious to talk. "I just loved her. Everybody in town did. This fall I was supposed to be an office aide for her over at the high school." She shook her head. "Why does bad stuff happen to people like her?"

Porter shrugged. "Things like that are tough," he replied evasively.

"So you're not related to her?" Porter detected a certain hope in the girl's eyes and tone, as though his being a relative would somehow make Allyson Huggins alive in a vicarious sort of way.

"Actually," Porter said slowly, carefully avoiding the girl's eyes, "I'm not related to Allyson Huggins. I'm sorry," he added in apology. He held up his key. "Thanks for the room." He slipped through the door and headed for his car, feeling guilty about his answer but rationalizing that he hadn't really lied. He wasn't related to Allyson. Not anymore.

Porter had only one travel bag, which he tossed onto the bed before locking the motel room and returning to his car. Walter's place was two miles north of town. Porter had gone there hundreds of times during the years he had lived in Panguitch. Porter had moved away, but Walter had remained and taken over his dad's farming and ranching business. At first he and his wife had lived in a trailer behind the family home, but eventually his parents had bought a house in town, and Walter and his young family had moved into the farmhouse.

Not wishing to postpone the inevitable, Porter headed for Walter's place. Suddenly the anxious flutter in his stomach returned in earnest. He hadn't even been thinking of Calvin Crosby, his other high school buddy, but as he approached the airport road, which jutted east a half mile before Walter's house, he glanced out across the valley toward the Crosby farm a mile in the distance and thought he spotted someone by a tractor in one of Calvin's fields. On a sudden impulse, he turned down the narrow paved airport road that went right past the Crosby place.

Porter pulled off the road and parked in the weeds and grass growing outside the fence surrounding the alfalfa field. Half the alfalfa was cut and lay in windrows. Porter knew that the man kneeling next to the tractor was Calvin. His back was to the road, so he didn't see Porter get out of the car, slip through the barbed-wire fence, and start across the field. Stepping quietly over the windrows, Porter approached Calvin's parked tractor.

"Hello, Calvin," he said when he was fifteen feet away.

Calvin jumped, startled by the sudden sound of his name. He pushed up from his knees and turned around. His first reaction was to smile sheepishly at his own skittishness, but as his eyes focused on Porter and recognition settled in, the smile slowly faded until it disappeared altogether.

"Hello, Port," he guardedly greeted his old friend. He stood his ground for a moment and then wiped his right hand on his pants, took a couple of steps forward, and held it out.

Porter clutched the proffered hand and shook it firmly. "Good to see you, Calvin," he said, grinning broadly, relieved to see a familiar face. "When I came down the highway, I saw someone out in the field fixing a tractor. I figured it had to be you." He shook his head and gazed around, jingling the keys in his pocket. "Looks like you're up to your ears in work. Isn't this early for a first crop of alfalfa?"

Calvin nodded. "We had a warm spring," he explained simply.

Porter coughed and dusted at hay leaves on the cuffs of his slacks. "I heard about your dad's heart attack. I wanted to come to the funeral. What's it been, two years?"

"He died five years ago this next month."

With an upraised hand, Porter shielded his eyes from the sun's glare and studied the field of alfalfa. "So the place is yours now?" He turned back to his old friend and grinned. "You used to say you'd never be a farmer. Too much work and not enough pay. You wanted to be a mechanic." He shook his head. "But here you are."

"Sometimes you've got to do what you've got to do," Calvin responded. He pointed to a white, two-story house with two gabled windows and a front porch running the full breadth of the house. A white plank fence ran in front of it. "That's my place. I built it a couple of years ago."

"Nice," Porter observed with genuine admiration.

"The white garage off to the side is a shop. I do some mechanic work there. Not as much as I'd like, but enough to keep in practice. It's a hobby more than anything. People bring their cars and trucks by, and I help them out." Calvin bobbed his head without smiling. "This isn't a bad way to make a living—in spite of what I used to think."

He studied Porter, looking him up and down. "Walter said you were coming," he muttered lamely, seeming to search for the proper words. He shrugged. "I wasn't expecting to . . ." He coughed into the back of his hand, looked down at the ground, and kicked at a clump of alfalfa with the toe of his boot. The hems of his jeans were frayed, his boots scuffed and worn. He had a faded New York Yankees ball cap on his head and wore a long-sleeved cotton shirt with the sleeves rolled to his elbows. His face was a sunburned brown with a few developing wrinkles at the corners of his eyes from constantly squinting into the glare of the sun. "Well, I wasn't expecting . . ." He cleared his throat. "I didn't think you'd stop here. You sort of surprised me coming across the field like that."

Porter laughed a nervous, strained laugh. "Why wouldn't I stop, Calvin? As much time as we've spent together."

Calvin forced a chuckle. "Well, it's been a while since you've dropped by. The last time you came to Panguitch, you were here one minute and gone the next," he reminded his old friend. "You didn't say hello to hardly anybody. At least not me. I figured this time you'd pop into town and be gone before anybody knew you were here."

Porter ignored the veiled accusation. "It's good to be back to the old town," he remarked, knowing that his words held very little sincerity.

"Is it?"

The question had a subtle barb to it. Porter's smile slowly vanished, and he heaved a sigh. "Actually, Calvin, it's not all that great to be back. I almost changed my mind when I hit the city limits." He turned and pointed toward Walter Henrie's place. "I still haven't made it over there yet." He smiled dourly. "I wasn't sure if I'd get halfway through town before I was dragged from my car and lynched. I guess that pretty well explains why I haven't made too many trips to Panguitch over the past few years. And since my folks moved away back in the mid-nineties . . ." Porter attempted a further explanation.

"Well, Port, can you blame folks?" Calvin cut him off. "People around here thought a lot of Allyson."

The question cut Porter, but he didn't want to show it. He wanted to stay upbeat. He smiled wanly and shrugged.

"You didn't come to the funeral. Most folks figured you'd show up for that." It was another pointed accusation couched in a simple statement.

"I didn't even know about the funeral," Porter responded honestly. "Nobody called me after the accident. Then I left town on business. My answering machine went on the fritz, so I couldn't get any messages. I returned home two weeks after the accident, a week after the funeral. I didn't know about any of this until last Sunday when Toni called me."

"It was a nice funeral, Port. The church was packed. The whole town closed down. Everybody loved Allyson." Calvin cleared his throat and added under his breath as an afterthought, "Almost everybody."

Porter noticeably winced at the last stinging words of rebuke. "Look, Calvin, I didn't hear about the accident or the funeral until this past Sunday afternoon. I came as soon as I could."

"The people around here didn't ever stop loving Allyson," Calvin commented, looking away. "In fact, the longer she was here, the more they loved her. She seemed to get better with time."

"Calvin, that's all water under the bridge. Things just didn't work out. I feel bad about it too, as bad as anybody."

"That's a stretch," Calvin retorted incredulously. He shook his head and looked away so he wouldn't have to make eye contact with Porter. "I sat in that funeral and thought of you, Port. I couldn't imagine anybody walking away from Allyson. She was genuine, Port. When that drunk hit her last month, he busted a hole in this town that nobody's going to fill. Ever."

"I hope they nail the sucker," Porter muttered angrily. "I don't even know who it was. I was in shock when Toni called me, so I didn't get the details."

"It was some guy from Nevada. He and his buddies had been camping, on a two-day drinking binge. This guy came flying down the highway for refills. Allyson was just leaving town from work when the guy crossed the center line. They say she didn't feel anything—died instantly. And the guy staggered away from his jacked-up 4x4 with just a broken collarbone and some cuts and bruises."

"I hope they lock him up and throw away the key," Porter said vehemently.

"I doubt that will happen. He'll get a good lawyer, end up doing a few hours of community service, and then walk away." Calvin kicked the clump of alfalfa again. "Lots of people at the funeral asked about you." He made no attempt to mask his bitterness.

Porter's cheeks and neck burned. He didn't want this meeting to turn nasty, but he was silently wishing he'd gone directly to Walter's place and avoided this unnecessary confrontation. Now he looked for a graceful way to retreat from the alfalfa field without appearing as though he were tucking his tail and running. "I didn't hear about the funeral," he mumbled lamely, not knowing what else to say.

"But would you have come?" Calvin asked quietly. "If you'd known in time?"

The question caught Porter completely off guard. He stared at Calvin for a moment, wanting to say something but not knowing what. He couldn't very well admit to Calvin, or anybody else for that matter, that being unable to attend the funeral had made things less complicated and awkward for him.

"That's what I figured," Calvin grumbled, observing Porter's hesitation.

"I didn't say I wouldn't have come," Porter countered warmly but without conviction. He wet his lips. "I'm not sure what I'd have done."

"Sure you are." Calvin shook his head.

"Look, Calvin, nobody wanted me there. I'd have just made people uneasy."

"I looked for you, Port. I figured you owed Allyson that much."

"How many times do I have to tell you I didn't know anything about it?" As much as he tried to stay calm and keep the anger out of his voice, Porter couldn't fight back the defensive coolness in his tone.

"Whatever," Calvin responded, shrugging his shoulders. He snatched a stalk of alfalfa from the ground and broke it into a half dozen pieces, which he dropped at his feet, and then he dusted his hands. He stared at his old friend for a moment. Porter returned his stare. It was as though both men were determined not to be the one to look away.

Calvin eventually capitulated, heaving a tired sigh and glancing across his uncut alfalfa. "It's probably just as well," he conceded. He pondered a moment. "As I listened to everything everybody said about Allyson, I thought about all the good times we'd had over the years. Allyson and I grew up together. You moved here the start of your sophomore year, so you didn't know her like I did. I remembered your first date with her. We were going to double. You planned to take Corrie Dunn, Rita Cooper's cousin from Cedar City. I wanted to take Allyson. Up till then you'd been happy to date all the hot girls, even if you had to go to Escalante or Richfield to find them. But that weekend you decided you wanted Allyson. Who knows why. You suggested we flip a coin, remember?"

Porter nodded once.

"You flipped the coin and claimed you won." Calvin studied Porter. "But you didn't win. You cheated."

Porter didn't confirm or deny the statement.

"I always knew you cheated that day, but I was okay with that back then. I figured Allyson deserved the best. And you had it all. I was glad Allyson got you."

"Calvin, that was about a hundred years ago."

"Actually, only twenty last May. It was the end of our junior year."

"We were a couple of dumb kids." He shook his head. "I figured you knew about the coin toss. It wasn't like I tried to hide anything."

"I knew. I thought about it at Allyson's funeral, wondering if things might have been different had I been the one to take Allyson. Maybe we'd have ended up together."

"You dated Allyson too."

"Yeah, but once she'd had that first date with you, you had her heart. Of course, I think Allyson was in love with you the first day you showed up at Panguitch High."

"Calvin, you're married with kids. Why go back to some high school romance? It's over. Finished!"

"Did you ever wonder why I didn't get married until I was thirty?"

Porter shook his head and in exasperation retorted, "No, Calvin, I never wondered. I had a life. I wasn't thinking about some dumb coin toss. That was high school. I did a ton of stupid things. Yeah, I cheated on the coin toss. You should have taken Allyson. Believe me, if that was the worst thing I had done in my life, I could die a happy man right now. Unfortunately, I've got a little more baggage than that, so I don't lie awake nights worrying about something that happened twenty years ago last May."

"Don't get me wrong, Port. I was happy for you. Because Allyson was happy. She waited for you until after your mission. You were the perfect couple, and I was envious. But I was happy, too. For both of you." He cleared his throat. "Then you left her."

"Calvin, I didn't come here to dredge up junk. I came to tell you hello."

Calvin ignored him. "At first I couldn't believe it." He shook his head. "But then you married Kerri, who had tons of bleached blond hair, a pretty face, and a knock-out figure—your signature girlfriend."

"Just leave it alone, Calvin. This isn't going anywhere."

"But apparently Kerri didn't hold your interest either." He kicked at the giant tractor wheel. "You know, Port, you were always looking for someone better. But whatever you were looking for was always someplace else."

Porter forced a strained smile. "Are you about finished?"

"Then there was some other girl . . . Frankie? At least you had enough brains not to marry her, but I hear she was a looker too." Suddenly he spun around and faced Porter. "Did you ever look at Allyson? I mean, really look at her? She didn't have Frankie's face or Kerri's figure, but Port, those girls weren't anything next to her. They were . . ." He shook his head, groping for the right descriptor. "They were empty fluff next to Allyson. Did you ever see that? Even in the beginning, did you ever see what Allyson really had?"

Porter rubbed the back of his neck and stared at the ground. "Obviously this conversation isn't going anywhere." He looked up. "I thought I'd stop by and say hello to an old friend. I didn't expect you to rub my face in the past. We haven't seen each other for several years, and now I come to say hi and you dump on me like this. Remind me not to come back for another ten or twenty years. Or ever!" He turned and headed across the field toward his car, his jaw clamped tight and his eyes blazing straight ahead. Calvin watched him go.

Porter reached the fence and tried to crawl through the strands of barbed wire without snagging his pants and shirt, but he had a struggle. When he finally slipped through, Calvin called out to him and began jogging after him.

"Port, wait up."

Porter fumbled in his pocket for his car keys, but as he pulled them out he dropped them. It took him a moment to locate them in the tall grass and weeds. By then Calvin was at the fence. Grabbing the nearest fence post, he swung himself over the top strand of wire as Porter was opening his car door.

"Port, hold on," Calvin called, his tone conciliatory. There was a softening in his voice, almost an apologetic pleading. "I was just spouting off."

Porter glared across the roof of his car at his old friend.

"Look, I wasn't expecting you. I knew you were coming to town, but I didn't think you'd show up here. Then all of a sudden I look up and there you are, like a ghost."

"No time to prepare, so you just told me what you really thought of me."

Calvin hesitated. "Maybe." He shrugged. "Probably." He shook his head and smiled grimly. "I won't lie. I've been thinking all those things."

"I didn't think they just popped out off the top of your head."

Calvin rubbed his eyes with his thumb and forefinger. "Yeah," he muttered, "I've wanted to tell you that stuff, but I should have picked a different time."

"Is there anything else you're dying to tell me before I rush over to the beating Walter and Toni will give me?"

Calvin chuckled, the first genuine show of good humor since Porter appeared. "Oh, there are probably some other things I could tell you, but I'd be beating a dead horse. Do you have a place to stay?" Calvin didn't wait for Porter to answer. "We can put you up. We've got a spare bedroom." His offer seemed sincere. "I don't know what kind of welcome you're going to get over at your ex-in-laws' place."

Porter smiled. "I stopped at the Blue Pine and booked a room."

"Don't waste good money on a motel room," Calvin muttered. "I'll call Burt and Glenna and tell them to cancel your room. They will."

Porter shook his head. "Thanks, but I'll keep the room." He sucked in a deep breath. "Well, I better head over to Walter's place and pick up . . . Alma." He didn't know why he hesitated, but just saying the name made him think of Allyson. She was the one that had picked out the name. Porter had wanted to name their son Bart, but Allyson had said that Bart sounded too much like a cowboy, and she had always liked the name Alma because Alma was her favorite Book of Mormon character. Even as a little girl she had decided that she was going to name her first boy Alma. "I hope the two of us can head out of here as soon as possible," Porter went on.

"I think it's a little more complicated than that, Port," Calvin said dubiously. He looked back at his tractor. "Have you considered leaving Alma here? This is his home."

"It's not *my* home," Porter answered quickly, a little too fiercely. "Walter knows better than to stand in my way."

"Nobody'll stand in your way. You've got all the legal rights to Alma. He's your son. But Panguitch is the only home he's ever known. You don't just barge in and jerk a sixteen-year-old kid around." He held up his hands as though to fend off an anticipated attack. "Port, I'm not trying to fight with you, but . . ." He gnawed on his lower lip. "These last few years, you let somebody else raise him. Why change that now?"

"He was with his mother. I stayed in contact. I called him. He's stayed with me off and on. I know that the last three years or so I haven't had as much contact with him as I should have. Twice during the past three years he visited my folks up in Montana. I was going to meet him there the last time, but . . ." Porter shook his head and decided to go a different direction. "He was planning to spend five or six weeks with me this summer. Allyson and I didn't want to be tugging him back and forth all the time." He raked his fingers through his hair and rubbed his neck. "I admit I should have had more to do with him lately. I don't deny that. But that doesn't mean I'll turn my back on him now."

Calvin took in a deep breath. "Well, Port, I have to admit I'd do the same thing. I don't know if that's right or wrong." He pulled his cap from his head and studied the sweatband, which was stained and dirty from hours of work in the sun. "There is one thing you should know. Last November, before his grandparents left on their mission to Nigeria, his grandpa gave him that old '71 Ford truck." He smiled and wagged his head. "It's mainly a pile of junk, but Alma had always wanted it. He wants to fix it up. He wants to have it ready to show off to Grandpa Henrie when he comes back from Nigeria next May."

"I don't have time for an old truck," Porter responded hastily.

"Now hold on. Alma has some pretty big dreams for that truck."

"I'll buy him a truck—a new one."

Calvin shook his head. "He likes the old one."

"Once he sees a shiny new truck, he'll forget all about the old one."

Calvin laughed. "Now, if it were me, Port, I wouldn't hesitate two seconds. You can buy me a new truck. In fact, if you want, we can drive over to Cedar City this afternoon and pick one out." He shook his head. "But Alma's different."

"That's because he hasn't seen a new one." Porter held out his hand to Calvin, and Calvin took it. "Well, I'm just postponing the inevitable." He glanced over his shoulder in the direction of Walter's redbrick house in the distance. "It's too bad we don't have time to run into town and grab something to eat. I noticed that the Cowboy's Smokehouse Café is still open."

Calvin grinned. "If you end up staying longer than you figured, give me a call. I'll even let you buy, since you're not getting me a new truck."

"Dinner'll have to wait for another time. I'm getting out of here as soon as I can."

"Will you be back? I mean, in broad daylight?" He grinned mischievously.

"Oh, jump in a lake. And tell Bonnie hello for me. She'd probably even talk to me—since she's not from here, she doesn't have so many prejudices." He grinned, waved at his buddy, climbed into the Mercedes, and drove away.

2

Loathing the thought of facing anyone else, Porter rapped lightly on the metal screen door and waited nervously. The inside door was open, so he could hear the sounds from within the house—the hum of a fan, the distant chug of a washing machine, a radio advertisement extolling the virtues of a soft drink. Turning his back to the door, he surveyed the front yard. There was a short, circular driveway with lawn on either side. Square, redbrick pillars joined by wrought iron formed a fence that ran parallel to the highway. That was an addition since he was here last. Everything else seemed familiar, except knocking on the door. Even before he dated Allyson, he had marched right through this front door like he was family. Being best friends with Walter, Porter had spent almost as much time at the Henries' place as he had at his own.

Porter gazed across the highway at the pastures and hay fields that stretched toward the hills on the far side of the valley. A big chunk of what Porter saw belonged to Walter and Toni. Turning back to the house, he realized with a blink of surprise that the barn located immediately behind the house was also new. It was made of the same red brick as the house and had a series of white rail corrals behind it. Walter was obviously doing well, Porter mused.

A burst of anxious flutters exploded in Porter's gut as he heard footsteps approach. Stiffening, he swallowed as Toni Henrie pushed the screen door open with a squeak. His immediate impulse was to avert his eyes from Toni's probing stare, but he willed himself to maintain eye contact, even though his stomach tightened into a hard knot of self-doubt. He opened his mouth to speak, but nothing came out.

After a moment's hesitation, Porter managed a nervous cough, which at least filled the silent void between them while Toni looked on, obviously as unnerved to find herself standing face-to-face with Porter as he was to find himself standing in front of her. Fighting to recover, he flashed a guarded smile. "Hello, Toni," he said. His voice sounding unnatural, even to him.

"Hello, Porter," she responded with obvious reservation.

It was as though their simple greetings had exhausted their conversational repertoire, because neither one managed to say anything more for several interminable seconds. This time Toni was the first to recover. "We didn't expect you this early," she remarked haltingly. "I mean, it's fine," she quickly added in a flustered attempt to disguise her blundering nervousness.

"I got an early start, and there wasn't much traffic between here and Eagar." He studied Toni for a moment. Though she was in her mid-thirties, she could have easily passed for a woman in her early twenties. She was short and petite, just under five foot two and tipping the scales at a light 110 pounds. She was generally calm and pleasant, but if something irritated Toni Henrie, Porter knew it could light a fire in her eyes and an even hotter one on her tongue.

Toni Foy had been the first girl Porter had met when he'd arrived in Panguitch. He had liked her right away and had even gone out with her a few times while they were in high school. She had also been Allyson Henrie's best and dearest friend.

"Come in," Toni invited, stepping back. "I guess I don't have to leave you standing on the front step." She touched her hair, but Porter knew that it wasn't for his benefit; it was merely an anxious gesture.

Porter looked down at his feet. "Oh, I don't want to bother you. I'll hang around out here if you don't mind. I just wanted you to know I was here. Is he around?" Porter cleared his throat and then swallowed. "I mean Alma. Is he here?"

"He, Walter, and Russell are hauling hay today." She nodded in the direction of the hay barn south of the house on the other side of a fifteen-acre field. "They'll be bringing the next load in any time now." Still holding the screen door open, she said, "I'll get you something to drink." Before he could turn her down, she ordered, "Porter, come in and sit down. I don't want to stand here with the door open letting all the flies in." She glanced toward his car. "I fixed a room for you. Bring your things in."

Porter shook his head and held up his hands. "I booked a room at the Blue Pine."

"I can unbook it easy enough. I'll tell Burt and Glenna you're staying here."

"No, Toni, everybody'll feel more comfortable if I'm in town."

"You mean *you* will."

Porter studied Toni. She, even more than Allyson's brother Walter, had been scathingly critical when Porter split with her lifelong best friend. Over the years, she and Porter had exchanged more than a few sharp words. Porter didn't have any illusions about how Toni felt about him, and he was confident that if he ever became curious to know more, Toni would gladly give him a blistering piece of her mind.

"I just finished fixing a jug of lemonade for Walter and the boys. I'll get you a glass. Then if you want to wander around outside, you can."

Porter awkwardly followed Toni into the house, where she led him to the living room and pointed to the sofa. While she left to get his lemonade, Porter fidgeted in front of the sofa, reluctant to sit down. He was about to sink onto the sofa when he spotted a photograph of a three-year-old boy standing next to a young mother sitting in front of a studio background. Porter felt a sudden knot in the pit of his stomach. He'd seen the picture countless times. He owned a copy himself, but he kept it in the bottom of a dresser drawer. In fact, he distinctly remembered the day he and Allyson had taken young Alma to the photographer in Provo. They'd had a complimentary coupon giving them a free eight-by-ten photograph. They had ended up taking several poses, most with the three of them together, but Porter knew that none of those would be on display here in the Henrie home.

He stepped closer to the picture and studied it. Allyson beamed with her arm around Alma. Her light blond hair was shoulder length and had a natural, wavy curl. Her dark eyes were full of life. Her smile displayed her straight white teeth. Her complexion was smooth and tan, because they had taken the picture at the end of the summer.

Porter was touched by her beauty. She didn't have a model's face, but she was beautiful in a way that captivated a person. She had captivated Porter years earlier.

Porter found himself wondering when Allyson's beauty had gone out of focus for him. Shortly after this photograph was taken, she had miscarried early in a pregnancy. It was the first of three such miscarriages over a period of two years. Those short pregnancies and subsequent miscarriages had taken a terrible toll on Allyson. She had gained weight, and her complexion had become poor, almost as though she had reverted to adolescence. Her emotions had become frayed, and she had eventually plunged into a deep depression. It was during that period that Porter had met Kerri Mead at work.

"She was beautiful, wasn't she?" Toni spoke unexpectedly from behind him.

Porter whipped around, embarrassed that Toni had caught him studying the picture. He felt his cheeks color. "Yeah, she was pretty."

Toni handed him the glass of ice-cold lemonade. Porter nodded his thanks and took a tenuous sip.

"It's hard to believe," she went on, stepping closer to the photograph and studying it herself, "but the older she got, the prettier she was. I mean, it's not that she was ever old—thirty-seven isn't old—but Allyson just had a glow about her."

Porter sensed that Toni expected him to respond in some way, but he was absolutely clueless as to what he might add to her observation. He took a long, slow drink of his lemonade.

"Do you have to take Alma?" Toni asked suddenly, completely changing the subject.

Her unexpected question made him choke on the lemonade. Wiping his mouth with the back of his hand, he responded, "He's my son, Toni."

She studied him coolly. "He's been your son for sixteen years."

"Toni, I don't want to . . ." He cleared his throat and took another sip of lemonade. "We could spend hours debating how things should have been. Believe me, I've had a few of those personal debates myself. I don't win very many of them." He shook his head. "I didn't come here to rehash the past." He wiped at the beads of steamy moisture on the outside of the glass. "Before now," he explained slowly,

"Alma always had his mother. That was the arrangement we made ten years ago."

"I always thought that that was the arrangement *you* made," she corrected him.

Porter forced a smile. "It serves no purpose to go there, Toni. When Allyson and I separated, we decided—and for the record, it was both of us that decided, not just me—that Alma would be better off here with her. I'm not saying it was right or wrong. That's just the way it was. I'm sure I could have taken a more active role in Alma's life. I'll be the first to admit that. But everything changed after the accident. He's my responsibility now."

"Is it the responsibility that's bothering you, Porter?"

Her well-aimed jab didn't miss the mark, but Porter chose to ignore its sting. "Toni, we don't have to fight here." His tone, though warning, was also pleading. "I came to get Alma and move on. I don't want to argue with you." He took another sip of lemonade. "Alma's mine. I don't need anybody's permission. I don't have to make a legal case. I don't need a court order."

"I'm not talking about legal. Nobody's suggesting that anybody scrounge up a lawyer. I couldn't care less about what some judge might say. And I sure don't care a hoot about your version of responsibility. But what does Alma want?" There was an edge to her voice, and Porter could see the fight in her eyes.

"You know, Toni, last April Allyson and I even talked about Alma moving to Eagar with me. That's why we had already made arrangements for him to spend six weeks with me this summer. There are more opportunities there. The high school's bigger. It has more to offer, academically and athletically. Eagar's a good town, a lot better than most of the places I've lived. Those are things Allyson wanted for Alma too. The accident has made things definite now, but Allyson and I had discussed a lot of this already."

"Just because you had a few phone conversations with Allyson doesn't mean you really know what she wanted for herself or for Alma."

Porter drank the rest of the lemonade and set the glass on the coffee table, wanting to say something but knowing that if he started he might say something he'd later regret. He was already burdened with regrets; he didn't need to add to his load, not today. Feeling trapped and at a disadvantage in Toni's house, he wanted to make a graceful exit. "Thanks for the drink," he mumbled. "I'll wait for Alma outside."

"Porter," Toni persisted, "Panguitch might not be much, but it's still Alma's home, the only one he knows. He doesn't know anything about Eagar, Arizona. He's never been there. If you want Alma with you, why don't you move here? I suspect you can do your Internet job as easily here in Panguitch as you can in Eagar."

Porter chuckled sardonically. "You're right, I can get on the Internet anywhere, but we both know I couldn't live in Panguitch. I'd get eaten up here."

"So I see that it's still all about what's convenient for you."

Porter chuckled again, but there was no humor in his low laugh. It merely disguised his simmering anger. "It's sure great to be back among friends." His tone dripped with sarcasm. "I can't understand how I managed to stay away so long." He started for the front door, railing himself for accepting Toni's invitation for a drink.

"Porter," she called after him, "Alma wants to stay here. We thought you'd be glad to let us have him. Allyson and Alma have lived in the trailer here on this place since they moved back. Alma and Russell are more like brothers than cousins. He's like a son to us, Porter."

This time Porter didn't resist the temptation to return the verbal fire. Ever since receiving Toni's phone call on Sunday—the call in which she'd had the unmitigated temerity to ask him to sign guardianship papers so that Alma could remain in Panguitch—he had been fighting down his anger and frustration. "Listen, I'm sorry I was out of town when Alma first called to tell me about the accident and the funeral. But that wasn't my fault. That's just the way things happened." He made no attempt to disguise his mounting irritation.

"Maybe if you'd been in the habit of calling Alma regularly, even while you were on business, you might have known sooner," she stated flatly.

"Let's just leave all of that alone. If you and Walter had really been worried about letting me know about Allyson, you could have called me every day."

"For your information, I was the one who finally talked Alma into calling you. That was three days before the funeral. He didn't want to. He didn't think you'd care. He didn't know if you should even be at the funeral. He was dealing with a lot right then. But I insisted that he call you. Every day after that until the day after the funeral, I insisted that he call. There was no answer. Once the funeral was over . . ." She shook her head and shrugged. "Well, after the funeral, there didn't seem to be a big rush. We had no idea where you were. We were thinking of Alma, what he wanted. He's the one who asked if he could stay with us. He was feeling a little displaced. With Allyson gone, he wasn't sure where he belonged. Walter and I wanted him to know that he had a place with us. And we honestly thought we would be doing you a favor, too."

"Well, try not to do me any more favors." Fuming, Porter left the house. He stormed across the highway, climbed through the barbed-wire fence, and stomped in the direction of the Sevier River a half mile away. He had always found peace and calm while wandering along the river bottom. He sought that peaceful calm now.

The sun was warm on Porter's back as he made his way through the tall meadow grass toward the low river bottom, which was a hundred yards or more across in most places. Lining the river were dozens of stumpy, silver Russian olive trees mixed with clumps of willows, patches of grass, and occasional thistles with white-and-purple blooms.

The river itself was fewer than twenty feet across and only a few inches deep in most places. The water moved slowly, winding back and forth among the meadows and pastures. An old bridge spanned it a little ways upstream, and Porter moved in that direction. He had been to that bridge many times with Walter, Calvin, and Allyson.

Spotting a large, gray rock below the bridge, Porter sat down on it and gazed into the cloudy water. A truck rumbled over the bridge, sending vibrations and dull echoes along the banks. For several minutes Porter sat still, letting the quiet and peace of this spot soak into his system, relax his taut nerves, and calm his troubled emotions. He found it ironic that he could immerse himself in such therapeutic tranquility here when a few hundred yards away there were swirling clouds of hostility threatening him.

The longer he remained at the river, the more peace he felt. He found himself reflecting on an evening two days before his mission to Santiago, Chile. From the highway he had seen Allyson strolling along the river. Secretly, he had sneaked to the bridge and hidden behind a clump of willows. When her back was to him, he had lunged from his hiding place and clutched her waist from behind, practically giving her a heart attack. She had screamed and almost fallen into the river, and Porter had responded by doubling over in laughter. Flustered and embarrassed, she had picked up a stick and whacked him.

For several minutes the two of them had rested on this same gray rock, tossing pebbles into the water and discussing trivial topics. Eventually Porter had told her that he expected her to wait for him. Although he was teasing, there had been a part of him that was serious. The few times she'd written to him on his mission, she'd kidded him about their playful pact at the river, assuring him that she was waiting faithfully—provided, of course, that someone else didn't come along with a more appealing offer.

When Porter returned from Chile, he had dated Allyson seriously. When he'd finally proposed to her, it had been here at the bridge with a dozen red roses strategically placed to make them appear as though they were growing naturally at the river's edge, just so he could pluck them and hand them to her, along with an engagement ring.

Porter was pulled from his silent reflections when he spotted Walter approaching the river from the opposite side, checking the barbed-wire fence running parallel to the road. Just as Walter came down the riverbank to search for a narrow spot to leap across the water, Porter called out, "I hope you're a better jumper than you used to be, or you'll end up facedown in the mud." He then stood and dusted off the seat of his pants.

Walter glanced at him and then leaped deftly across the water to a small island in the middle of the river. From there he jumped the remaining six feet to the opposite bank. "You never know what this old river is going to wash up," he remarked pleasantly. "Hiding under the bridge?" He grinned. "Who's chasing you?"

Porter squinted against the glare of the afternoon sun. Taking a couple of short steps forward, he held out his hand to his ex-brother-in-law. "I'm getting the feeling that the whole valley is chasing me, Walter. This seemed as good a place to hide as any."

Walter wiped his hand on his pants and shook Porter's hand. "We weren't expecting you till tonight," he remarked. "Toni said you'd come down this way. I needed to check a couple of breaks in the fence. I assume the Mercedes up at the house is yours." Porter nodded, and Walter smiled. "That Internet business must be doing all right."

Porter's cheeks colored. "Oh, things are moving fine. But the Mercedes is five years old. I got it used a couple of months ago. I found it on the Internet. Some old guy in Denver had it and wanted to get rid of it."

"So how much does a five-year-old Mercedes set a guy back?"

"The guy gave me a good deal."

"That's not an answer," Walter persisted playfully.

"It was under thirty-five." Porter was reluctant to admit to the price tag.

"Sounds like a chunk of change for a used car."

Porter wished to divert the talk from his Mercedes. "You're not doing so bad yourself. Your place looks good. I like your new barn. It sure beats that old broken pile of junk your dad had all those years."

Walter chuckled. "I probably built that barn for about half of what you paid for that old used Mercedes." He pointed to the house. "Let's head up that way." The two of them started walking. "Don't step in a mud hole or worse," Walter warned. "Did Toni show you your room?"

Porter smiled wanly. "Actually, I booked a room at the Blue Pine."

"No problem. We'll give Glenna and Burt a call. They'll wonder why you booked a room there when we're right here."

"Toni's glad I'm staying at the Blue Pine." Porter was relieved that Walter hadn't attacked him like Toni. Walter had always been less emotional than his wife. In fact, the time that he and Porter had almost come to blows had been more Toni's doing than Walter's. Porter had driven to Panguitch to pick up Alma for Christmas break, and Toni had aggravated the situation by angrily pushing her way into the exchange, making accusations about Porter, who had brought along his latest girlfriend, Frankie Phillips. Porter had realized too late that bringing Frankie had been an insensitive and callous blunder on his part, but once he was in Panguitch, his macho pride hadn't allowed him to back down in the face of Toni's biting criticism. Besides, he had felt obligated to prove to Frankie that he wasn't about to be bullied by his former in-laws.

Tempers had flared, harsh words had been exchanged, and Walter had jumped into the fray, attempting to defuse an ugly confrontation. Before he knew it, he and Porter were on the verge of fisticuffs, which would probably have suited Toni fine. Allyson was the one who finally pushed between them and suggested that Porter leave. With that inauspicious beginning, nothing else had gone right during the long Christmas break, which had turned out to be the last Christmas Porter had spent with Alma. It had also turned out to be the last time Porter ever picked Alma up in Panguitch. From that time on, all other exchanges, the few there were, took place at mutually agreeable neutral locations.

"I'm hoping Alma and I can leave first thing in the morning," Porter explained, hoping to receive Walter's approval.

Walter pondered a moment. "Port," he said slowly, thoughtfully, "Alma's been a little upset ever since Toni talked to you. He might need some time."

"Time for what?"

Walter hesitated. "Time to get reacquainted with you. Time to get a handle on his emotions. Most kids would have been blown away by everything that's happened. He's held up really well. He's a tough kid. But under the surface he's still pretty upset, a little fragile."

"Any kid would be upset if he lost his mom."

Walter cleared his throat. "He's handled Allyson's death pretty well. He's spiritually mature and sensitive. I think he's finally at peace with it. But there's still some grieving that he's got ahead of him. That'll just take time." Walter cleared his throat. "He's not all that excited to head off to Eagar. That might be home to you, Port, but it doesn't mean anything to Alma. Leaving Panguitch has hit him pretty sudden. Sunday when Toni called you, we all kind of figured . . ." Walter shook his head and snatched up a fistful of long, stringy meadow grass. "Shoot, Port, we all just kind of figured you'd let Alma stay here. That's why Toni brought up the guardianship papers. Alma moved out of Allyson's trailer into Russell's room. He's just part of the family."

"I'm his dad." Porter felt his anger stir, but he sensed that Walter didn't want an argument any more than he did. "I plan to explain everything to Alma."

"It doesn't have anything to do with an explanation. He knows you can take him. He hasn't said he's not going. But tomorrow might be pushing things a little hard."

"And what am I supposed to do in the meantime, stay holed up at the Blue Pine, eating chips, drinking soda, and watching TV?" Porter muttered, turning away.

"That's why Toni fixed you a room, so you wouldn't run up a motel bill."

Porter laughed humorlessly. "Walter, I wouldn't dare sleep in your house for fear Toni'd creep into my room brandishing a butcher knife."

Walter laughed. "Will you stay if I lock up the knives?"

"Walter, the knives don't scare me. Toni scares me. Lock up Toni."

For a long time both men swished through the grass, caught up in their own private thoughts. Finally Walter heaved a sigh. "Port, Alma has this old—"

"Truck," Porter cut in.

Walter gave him a quizzical glance.

"I stopped by Calvin's place. He told me about it." He slapped at a burr on the cuff of his pants. "I'll buy him a truck."

"Port, he doesn't want just any truck."

Porter threw his arms in the air and let them drop to his side. "Fine, he can keep his old truck. He can leave it here, and it will be his. In the meantime, I'll buy him a truck that he can run around in." Porter shrugged as they crossed the highway. "Well, I guess I'd better find Alma and see what I'm up against."

"He and Russell just finished putting away their last load of hay," Walter explained. "Alma's probably out at the barn looking over his truck."

* * *

When Porter reached the barn, he spotted the old, faded, red-and-white, long-bed truck, its sides speckled with rust. It looked older, more worn and beat up than he remembered it. Protruding from under the truck were two legs dressed in dusty denim jeans and wearing scuffed work boots. He couldn't see the body and face attached to the legs, but he assumed they belonged to his son.

Porter ambled over to the truck and leaned against it. He coughed, not because he needed to but to subtly announce that he was there. When that failed to elicit a response, he drummed his fingers on the fender and then spoke. "Hello, Alma." Again, there was no answer. He heard the dull clang of tools on metal as well as an occasional grunt. "Walter said I'd find you here." There was still no response from under the truck. "I hear you've turned into quite the mechanic." Porter waited. Nothing. He groped for something else to say. "I'm sorry about your mom, Alma," he offered sympathetically. "I wish I'd known sooner." The clanging and grunting from under the truck continued.

For the next several minutes, Porter commented about the truck, the farm, and Alma's school, but everything was a one-sided conversation. Finally, exasperated and out of small talk, Porter remarked as casually as he could, "I was sort of hoping we could head out of here first thing in the morning."

"To Arizona?" Those were Alma's first words, and they dripped with disgust.

Porter hesitated. "You'll like Eagar. They've got a football team, and a good track team. There are opportunities there that you'll never get here in Panguitch."

"Are you making me go?" It was more an accusation than a question.

Porter pursed his lips and scratched at a speck of mud on the truck's fender. "I'd prefer you came willingly." When Alma didn't reply, Porter cleared his throat and looked around the barn. The muscles along his jaw tightened some. "I don't want to get in a big fight over this."

Another long silence ensued. "What about the truck?" Alma finally asked. "If I go, the truck goes."

Porter pushed away from the truck. "We'll work something out," was his muttered concession.

In the late afternoon sunshine, Porter strolled to his car. He glanced at his watch. It was only four thirty, and he had no idea what he was going to do to kill time the rest of the day or where he was going to kill it. There wasn't even a movie theater in Panguitch. He jerked up on the door handle and pulled open the door. At the same time, the screen door squeaked open and then clattered closed. Toni came down the front walk toward him.

"Porter, I'm sorry I got all over your case," she apologized as she approached. She folded her arms across her chest and shook her head, tears brimming in the corners of her eyes, but Porter knew the tears weren't for him. "You have no idea how close Allyson and I were. Every time I think about her . . ." She gulped and touched the corner of her eyes with the tips of her fingers. "I want you to stay here." She pressed her lips together and then took a deep breath. "I'll have dinner ready in an hour or so."

"Well, Calvin and I were heading in to the Cowboy's Smokehouse Café," Porter returned, frantically fabricating a believable excuse. He knew that dinner with Calvin was a wild stretch, but he also knew that dinner with Walter and Toni's family would be a complete disaster.

"You and Calvin can go to dinner another time." Toni turned and started back to the house. "I'll call Bonnie and tell her you're eating here."

"Toni, Bonnie doesn't know anything about it. I just talked to Calvin in the field." He imagined Toni getting Calvin on the phone and trying to cancel a nonexistent dinner appointment. He cringed to think of Toni catching him in a lie.

"I'll get him on his cell. That'll save you a trip," she called over her shoulder.

Porter leaned against his car while he cooked in the sun, wondering how Calvin would respond to his fabricated dinner invitation. Frustrated and agitated, he fought back the urge to lunge into his car and speed away, leaving Toni to figure out the whole mess.

Soon the screen door squeaked open again. "Calvin always was stubborn and pigheaded," Toni called out. "I even invited him and Bonnie to come here." She sounded disgusted and out of patience. "He prefers the T-bone steak you promised. He said to pick him up around six thirty." She waved Porter away and slipped back into the house.

"What was that all about?" Walter asked, coming up behind Porter.

Porter turned to him. "Toni's trying to talk me into staying for dinner." He cleared his throat guiltily. "But I'm taking Calvin to the café." He grinned sheepishly. "Do you want to come?"

Walter smiled weakly and shook his head.

"You know," Porter went on, "everybody around here but you has lambasted me."

Walter chuckled and folded his arms while he rocked gently back and forth on the balls of his feet. "You don't need to hear anything from me, Port."

"Oh, go ahead, hammer me while I'm still down and numb. Don't spare me. Let's hear your take on my miserable life. Everybody else has taken a swing at me."

Walter stopped smiling, but he didn't look at Porter. "I don't have this aching urge to get anything off my chest. Sure, I've cussed you and discussed you in my mind. But no need to dredge any of that up now."

"Now you've got me curious. Come on, I can handle it."

Walter squatted down on his heels and picked up a stick from the ground. He made a square in the dirt and proceeded to draw straight lines across it like miniature plowed furrows in a tiny field. "Port, you and I were always friends. Best friends. The brother I never had. I didn't look up to anyone the way I looked up to you."

Porter waited for him to go on, but he didn't. "All right," he nudged, "where's the big *but*—you know the one: 'you were my best buddy . . . *but* . . .'"

"I didn't throw in any *buts*."

"You have them, though. What are they?"

Walter had finished making his furrows across his tiny square field. He held the stick in both hands while he pondered. Slowly he reached out with the stick and scratched out his work. "You were my best friend." He paused. "But Allyson was my little sister. Even if she hadn't been my little sister, I would have known she was different. You knew she was different. That's why you married her. No, she didn't have the most gorgeous face in the world. Pretty, but not gorgeous. She didn't have a movie star's figure, either. She was deeper than that." He clenched his fist and pressed it to his chest. "In here she was different. She deserved the best. I was glad you got her, because I wanted her to have the best, and I had a pretty high opinion of you, Port."

Walter heaved a sigh. "Just the other day I tried to figure out the difference between you and Allyson. I think I finally figured it out. Allyson could have lived anywhere and made that corner of the world a better place simply because she was there. She would have thrown her whole heart and soul into making the dingiest corner something special. You, on the other hand, were always looking over the fence, searching for something bigger and better. Neither one of you was satisfied with the way things were, but your solution was to search for the perfect place while Allyson's solution was to make every place a little better—the perfect place."

He began drawing in the dirt again, this time haphazardly. "I don't know what happened, Port. I tried to figure things out ten years ago. For the life of me I couldn't make sense of anything you did. I doubt you can. I know you leaned toward the fast lane, the big bucks, your name in neon lights. Allyson would have been happy to follow you back here to Panguitch so you could clerk in the hardware store or check the water meters for the city. She would have supported whatever you did. You're probably making pretty good money, but it won't matter how much money you make. You'll never make enough to compensate for losing Allyson. You sold yourself short, Port. You cheated Allyson. You cheated me. You cheated Alma. You cheated everybody."

He swallowed, broke the stick in two, and flung the two pieces aside. "But," he added slowly, thoughtfully, "the sad thing is that I'm not sure even now that you realize what you cheated all of us out of."

He stood up and glanced at Porter, who was staring at him with a pained look on his face. Walter shrugged. "Those are the big bad *buts*. You're the one who wanted to hear them."

3

With a couple of hours to kill, Porter returned to Panguitch, parked his car at the Blue Pine, and made a quick tour of the town on foot. Downtown Panguitch was much the way he remembered it—nothing much going on—and ten minutes was more than enough time to stroll along both sides of the business section of town. After that, he decided to take the ten-minute walk over to Panguitch High School, home of the Bobcats. On the way he paused in front of the old, yellow-brick high school building where he had attended classes right up to his senior year, the year the new high school had been completed. The memories flooded back.

When he'd first arrived in Panguitch, he'd been disappointed that the high school didn't have a football team. Back in Logan, Utah, he had played junior varsity football as a freshman. He had dreams of being a football star, but those dreams were dashed when he discovered that there wasn't even a football team to try out for at his new school. His parents had discussed sending him to live with an uncle in Salt Lake so he could play football there, but by then Porter had become close friends with Calvin and Walter, and he didn't want to leave.

Basketball had never been Porter's main love, but basketball was what Panguitch offered, so he tried out for the team and landed a varsity spot as a sophomore. He ended up making the 1A all-state team his junior and senior years.

He pitched for the Panguitch Bobcat baseball team and earned all-state honors as a senior. He even ran track when it didn't interfere with the baseball schedule. He managed to set school and state records in the one hundred and two hundred meters. But through it all, he always wondered what he might have done in one of the big schools with some good coaching.

Porter left the old high school building and ambled over to the new campus. When he reached the chain-link fence surrounding the athletic field, he admired the all-weather track that the school now had. He wondered if any of his track records still stood.

For a moment he had an urge to sprint down the rubberized track, but he resisted the temptation and contented himself with a simple walking lap, remembering his glory days when he first set the school record in the hundred meters. Trina Ipson, one of the senior cheerleaders, had been waiting on the grass at the finish line when he'd burst through the tape and the timekeeper had announced that he had set a school record. Trina had been more than a little impressed and had thrown her arms around him in a crazy, uninhibited embrace. Allyson had been there that day too, but she had remained shyly behind the outside fence. She hadn't said anything to him until that evening, when he and Walter walked up the Henries' front walk. She was sitting on the front steps with a book in her lap and offered him a simple but sincere "Good job, Porter."

Porter peered through the glass doors leading into the gym area, where the trophy cases were filled with the fruits of the school's long history of athletic achievements. He'd helped earn some of those trophies, but he had no way of being able to tell which ones.

Leaving the high school, he walked several blocks to the edge of town, where the new baseball complex had been built—a three-diamond playing field. He was duly impressed. Most towns—even larger ones—couldn't boast of playing fields as nice as these. The lawns were well-watered, trimmed, and cared for. He sat in the new silver bleachers and wondered what it would have been like to play on fields like these. He closed his eyes, and for a moment he heard the cheers from an imaginary crowd as he struck out one batter after another.

He was surprised by how fast the two hours passed. When he finally pulled up in front of Calvin's home, he was thirty minutes late. "Hey, Calvin," he apologized sheepishly as his old friend climbed into the Mercedes, "I'm sorry about this whole mess. I didn't mean to put you in this bind. I told Toni not to call. I mean . . ."

Calvin burst out laughing. "As soon as Toni said you and me were having dinner in town, I knew you were up to your ears in trouble. I could hear the alligators snapping at you in the background." He laughed loudly. "But I played it cool for you. After all, we *had* talked about grabbing a steak at the café. You didn't stretch the truth too much, at least not by your liberal standards." He slapped Porter on the knee. "And I get a free dinner out of it. T-bone, if I remember correctly."

"I owe you one, buddy," Porter acquiesced gratefully. "You can have two T-bones. Shoot, I'll buy you the whole dinner menu if you want it."

"One steak's enough for me." Calvin touched the leather bucket seat. "But after bouncing around on an old tractor all day, I thought a ride in your fancy Mercedes would suit me just fine."

"Hey, man, I'll let you drive this thing if you want."

Calvin shook his head. "I'm fine with just the ride."

The Cowboy's Smokehouse Café was kitty-corner from the Blue Pine Motel. It was an ancient, two-story, pale redbrick structure with a tall, narrow storefront, the likes of which one might find along the main streets of hundreds of small towns. Porter parked in the motel parking lot, and he and Calvin ambled across the street to the café and stepped through the door propped open by a silver, ten-gallon milk can. The varnished hardwood floor creaked as they walked to the left side of the dining area. Sitting down at a small table covered with a green vinyl tablecloth, Porter looked around. Little had changed since his last visit years earlier.

One section sported several deer heads mounted on the wall along with one giant elk and a moose, both of which sported handsome racks of antlers. One full wall was papered with literally thousands of business cards left by appreciative customers over the years. Cowboy art and western memorabilia covered the walls, and in one corner stood a life-size, cardboard cutout of John Wayne, complete with a .45 on his hip and a Winchester in his hand.

The chill that had existed between Calvin and Porter earlier in the day was gone. They were old friends again. From the back corner of the café, a radio moaned some popular country western song, and ceiling fans whirled noiselessly overhead—the café's feeble attempt at air conditioning. Porter glanced toward a small, square, dry-erase board that advertised the Special of the Day—pork loin for $11.95.

"What'll it be?" Porter asked Calvin before the waitress had even brought their menus. "I'm buying."

Just then the waitress stepped over to their table. Porter looked up and grinned. "Annie Houston?"

The waitress, who was in her mid-thirties, froze three steps from the table. Her mouth hung open for a moment, but then she smiled. "Porter Huggins?" She shook her head. "I heard you were coming," she marveled, stepping to the table and setting two menus in front of them. "I didn't expect you here. And just for the record," she added as an afterthought, "it's Annie Miller now."

"So you didn't marry Carl Hatch?"

She heaved a sigh and shook her head. "Carl married some girl from Escalante. They've got six kids now." She blushed. "Of course, I'm not too far behind. I've got five, but I think that about does it for me."

After a few pleasantries and some quick questions to fill in the gaps of the past twenty years, Porter ordered T-bone steaks for Calvin and himself, and Annie left them. Porter was able to relax and partially forget that he was a Panguitch pariah.

"Didn't you date Annie?" Calvin asked, taking a sip of ice water.

"I took her out once, that first year I lived here."

Calvin chuckled as he played with the salt and pepper shakers. "I still remember the day you pulled into town," he mused. "You gave 'cocky' a whole new dimension."

"Self-assured," Porter countered with a guilty grin, holding up a forefinger.

"Bull! You were flat-out cocky. I wanted to bust you in the mouth."

"You did that first day over at the church when we were playing basketball."

"But that was practically unintentional. It was what you used to call a good foul."

"A cheap hit. And you stood there with that dumb, sad look on your face like you were really sorry."

Calvin laughed as Annie set their salads in front of them. "But I finally got so I could stand to be around you."

"I stopped being cocky."

Calvin shook his head. "No, you're still as cocky as ever." He grinned.

"I can't help it if I'm talented. What can I say?" Porter joked.

"Talented? Like in the regional playoff game when we were sophomores?"

"Oh, don't drag up that mess."

"Five seconds left, the score's tied, and you've played about two minutes the whole game, but you were a hot outside shooter, so Coach Miller figured he'd pull you off the bench and get the ball to you. He figured everyone would be watching Sevy and Cooper so no one would have an eye on you. You were so excited you were drooling all over the gym floor. This was your big chance."

Porter watched his friend relate the story, knowing that he was enjoying every detail.

"You race onto the court, Heywood tosses you the ball, and all you can think is that you're in the clear. You dribble twice, and from the top of the key you shoot that basket. Nothing but net. You're jumping up and down going crazy, waiting for everybody to mob you on the floor. The crowd's going wild, screaming their guts out, and your team's just standing there on the edge of the court with their mouths open. They can't believe you nailed that twenty-two footer— and sent the *other* team to the state playoffs." Calvin slapped the table and howled. "You oozed talent that night." He shook his head. "Remember that night?"

Porter fought back a grin. "No," he muttered dryly, "I've never thought of that shot again since that night."

Not wanting to let the memory go, Calvin piled it on. "I can still see you jumping around on the court, clutching your head and grinning and thinking you were the new school hero. Even after Coach Miller pointed to the scoreboard, you didn't get it." Calvin shook his head and pretended to hold a microphone in front of Porter's mouth. "Mr. Huggins, can you tell us what you were thinking when you finally realized you'd sent Parowan to the playoffs?"

Brushing the imaginary microphone aside, Porter grumbled, "Hey, Calvin, do you think we can move on to something else?"

Calvin nodded sagely and stroked his chin with his thumb. "Port, you were a tough act to follow. Let's see." He put his hands behind his head and stared up at the ceiling fans whirring softly overhead. "Prom, our senior year. You took that girl from Richfield because you wanted to make all the Panguitch girls jealous."

"Isn't there something else we can talk about, Calvin?"

"Since it had been raining, you didn't want to get your black shoes muddy, so you slipped on your white tennis shoes and drove all the way to Richfield to pick up your date. You thought you were so hot strutting into the prom with that girl on your arm. The prom was half over before you realized you were still wearing your old tennis shoes." Calvin grinned. "Did you ever ask that girl out again?"

"I haven't even driven through Richfield since that night. I've been afraid I'd run into that girl. *Now* can we talk about something else?"

"All right, where the heck is Eagar, Arizona?"

"Northeastern Arizona, a few miles from the New Mexico state line. I used to think I'd rather die than live in a little town." Porter shrugged. "But I've changed a lot, especially the last few years. Eagar suits me fine," he finished quietly.

"You lived in Colorado for a while. What made you move to Eagar?"

"Did you know that John Wayne once had a big ranch just outside of Eagar?"

"Oh," Calvin deadpanned, "so you moved to Eagar to be close to the ranch of your good buddy John Wayne. Even though he's dead and his ranch belongs to somebody else now."

"Real cute." He pondered a moment. "It's really pretty country up there. Tons of pines and aspen forests. There's a nice ski resort about twenty miles from Eagar."

"Oh, so you ski now?"

"No."

"Am I missing something? You still haven't told me why Eagar, Arizona."

Porter considered the question for a while, then became serious. "I was looking to start over." He shrugged again. "I drove through

Eagar a little over a year ago and saw a place for sale. I figured Eagar was a good place to make a fresh start."

Calvin nodded and then added solemnly, "And I'll bet it's a real comfort to be that close to John Wayne's old ranch." He burst out laughing and slapped the table.

Long after their food was gone, they continued to laugh and reminisce. Finally they sat quietly with their forearms resting on the edge of the table as they stared at their empty plates and glasses.

"When do you figure on pulling out?" Calvin finally asked.

Porter heaved a sigh and shook his head. "I talked to Alma for a few minutes this afternoon. It was a little bit of a one-sided conversation."

Calvin clasped his hands in front of him and pursed his lips. "Port, he's sixteen. Do you remember what it's like to be sixteen? Shoot, his mother was killed a month ago. He doesn't really know his dad, and a lot of what he does know isn't all that great. He's supposed to move to some out-of-the-way place in Arizona, and believe me, he won't be impressed with John Wayne's ranch or the ski resort. That's a lot to dump on a kid."

Calvin picked up his glass and drank the last few drops of ice and water that lingered in the bottom. "I talked to Alma the day before Toni got in touch with you. He told me Toni was going to ask you to sign over guardianship to them."

"Toni and Walter are the ones who put all that junk in his head."

"Hey, they'd love to keep Alma with them, but don't blame them for the mess."

"And why not?" Porter countered irritably. "They put on a show of being nice, especially Toni, inviting me to stay the night and have dinner. All along I knew she'd like to tear my eyes out. She's a hypocrite."

Calvin shook his head ruefully. "Walter and Toni are good people. Their basic nature is to be nice—to everyone, even you. But, Port, you've got to understand that it was Walter and Toni—mainly Toni—who helped Allyson put herself back together after you left her. Allyson returned to Panguitch one busted up girl. And where were you? Off having a great time with Kerri Mead. And while Kerri was entertaining you, Toni was here nursing Allyson. For the first six months, Allyson hardly went out in public. Not even to church. I saw her a time or two walking down by the river, but she was too ashamed to talk to me—to talk to anybody. Her marriage had gone to the dogs, and she blamed herself. She beat herself up pretty bad over something that wasn't her fault. But Toni hung with her until she was back on her feet and realized she had a life ahead of her. She finally realized that she could mope around and mourn the rest of her life or she could move on. And she moved on. She was a little overweight, so she started jogging and slimmed down. She took pride in herself. She got a job as a secretary at the high school. The rest is history."

Calvin ran his tanned, calloused hands over the vinyl tablecloth, brushing a few crumbs onto the floor. "Forgiving you, Port, might not be too high on Toni's priority list right now. Maybe you've changed a lot since you dumped Allyson, but time doesn't heal everything. Maybe Toni does want to tear your eyes out. She won't do it, though. Instead she'll fix you a room and invite you to dinner, because deep down she's a good person. She's fighting back some bitter feelings toward you, but believe me, Port, she'll keep making the effort."

"Look, I appreciate what Walter and Toni did for Allyson and Alma," Porter offered grudgingly, "but they don't have the right to steal my son from me now."

"They didn't think you wanted him. It's not like you've been deeply involved in his life. Oh, he's spent some holidays with you, but in the last few years, even those haven't been too regular."

"I tried to get him to come more often," Porter defended, "but he always had other things going—ball games, dances, Church activities. It didn't matter when I invited him, he seemed to have something else more important than seeing me. And I didn't want to force him. I could have, you know."

"How often did you call? Did you ever write?"

Porter hesitated. "I'm not much of a letter writer. I called some." He shook his head. "The phone calls were . . . Well, let's say they lacked a little enthusiasm. I got the impression that Alma was looking at the clock, counting the seconds until I hung up. So I haven't been all that involved. That's the way I thought he and Allyson wanted it."

Porter swallowed hard and stared out the open front door of the café. "And I'll admit that I felt guilty. About three years ago, after I broke things off with Frankie, I got my head screwed on straight." He wet his lips and narrowed his eyes. "It was then that I really realized what a mess I'd made of my life. And theirs. I didn't feel I had a right to intrude much. I started being really regular with the child support payments—something I hadn't always done. But I still didn't think I could pressure Alma into seeing me. I always remembered his birthday and Christmas and things like that."

"Yeah," Calvin commented quietly. "Walter told me once that Allyson always knew how guilty you were feeling by the size of check you sent Alma for Christmas or his birthday."

Porter turned to his friend and studied him for a moment before looking away again. "I didn't know it was so obvious," he muttered.

Calvin heaved a sigh. "All I know is that Alma didn't think you gave a howling hoot for him. That's a pretty big burden for a young kid to pack around with him. It's bad enough that you abandoned his mother. It's a whole different thing for a kid to realize that his own dad doesn't really care for him."

"That just isn't true. I don't know what Allyson told him, but—"

"Get one thing straight," Calvin interrupted. "Allyson didn't badmouth you, especially not around Alma. She wanted him to respect you as his dad. I've heard some other people badmouth you—heck, I've done my share—but Allyson didn't."

"She was a real saint," Porter muttered cynically. "I was the devil incarnate."

Calvin let the shadow of a smile touch his lips. "I don't know what you are, Port. Not anymore. We've been apart too long. But I'll swear by Allyson's character. She was genuine. So's Alma. But his version of reality says you didn't give a hang about his mother and you probably don't give a hang about him." Porter started to protest, but Calvin held up his hands. "I'm not talking about *your* reality. I'm talking about his."

"I wanted to do more with him. I tried."

"You should have tried harder. You gave up too easily. That's why he naturally figured you didn't care. That's also why it just blew him away when you said you were coming to get him. He's a sensitive kid, Port. He really is."

"He seemed pretty ornery this afternoon."

Calvin took a toothpick from a plastic cup on the table and began to work on a back molar. "Port, he's the spitting image of you when you were sixteen—without being cocky." He smiled with the toothpick in the corner of his mouth. "He's a better athlete than you." With his tongue, Calvin flicked the toothpick to the other side of his mouth. "But on the inside he's all Allyson. He's got her heart, her sensitivity, her goodness."

Calvin took the toothpick out of his mouth. Holding it between his thumb and forefinger, he gazed toward the front windows. "Last year for prom, Tracie Owens got asked out for the first time. She was a senior but had never had a real date. One of her friends arranged for her to go with a cousin in Escalante. Three days before the dance, Tracie had an appendectomy and ended up staying home the night of prom."

Calvin cleared his throat and stared down at the table. "What would you have done had she been your date, Port?" Calvin shook his head. "I would have probably done the same thing as you. But Alma's not a chump like you and me. He's got class. Keep in mind that Alma was a sophomore this past year. Tracie wasn't his date. She's not what you'd call a real looker. But Alma found out about her operation. He showed up to her place all dressed up. He gave her a corsage. He brought a CD player and some music. He ordered steak dinners from the Cowboy's Smokehouse here and took them over to her place. He stayed there with her until midnight, eating, playing music, talking, just making her feel like a thousand bucks."

Calvin chuckled. "I don't know what the kid from Escalante was like. I don't know what the prom was like. But by the time Alma left Tracie Owens's place that night, she was glad she'd had that appendectomy and stayed home from the dance."

Calvin put the toothpick back in his mouth and smiled wanly. "That's the kind of thing Allyson would have done."

Porter's brow raised slightly as he stared at his friend.

"I don't know what Alma is thinking or what he plans to do," Calvin went on, "but he won't hurt you, Port, not intentionally. He might do things you don't understand. Maybe he won't even understand. But he won't try to hurt you. That's just not part of Alma's nature."

Much earlier, Annie Miller had set the check on the corner of the table. Now Porter laid two twenties on top of it and stood. Calvin followed him out of the café. In the car, Porter remarked quietly, almost apologetically, "You know, Calvin, I really didn't know you'd liked Allyson so much. I mean, I knew you liked her, but . . ." He shook his head and shrugged, not knowing what else to say.

Calvin didn't respond immediately. He rubbed his hand along the dashboard and then dropped both hands in his lap. "Like I said before, I didn't get married until I was thirty." He shrugged. "I know I was just a dumb farmer—a little backward, not much of a socialite. I'd gotten over my infatuation with Allyson a long time before, but I was here when she came back, and I was still single." He looked over at Porter. "I fell in love with her again. At first I told myself that I couldn't go out and marry my best friend's ex-wife." Calvin shook his head and looked away. "But after a while I didn't care whose ex she was. I took her out a few times, nothing serious. We had a good time. I wasn't thinking of marriage yet, but I was definitely interested in exploring all the possibilities."

Calvin smiled and shook his head. "Allyson must have read me like a book, because one day while I was working, she walked out to the field. She was as gentle as she could be, but she told me that she could never . . ." He swallowed hard. "She told me that she didn't want to hurt me, but she wasn't going to see me anymore, not as anything more than a friend." Calvin smiled and turned to Porter. "She didn't say it, but I knew she still loved you, Port, even then. And she was never going to be disloyal."

Porter winced noticeably, as though pricked suddenly by a red-hot poker. He felt a stabbing pain twist through him, followed by an overwhelming rush of regret.

"Allyson seemed to take my heart in her hands and gently cut off all the romantic strings hanging out and then hand it back to me. It didn't happen that same day, but over the next few days she doctored my romantic wounds." Calvin smiled. "Only Allyson could have done that. We were still friends, but the romance was gone. She was like my sister. She's the one who introduced me to Bonnie. Bonnie and I still joke that my old girlfriend was the one who set us up."

Porter and Calvin were quiet as they drove home. When Porter stopped in front of Calvin's house, Calvin held out his hand and Porter shook it warmly. "Next time don't take so long in coming back." He opened the door and started to step out, then reconsidered, staring straight ahead. "Port, I know you're not crazy about that old truck, but Alma's got a lot of memories wrapped up in it." He cleared his throat. "If you're serious about winning Alma over, I suggest you find a way to get that truck to Eagar, even if you have to put your shoulder to the back fender and push it there yourself."

4

After dropping Calvin off, Porter had planned to drive back to the Blue Pine, but as he was coming up the airport road, he saw a light in Walter's barn. He had a hunch that Alma was there, working on his truck, so he decided to make one more attempt to crack the icy wall between them.

Porter pulled into Walter's driveway and wandered in the direction of the barn. As he approached, he saw that the truck's hood had been propped open with a hoe handle. Alma leaned over the fender with his arms elbow-deep in the black engine cavity. Using a long orange extension cord, he had hung a single-bulb shop lantern from the hood.

For the first few moments, Porter hung back in the shadows, his heart aching as he watched his son. He couldn't see Alma's face until Alma finally turned and reached for a greasy rag lying on top of the radiator. He had a small nose and a straight, hard jaw. His hair, eyebrows, and dark brown eyes were like Allyson's, but his thick neck and muscular shoulders and arms gave him the unmistakable aura of an athlete.

"So you're still working on the truck," Porter finally said, stepping from the shadows into the circle of yellow light.

Alma glanced up but quickly turned back to his work.

"Do you need a hand?" Porter asked clumsily, not knowing what else to say and yet feeling silly for making such a ridiculous offer. He knew there was practically nothing mechanical he could do to help his son.

But that didn't matter, since Alma didn't want his help anyway. Alma just shook his head and continued working.

"Calvin says you're quite the mechanic. You couldn't ask for a better teacher than Calvin."

Alma grunted.

Porter didn't know if that was a yes or just part of his work. "I remember driving this old thing." He reached out and hesitantly touched the grille as though it might burn him. Alma glanced toward his hand, so Porter pulled it back and pushed it into his pocket. "I remember taking you for rides when we were visiting your grandparents." Porter forced out a weak laugh that was far from genuine. "Do you remember that?"

Another grunt.

This time Porter was relatively certain that the grunt was an answer, but he didn't know if it was an affirmation to his question or not. Alma looked busy under the hood, but Porter wasn't sure if he was actually making repairs or merely keeping himself occupied so he didn't have to talk.

"Does it still run?" Porter ventured, hoping that Alma would answer in the negative.

"On a good day."

Porter swallowed, encouraged. "Would it make it to Eagar?" he asked, already knowing the answer. "That's about five hundred miles."

Alma backed out from under the hood, but he kept his hands on the fender and stared down at the engine. "Not without a lot of serious work."

Porter decided to be bold. "I can buy you a truck, Alma. I'm wrapping up a business deal right now, and when it's finalized I could put a nice down payment on about any truck you want."

"I've got a truck."

"I can buy you a good one, a new one."

"I like this old one."

Porter fidgeted. "If it doesn't run well enough to make it to Eagar, I don't know what we can do." He coughed nervously. "Maybe Walter will keep it here and later—"

"I'm not leaving the truck behind."

"What are we supposed to do, push it?"

Alma considered that option. "If we have to," he finally answered. He wiped his hands on the greasy rag. "I'll work on it some more."

"How long will it take?"

Alma breathed deeply and shook his head. "I don't know," he answered quietly.

"I can't wait around indefinitely. If you're talking about a day or two, then—"

"Come back when it's fixed."

"I was planning for us to leave together."

"Then we'll have to figure out a way to take the truck." His tone wasn't exactly defiant, but it held the unmistakable tone of a challenge.

"Look, Alma, I didn't come here to argue." Porter turned to the side and rubbed the back of his neck and closed his eyes. "Ever since I drove into town, I've been arguing with somebody. I don't want a fight. I don't want to argue. I just came to take you back."

"Why?"

The question was a blow out of nowhere, and it jarred Porter into speechlessness. "Why?" he repeated after a few seconds. Out of the corner of his eye he saw Alma studying him, waiting for a response. "Because . . . you're my son," he stammered.

"And you barely found out about me?"

Porter shuffled his feet in the dust and bits of straw covering the wooden barn floor. "Alma, your mom and I had an arrangement." Even to him his voice sounded strained and taut. "I'm not saying that it was the best arrangement."

"Why don't you just leave that arrangement alone? It worked before."

"Because your mom isn't here now," Porter answered quietly, evenly. "And now you're my responsibility. It's my turn to take you."

"That's what I am—a responsibility, your turn?"

Porter took a deep breath and exhaled slowly. "Alma, I don't know what your mom told you. I mean about us—about her and me—and about why things didn't work. I know I never talked to you much about all that, even when you'd visit."

"I guess it's about time I heard your side."

"Alma, there are a lot of reasons a marriage doesn't work out." Porter wet his lips and pressed on. "I'm not saying it was anybody's fault. I'm just saying—"

"Are you saying that part of this was Mom's fault?" Alma's question crackled with unmistakable anger. Porter immediately sensed that he had touched a raw nerve. "Didn't you walk out on her?" Alma gripped a wrench with both hands. "Don't make this whole thing sound like it was nobody's fault," he added hoarsely, "that nobody was to blame." He tossed the wrench at the tool chest at his feet and missed.

Porter held up his hands in surrender. "Okay, okay!" he called out. "It was my fault. I walked out. I'm just saying—"

Alma cut him off. "I really don't want to know. I'm sorry I brought it up." He started gathering his tools. "I'm not in the mood to hear a bunch of lame excuses."

As Porter watched Alma pick up the tools, he started to wish that he'd followed his first impulse and driven straight to the Blue Pine. "Look," he said, "I'll just hang around Panguitch until you're ready to go." He studied the truck for a moment. "I don't know how we'll take the truck, but I'll find a way, even if I have to push it to Eagar myself."

At that moment Porter hated the truck. It was an additional dilemma he hadn't counted on. He felt that his plate was already over-flowing with more problems and challenges than he was in the mood to deal with. The truck was an unnecessary complication. Had he had a sledgehammer, he would have relished the idea of pounding the truck into a pile of scrap metal and carting it off to the nearest junk heap.

Instead, Porter cleared his throat. "You need to understand that I don't know anybody in Eagar who would be able to help you fix up this truck. It'll just be you."

"I figured maybe you'd lend a hand," Alma responded sarcastically. "Calvin said you two used to work on your car all the time."

Porter attempted a smile but failed. "Yeah, Calvin worked, and I watched. My total contribution was running into town for soda pop. If we had a big job, I'd pick up hamburgers and fries." He dropped the fake smile and folded his arms. "I don't want you to have any illusions. I'm no mechanic. I can put gas in the car, and I can check the oil and the fluid in the radiator, but I break out in a rash just thinking about actually working on a car. That's why I'd just as soon buy you a new truck and forget about this one."

"I'm not like you," Alma answered sullenly. "If something's broken, I stick with it until it's fixed. I don't buy a new model just because the old one has a few problems."

"Do you really know how to fix this thing?"

"Give me a little credit. I can figure out what needs to be done."

For a long time Porter and Alma stood by the truck without speaking. Alma stared down into the engine cavity, the muscles along his jaw tense. Porter would have preferred to simply force Alma to go with him—without the truck—but a more reasonable side of him whispered that beginning life with Alma in Eagar in the middle of a major conflict wasn't the best way to handle things.

"Well, like I said," Porter muttered in defeat, "we'll take the truck to Eagar." He turned his back on the truck and stared into the blackness of the night. "I don't know how long it will take you to get your things ready or how much time you need to say your good-byes. Maybe you need a day, or two days, or a week. You tell me." Porter started to move away.

"I can leave in the morning," Alma responded before Porter had taken two steps. "I don't want to drag things out."

Porter stopped and turned. "You can have more time than that," he offered in a softer, more conciliatory tone. "I can hang around awhile."

"For what? If we're going, let's do it."

A moment later Porter rapped on Walter's front door. Walter, dressed in a pair of sweatpants and a T-shirt, invited him in.

"I won't take long," Porter apologized as he stood just inside the front door. While he stood there, Toni came from another room and curiously peered into the entryway without saying anything. "Alma and I want to leave in the morning. There's only one hang-up." He wet his lips and pressed them together, staring at Walter. "That old truck won't make it out of the yard without breaking down or blowing up—which would be fine with me—but Alma doesn't think he can live without it."

Porter glanced down at the floor as he prepared to make his request. "You've got a heavy-duty flatbed trailer out there. Could we load the truck onto the trailer and have you pull it to Eagar first thing in the morning?"

Walter didn't answer immediately.

Sensing reluctance or outright refusal, Porter grabbed for his back pocket and pulled out his wallet. He extracted two hundreds and a fifty. "Here's for your time and the wear and tear on your truck and trailer." He held the money out. "I'll pay for the gas too. If that's not enough, I'll pay you more."

Walter shook his head. "I don't want your money, Port. I'll get the truck to Eagar, but I'm in the middle of hay season. Give me a few days and—"

"I could wait if I absolutely had to, but Alma says he's ready to go tomorrow. And Panguitch is about the last place in the world I'd want to spend a few days in, even if I had them to waste."

"Look, Port, you take half my help when you leave with Alma. He and Russell are the best hay-hauling crew in the valley. Now you want me to drop everything and make a trip to Eagar myself. I can't do that right now. I've got to get that hay out of the field in case it rains."

For a moment Porter and Walter stared at each other, Porter still holding the three bills in his hand. Finally, Porter nodded. "I'll find somebody else then."

"I didn't say I won't," Walter countered. "In a few days the hay will be up." He hesitated, seeming to debate something in his mind. "Look," he burst out in frustration, "you come barging in here and want everybody to drop everything and make accommodations for your schedule."

Porter smiled humorlessly. "Ever since I got here, everybody's been jumping all over me." He held up his hands in partial surrender and then countered. "Maybe I deserve most of that. But I've kept my cool pretty well. I've bitten my tongue a few times, but I've had a right to be a little bent out of shape. Somebody could have called me right after the accident, and I could have canceled my trip and been here for the funeral."

"Look," Walter said pointedly, "for your information, notifying you wasn't exactly high on our priority list right after the accident. It wasn't like you'd shown a lot of interest in Allyson. We called you before the funeral, when we got around to it. It's too bad you were away from home at the time."

"Look, I'm just saying that I've been blamed for not being here for Allyson's funeral. But that wasn't my fault."

"You should have been here a lot of other times too. But you weren't. Those times were your fault."

Porter took a deep breath and ran his open hand over his mouth. Then, dropping his hand to his side, he started again, this time his voice lower and his emotions more controlled. "Since I got here, everybody's been telling me that they don't understand why I did this or that or why I don't do this or the other. Everybody blames me for not being more involved in Alma's life. Well, now I'm trying to get more involved. I'm trying to take him with me, for good. But I get criticized for doing that and told I'm doing it all wrong. Well, I can't go back and change the past." He shrugged, and his shoulders sagged slightly. "Believe me, I'd change a whole lot of things if I could, but changing the past doesn't happen to be one of my options."

He held out the $250 again. "Will you help me get the truck to Eagar? Or do I need to find somebody else?"

Walter studied his ex-brother-in-law before finally answering. "All right, I'll get the truck to Eagar. Tomorrow." He stared down at the money. "Keep your money."

"Take the money, or I get somebody else," Porter said evenly.

"I'm doing this for Alma, not for your money."

"Then I'll rent a lousy U-Haul or something. I'm not looking for charity."

Before Walter could respond, Toni, who had witnessed the entire exchange from behind the two men, stepped forward and snatched the three bills from Porter's hand. "Oh, for crying out loud. You're both as stubborn and mule-headed as you can be. We'll take the money," she said to Porter, "and Walter will haul the truck to Arizona." She shook her head while continuing to stare at Porter. "But," she added firmly, "the money isn't the reason Walter is taking the truck to Eagar. I'm only taking your money because you're so pigheaded."

Porter gritted his teeth and turned to the door. "I can't wait to see this town in my rearview mirror," he muttered.

5

The next morning when Porter pulled into the Henries' yard, the truck was already loaded and chained down on the trailer, and the trailer was hitched to Walter's diesel truck. Walter, Toni, and their four children were gathered on the front lawn around Alma, telling him good-bye.

Porter took his time getting out of the Mercedes, and no one spoke when he approached. All of them kept their gazes down, seemingly embarrassed or annoyed by his arrival. En masse they moved to the diesel.

"Looks like everything's ready," Porter remarked, surveying the truck and trailer. Turning to Alma, he inquired casually, "Do you need help bringing your things out?"

"Everything's loaded. We were just waiting for you." He jabbed a thumb at the trailer. "I'll ride with the truck." He pulled open the diesel's door and stood by the cab.

Porter hesitated but recovered quickly and tossed his car keys to Walter, who scrambled to catch them. "I guess you're driving the Mercedes," he announced. "I'll drive the diesel with Alma."

Walter was about to protest, but Toni touched his arm. "All right," he conceded, swallowing his objections, "you lead, I'll follow."

There were several quiet good-byes before Alma finally climbed into the truck next to Porter. Then Porter started the engine, put the truck in gear, and started moving slowly toward the highway. Alma waved to Russell, Toni, and the other kids while Porter kept his hands on the steering wheel and his eyes straight ahead.

"I'd like to stop at the cemetery," Alma spoke up after less than a mile. "It's on the other side of town."

The cemetery was half a mile off the main highway. A straight, paved road led to its open gates. Porter pointed the diesel down the narrow road while Walter pulled off the highway and waited for them.

"Where's the gravesite?" Porter asked delicately as he drove over the cattle guard at the cemetery entrance.

Alma pointed to the far side of the cemetery, where the neatly arranged headstones were surrounded by grass, trees, and shrubbery. "It's in the far corner," he explained. "Leave the truck here. I'll walk. You can turn the truck and trailer around while I'm gone."

"I've never been to your mom's grave. Do you mind if I walk over?"

Looking across the field of headstones, Alma answered, "I planned to go alone."

Porter nodded and looked away. "Take your time," he offered, smarting from his son's unmistakable rejection.

Alma stayed at his mother's grave for most of twenty minutes. When he returned to the truck, his eyes were red and swollen, but he tried to hide that fact by keeping his head down and staring out the window as soon as he climbed into the truck.

For the first ten minutes the only sound came from the deep growl of the diesel engine as the truck pushed its way down the highway. Porter hoped Alma would say something, but he instinctively knew that if there was going to be a conversation, he'd have to initiate it.

"Calvin said you were quite the athlete," he finally ventured, trying to sound as casual as he could as he chose what he thought was a neutral topic. Staring straight ahead, he held the steering wheel with his right hand and rested his left arm on the sill of the open window.

There was no response from Alma.

"He said you run a mean one hundred meters. He thinks you could qualify for state this next spring."

Alma continued to stare silently out the window. A couple more miles went by.

"I understand you're a good student. The last I spoke to your mom, you had straight A's."

The silence continued.

"Walter said you were a mighty fine worker."

No response.

"I think you'll like Eagar. They've got a good school. I figure you won't have any trouble being a varsity starter on their football team. You'll catch on fine. The school needs a good running back."

Still no answer. The minutes and the miles slipped by monotonously.

"In some ways Eagar is like Panguitch—small town, everybody knows you, a little backward, definitely out of the way. There are a lot of good kids there. In fact, I'm pretty sure there are a few cute girls about your age in my . . . *our* neighborhood."

Alma slumped down in his seat and leaned his head back but kept his eyes riveted to the passing scenery.

Less than an hour into their nine-hour trip, Porter wondered how long he could keep fishing for conversation and coming up empty. "You know, we've got quite a ride ahead of us. Talking helps pass the time."

"So does sleeping," Alma mumbled, closing his eyes.

Porter nodded and stared at the endless strip of asphalt ahead of him. "I figured this trip would give us a chance to catch up on a few things."

Alma's only reaction was a low grunt. Porter couldn't tell if that was a response or just a simple grunt without significance. He thought wryly that he needed to learn what each of his son's grunts meant or they'd never be able to communicate at all.

"I'd like to find out more about you." He waited for a reply, but none came. "So," he sighed, "do you want to talk or do you prefer to sleep?" Again there was no response. "Surely you can at least answer my question," Porter pressed, feeling irritated but being careful to keep his tone good-natured.

"I'm still thinking," Alma replied.

"Oh, so you just need some think time before you say anything," Porter said, attempting some subtle humor. "You're still thinking about my first question, the one I asked as we were leaving Panguitch." He chuckled and heaved a sigh. "Do you think you'll have a response to that first question before we reach Page? Or do you need a whole lot of think time?"

Alma didn't reply, and Porter abandoned all attempts at more conversation. Ten minutes later, as they were driving through Kanab, a small town on the Utah/Arizona border, Porter heard the slow, heavy breathing of slumber and looked over at his son. Alma had stuffed a sweatshirt between his head and the door and was sleeping soundly. "Maybe I should have just driven the Mercedes," he muttered to himself. "At least that way one of us would have been happy."

An hour and a half later they pulled into Page, Arizona. Porter glanced at the fuel gauge. The truck still registered more than half a tank, but Porter wanted an excuse to stop. On the far edge of Page, he spotted a convenience store with half a dozen fuel pumps in front, one of them diesel. Porter turned off the highway and pulled up beside the diesel pump. Alma stirred, opened his eyes, and slowly sat up, stretching.

"Do we need to fill up already?" Alma questioned, glancing around. "We had a full tank when we left Panguitch."

"I'll top it off. Plus, I need to stretch my legs and back. Hey, I'll buy you a soda or a fruit drink. If you want something to eat—"

"I've got money," Alma answered before Porter could finish. For a moment he stretched next to the truck, and then he ambled back to where Walter had parked the Mercedes, and the two of them strolled toward the convenience store. Porter couldn't pick up any of their conversation, but he could tell that both of them were laughing and talking freely. He turned away, envying the ease with which Walter interacted with his son.

Porter leaned against the truck and watched the diesel pump as the numbers rolled past, calculating the gallons as well as the price of the fuel. When the pump shut off automatically, he continued leaning against the truck and stared vacantly at the pump for a few minutes. Lethargically, he hung up the hose, replaced the fuel cap, pocketed his credit card receipt, and returned to the driver's seat. He had anticipated entering the convenience store to get something to eat and drink and perhaps to buy something to help thaw things between Alma and him. But those hopes had quickly dissipated as he had watched Alma and Walter enter the store together. It was clear that he was the odd man out, and the possibility of improved relations during the remainder of the trip didn't seem promising. He even wondered if Alma would choose to ride in the Mercedes with Walter. Closing his eyes and slumping down in his seat with his head leaning back on the truck's headrest, he considered the possibilities before him, finally concluding that if Alma chose to ride with Walter, then he would drive the truck alone. He saw no point in fighting a seemingly losing battle all the way to Eagar.

The passenger door opened, but Porter remained where he was with his eyes closed. He heard and felt Alma slide onto the seat without speaking. The door slammed closed. Porter heard the sudden hiss of a soda pop bottle opening and then the low gulp as Alma swallowed. Just before Porter opened his eyes and sat up so he could turn on the engine, Alma spoke.

"I bought you a root beer."

Surprised, Porter opened his eyes and glanced over at his son, who was holding out a cold bottle of root beer. Slowly, Porter pushed himself up straight, studied the proffered bottle, and then glanced at Alma, who stared straight ahead while extending the soda to his father.

"Thanks," Porter replied, still shaking off his surprise. "I'm always partial to a cold root beer on a hot summer day." He took the bottle, opened it, took a quick sip, and then looked over at what Alma was drinking—root beer. "I see you've acquired my same habit. Did your mom teach you that?" he inquired, trying to joke.

Alma shook his head. "Actually, you're the one who got me hooked on it. That's all we ever used to buy."

"Oh," Porter mumbled, taking another quick sip, wishing he had remembered that particular detail. "I remember that now."

For a moment Porter thought that perhaps the chilly silence between them was finally broken, but as soon as Porter pulled onto the highway, the conversation died away. Porter made a couple of weak attempts to get it going again, but it was a losing proposition. Alma refused to take the conversational bait, and they rode down the highway watching the scenery but not exchanging any words.

They drove in silence for most of an hour. Then Alma shocked Porter with an unexpected bombshell: "Are you a member of the Church now?" The question was asked casually, like an inquiry into the weather, but Porter suspected that it was loaded with an entire field of ramifications. He was certain that Alma had ruminated on that question long before finally posing it.

Porter gripped the wheel and took a moment before answering. "Yes, I'm a member." He shifted uneasily in his seat.

"Do you go to church?"

"Yeah."

"Regularly?"

"Every Sunday." He tried to laugh, but it was a failed attempt.

"When did you get rebaptized?"

There was a prolonged pause.

Finally Alma remarked indifferently, "I guess you don't have to answer that if you don't want to." With his arm out the window, he drummed his fingers on the side of the truck. "You said you wanted to talk, though. You know, get to know each other better."

"What made you think I needed to be rebaptized?"

"There's a lot I don't know about you. But I know that."

"I'm glad your mom made sure you got that particular juicy detail," Porter responded, unable to keep his words from sounding like a disgruntled grumble.

"Mom didn't tell me. There are others who know what happened," Alma said pointedly.

Porter continued to fidget. "I guess I was just hoping . . ." He cleared his throat and tugged on his right ear lobe. "Well, I would have preferred that you didn't know that part of my past."

"That you got rebaptized or that you needed it in the first place?"

"Look, Alma, I'm not happy about a lot of things in my past. I wish there were a little switch in my brain I could flip that would black it all out."

"So you've got your life all together now?" There was definite doubt in his tone.

"Do we ever get our lives all together?"

Alma pondered a moment and then remarked casually. "You look different now." Porter didn't comment or question, so Alma pushed on. "You used to have that funky goatee, and your hair was longer—at least a lot longer than it is now."

Porter glanced over at him and smiled. "You make me sound like a crazy rock star. I did have a goatee—trimmed and professional looking—but I don't remember my hair being terribly long."

Alma shrugged. "It was hanging over your collar and over your ears."

"Well, I guess I wanted a more professional look," Porter joked. "Actually, this is how I used to have my hair cut when I was your age."

Alma nodded. "Yeah, I've seen some of your old pictures." He cleared his throat and posed another question. "How long have you been going to church? I know there was a time when you weren't exactly active."

"There was a time when I wasn't exactly a lot of things. I always took you to church when you visited."

"Yeah, but was that for my benefit or yours?"

Porter wanted to insist on a change in the topic of conversation, but he intuitively knew that if he pressed for a change, there would be no conversation at all. He also reasoned that sooner or later he would need to discuss some of his past with Alma, although this wasn't his preferred time. "I never stopped going to church completely." He reconsidered that explanation and tried to clarify. "Well, I guess I did there for a little while, after being . . ." He swallowed and cleared his throat. "After being excommunicated," he added softly. "But about three years ago I started going back to church. I mean, going back regularly, never missing. I'd just moved to a small ward in Durango, Colorado. Some good people helped me. About a year later I was rebaptized."

"So you're back to normal? As far as the Church is concerned, I mean."

Porter swallowed, trying not to recall all of the bad memories. "Pretty much."

"With all those good people in Durango, why'd you move to Eagar?"

Porter took a long time to answer the question. "I guess I wanted a fresh start."

"So nobody in Eagar knows about your past?"

Porter breathed deeply, finding it more and more difficult to answer Alma's hardball questions. "The bishop does. I've been completely open with him."

"But if he's like most bishops, he probably hasn't published your personal information in the ward bulletin, so it's a pretty safe bet to say nobody else in Eagar knows much about your past. Unless you've told them, which is doubtful."

"Generally I don't make my past indiscretions a topic of conversation," Porter remarked dryly. "Of course, I don't hang around with a lot of people in Eagar. I'm pretty wrapped up in my work, so I keep to myself a lot." He smiled plaintively. "I guess I've turned into a bit of a recluse. That would shock a lot of people," he muttered. "But it's true. And I'm fine with that at this stage in my life. I've gotten so I like my privacy."

"You were married a few times. Where are those other women now?"

Porter cleared his throat. "I only married one other woman besides your mom—Kerri Mead. Later I was engaged to Frankie Phillips. You met her once. We ended up breaking things off. The last I heard, which was about three years ago, Kerri was in Nevada and Frankie had just moved to southern New Mexico. I haven't felt a need to stay in touch."

"Do you date much?"

"This is starting to sound a whole lot like a bishop's interview," Porter said wryly.

"Just getting to know you," Alma retorted in a flat tone. "After all, talking makes the time pass quicker." A faint smile tugged at the corners of his mouth. "We can always sleep. At least I can. You'd better keep your eyes on the road."

Porter adjusted the rearview mirror and reluctantly replied, "Right after breaking things off with Frankie Phillips, I went into a dating slump." He smiled ruefully. "Some people probably figure I'm still in that slump."

"So you were a pretty wild dating machine before then?"

Porter stared somberly ahead. After a few seconds, Alma offered a half-hearted apology. "Sorry. You were telling me about your dating days."

"After Frankie, I took a hard look at myself and wasn't exactly impressed." Porter glanced over at Alma, who was staring out the side window. "Do you care about the answers to these questions, or are you just interested in making me squirm?" he asked pointedly.

Alma considered the question. "I want to know," he replied honestly. Then, with a wry grin, he added under his breath, "But I like to see you squirm, too."

Porter cleared his throat loudly. "I've dated a little bit during the past few months," he resumed. "It's not exactly easy for a thirty-eight-year-old guy to snag a date, though. The women who are close to my age have been married before and have a bunch of kids, and the women who haven't been married are either really young or really ugly—or both." He chuckled at his own joke.

Alma remained solemn. "You've been married before—twice—and you've got a kid. How are you different from them?"

Porter wondered if silence was preferable to Alma's sharp verbal barbs.

"So there's nobody in Eagar that you're seeing? Are you afraid somebody there will find out about your past?"

Porter's cheeks colored. "Alma, I don't care what people in Eager think about me. I am what I am. I did what I did. My past is what it is. I can't change it. That doesn't mean I like everything that's in my past, but I don't go around hiding it under the nearest rock. I don't know what people in Eagar know about me. Some of them would be scandalized if they knew very much."

Alma shrugged as though satisfied with the answer. "I'm glad there's no wife or girlfriend back in Eagar. I always felt sorry for kids who had stepmoms. I'm glad you didn't do that to me."

"There's no stepmom."

"You said you've dated a little bit in Eagar. With lots of women or just one?"

"I've dated more than one."

Alma heaved a sigh. "You know, trying to get a straight answer out of you is like trying to squeeze water out of a rock."

"There is a girl in Eagar that I've dated recently," Porter conceded. "It's nothing terribly serious. Not yet." His cheeks colored slightly, but Alma didn't appear to notice. "I mean, we're not talking about marriage or anything like that. We've become pretty good friends, though. We're in the same ward. We go to church together, that sort of thing."

"Eagar must be a wild place," Alma chuckled. "A hot date is going to church." He shook his head and added, "And I thought Panguitch was dead." He took in a long breath of air. "So how serious are things with this *one* woman?"

"I think you'd like her, as a person, as a friend." Porter gnawed momentarily on his lower lip and then went on. "Her name's Darbie. Darbie Montgomery."

"Has she been married before? Does she have a bunch of kids?"

Porter shook his head.

"So she's either really young and pretty or she's pretty old and ugly."

"You can decide that for yourself." Porter shifted in his seat. "She's single, twenty-eight, teaches English at the high school, jogs, hikes, bikes. She's not drop-dead gorgeous, but she's nice looking and just an all-around good person."

"What's the catch?"

"The catch?" Porter was genuinely perplexed.

Alma shrugged. "If she's so wonderful, why's she twenty-eight and single and hibernating in Eagar?"

"She's only been in Eagar for a year. Her aunt owned a second home there, just down the street from me. Darbie had been teaching school in Salt Lake. For a long time she was engaged to a guy, but things didn't work out, so she wanted to try something new. Round Valley High School had an English opening, and Darbie's aunt had a house that was available, so Darbie moved to Eagar for a year. She liked her first year and has decided to stay on for another one."

"So you both moved to Eagar because you were on the run?"

"What do you mean, on the run?" Porter questioned, stung by the accusation.

"You were both trying to get away from your pasts."

Porter was about to protest, but Alma went on.

"Are you going to introduce her to me?"

"When the time's right. I'm sure you'll meet her." He cleared his throat. "She's not there right now. She won't be for two or three more weeks. Actually, I haven't seen a lot of her during the past month. Early in May I took an eleven-day business trip. When I got back, she was pretty tied up with the end of school—tests, papers to grade, report cards, dances, and parties. So church was about the only time I saw her. She was a chaperone on the high school senior trip for a few days, and then she left for Salt Lake as soon as school was out. She plans to spend three or four weeks with her mother before returning to Eagar."

There was a prolonged silence, and then Alma spoke again. "I think I understand about you and Mom. I don't agree with any of it, but I know why you decided to take off." He paused, looking a bit embarrassed to go on. "What about me?" he finally managed. "You walked away from me too." He cleared his throat and stared at the dashboard. "Did you ever wonder about me? Besides the birthday and Christmas cards and the few visits."

Porter gripped the steering wheel. "Sure I did, but I didn't know what to do about it. I didn't want you to be one of those kids that's bounced around from one parent to the other. And Allyson was the better parent. I knew that. I think you do too."

"So it was just convenient to walk away from me too. That way I wouldn't get bounced around, and you wouldn't have to do the bouncing. Is that it?"

"I thought about you, Alma, I really did," Porter explained painfully, but even as he struggled to explain, he knew his explanation was going to ring lame at best.

"Yeah, I got the birthday cards. And the money. The money was always nice," Alma intoned sarcastically. "I even wrote you a few thank-you notes. Of course, you could probably tell that most of those were written while Mom threatened me."

"They were a little short. Especially after you got older."

"Do you blame me?"

Porter shook his head. "Not really. I don't know that I expected much."

"Did you ever wonder what I was doing?" He shrugged. "Sports, school, work?"

"Not as much as I should have. I got involved in work and other things." It pained Porter to admit all of this to his son. "There is no question that I lost my focus."

Alma was quiet for a moment, and then he remarked, "When I was little I used to think you really did want to come get me." He smiled wanly. "I concocted some pretty good excuses for you. When I was younger, it was easy to blame Mom. After all, she was there, the one making all the rules." He swallowed. "But you didn't have any good excuses, did you?"

"Not good ones," Porter conceded softly.

Alma nodded and smiled bitterly. "Yeah, I figured that out three or four years ago." He coughed and pushed on. "So why didn't you just leave me with Uncle Walter? Why'd you come for me after all those years of work and other important distractions? Did you get tired of sending birthday cards?" he questioned sardonically. "Postage was getting expensive? You figured I'd want bigger checks for my birthday?"

"I got tired of not being a dad." Porter chewed on his lower lip. "Alma, sometimes you start down a road, and after you've traveled a little while, you realize you're on the wrong road. What's strange, though, is that even after you realize it's the wrong road and it's not taking you where you want to go, you still stay on that road." He shook his head. "Men especially have a tough time asking directions, and even when they've got the right directions, they stay on the wrong road. Maybe they figure if they stay on that wrong road long enough, it will magically turn into the right one or will intersect with the right one. I don't know what it is. I was on that road for a long time, and for a long time I refused to admit that it was the wrong road. But even after I knew it was the wrong road, I still stayed on it. Don't ask me why, because I don't have a clue. Maybe it's a guy thing. Guys are just naturally a little stupid."

They were quiet again, and then Alma asked, "Did you ever think that the two of you might have . . . well, you know, eventually gotten back . . ." He coughed rather than finish the question, but Porter knew the question even without Alma verbalizing it.

"I've wondered that myself," he answered hoarsely. He wet his lips. "I ran into your mom last January. I don't know if you knew that."

Alma looked over at Porter, surprise evident in his eyes.

Porter continued. "She was in Salt Lake at some school in-service or training. I was there on business. We just happened to see each other on the street. We talked, probably for fifteen or twenty minutes. I wanted to ask her to lunch." He shook his head. "But I was afraid she'd turn me down, so I didn't." He pressed his lips together, remembering. "The next day I wandered up and down the street, hoping I'd run into her again. I didn't, and I didn't know where she was staying. I've wondered since if things would have been different had I asked your mom to lunch that day. I wish I could say yes. I'd like to think that I would have swallowed my pride and patched things up. But I guess we'll never know."

"Would Mom have given you a chance, more than just lunch together?"

Porter thought long and hard on the question. "I don't even know if she would have had lunch with me. I certainly wouldn't have blamed her for telling me to take a hike. I did a lot of dumb things, Alma, a lot of things I'm ashamed of. She would have had a lot to forgive."

"I know that when you walked out on her you—"

Porter held up his hand, cutting him off with a brusque retort. "I won't dredge up the past, Alma." He shook his head, looking away. "It serves no purpose for you or me to go there. That's not a part of me anymore. Maybe it was once, but not now. Never again!"

For the rest of the way to Flagstaff, Alma was quiet, which Porter found to be a welcome change after his pointed grilling. In Flagstaff, they grabbed some hamburgers with Walter before taking I-40 east. Once they were back on the road, Alma dozed, but this time Porter didn't disturb his son's slumber; in fact, he hoped Alma would stay asleep until they reached Eagar. Fortunately for Porter, he did.

"There it is," Porter announced when he saw the twin communities of Springerville and Eagar lying in the afternoon sun in a bowl-shaped valley surrounded by low, rolling hills covered with shaggy junipers and ponderosa pine. Eagar was quaintly laid out with straight, wide streets lined with tall trees. "What do you think?"

"What's the big dome thing down there?" Alma asked curiously.

"Round Valley High School has its own domed football field."

"You mean like the whole thing's inside?"

"Amazing, isn't it?" Porter smiled. "They're very serious about their football. If you play for the Elks, that's where you'll be playing, just like in the pros. The 2010 Super Bowl is going to be played in that dome." When Alma glanced over at him dubiously, Porter grinned and shook his head. "Just kidding."

Porter drove straight to his house, which was on the far side of town, nestled at the foot of the juniper-covered hills. The house was on School Bus Road, just east of a large meadow surrounded by a barbed-wire fence that was woven with wild rosebushes and honey-suckle vines. On the opposite side of the meadow was a stand of massive poplar and silver poplar trees with a narrow ditch running through them. Under the trees was a tangle of bushes, vines, and grass.

The area just off School Bus Road was residential but still rural, with houses scattered among the trees, bushes, and other vegetation. There were meadows, corrals, large gardens, and huge lots, giving a sense of wide-open, country freedom.

"It's a whole lot like Panguitch," Alma observed. "Was that on purpose?"

Porter looked around, wondering that himself for the first time. "I guess it is a lot like Panguitch. Pretty, isn't it? I fell in love with this place," he declared as they pulled up in front of his house, "when I first spotted the big For Sale sign out front."

Porter's home was less than five years old, a tri-level set back next to a stand of aspens, Douglas firs, and ponderosa pines. There was a well-trimmed yard in front. On the west side of the house and set back a hundred feet or so from the street was a shed that was much older than the house itself.

Within a few minutes of arriving, they had the truck unloaded from the trailer and Alma's things piled on Porter's front lawn. Then the three men busied themselves checking the truck, making sure all the chains and tethers were back on the trailer, and surveying Alma's belongings to make sure everything was accounted for, including his heavy tool chest. When they had finished, the three of them stood awkwardly on the lawn.

"Come in and rest up," Porter invited Walter.

Walter took a deep breath and exhaled slowly, shaking his head. "I'll be heading back."

"I figured you'd stay the night," Porter replied. "I've got plenty of space. You can have your own room."

Walter shook his head. "I can't afford to miss another day of work."

Porter soon found himself a silent observer as his son and former brother-in-law said good-bye to each other. The two stood next to the truck with their hands in their pockets, making one final inspection, careful to look anywhere but at each other.

Finally Walter kicked at the ground with the toe of his boot and sucked in a deep breath. "Well, I better hit the road." He held out his hand. "You take care of yourself."

Alma slowly accepted the proffered hand and squeezed it firmly, and then both he and Walter, as though on cue, pulled in for a tight bear hug. When they finally released one another and took a short step backward, they dabbed at their eyes with their fingers and the backs of their hands.

"I'll miss you, Alma. Home won't be the same without you there."

Alma nodded his acknowledgment, his chin quivering ever so slightly, while he kept his gaze on the ground. He swallowed hard, dug his hands into his pockets, and shook his head. "I'll miss you too, Uncle Walter," he managed to say, his voice breaking.

Walter put his hand on his nephew's shoulder. "This is your home now, but you remember, our place is also home. We're family. Don't you forget that."

As Porter watched the scene before him, he was envious—envious of the days, weeks, and months that Walter had had with Alma, envious of the love and admiration that had obviously developed between them, and envious of the emotions that their parting created within each of them. As he stood on his front walk, he wondered how Alma would respond if circumstances were reversed—if they were back in Panguitch and he was telling Alma good-bye and returning to Eagar. It pained him because he knew there would be no hugs, no tears, no expression of disappointment.

For several minutes after Walter pulled away in his diesel, Alma and Porter stood on the front walk, staring down the street where he had disappeared. "Well," Porter finally ventured, "I'll show you inside."

For a moment Alma didn't move, and then slowly, almost lethargically, he picked up his bags, staggered into Porter's house, and stopped just inside the door. Porter watched as he took in the home's interior. Although Porter was a bachelor, he wasn't a slob. He liked things clean and orderly. And he knew that his home was much roomier and more modern than the two-bedroom trailer Alma and his mother had shared. Their furniture had always been clean, but it was old and worn. Porter's was new and hardly used, and suddenly he felt self-conscious about it.

"Well, this is it," he remarked casually as Alma continued to look around with his brows knit together. "It's no Taj Mahal, but it will do in a pinch. Feel free to go where you want, do what you want. This is your place. Get comfortable. You can take a bedroom upstairs—" he pointed to a series of stairs going up to the third level—"or take one in the basement." He pointed to another set of steps that descended to a large family room. "There's a door just around the corner that opens on some more stairs. There are a couple of bedrooms and a bathroom down there. What's your preference?"

"Where's your room?" Alma inquired.

Porter pointed up the stairs. "I stay in the master bedroom. My office is across the hall in the room looking out over the back lawn."

"I'll take one of the rooms downstairs."

Porter nodded and shrugged. "I'll put a desk and chair in there for you. If you need another dresser, I can get you one. The bed's new. The family room is right there. There's not much in it now. I thought I'd get a pool table or a ping-pong table. Do you like pool or ping-pong?"

"I didn't have much time for games. Besides, it's a little tough setting up a pool table in a two-bedroom trailer."

"There's a big-screen TV in the family room. And I've got a little nineteen-inch TV in storage. If you'd like, I'll put that in your bedroom."

Alma shook his head. "I'm not a big TV fan. Didn't have time."

Porter pulled the corners of his mouth down in a frown and shrugged. He looked around and then pointed to his right. "The kitchen's right through there. If something's not there that you want, we'll get it. I'm not much of a shopper, so we might need a few things." He smiled sheepishly. "I eat out a lot."

"We hardly ever ate out, but I shopped a lot for Mom. She didn't have time."

"Great. You'll be our designated shopper. I'll put the debit card and PIN number in the cupboard. Whenever you want something, buy it. Do you cook?"

"A few things."

"All right, you can be the designated chef." Porter looked around. "I tend to be a bit of an organizational freak," he mentioned apologetically. "I like things clean and in their place. Some might think I'm a bit fanatical." He shrugged. "I don't care if you squeeze the toothpaste tube from the middle, but if you squirt toothpaste on the counter, I'd appreciate it if you'd clean it up. When you fix something to eat, clean up after yourself, because I don't hire a maid here. You know, little things like that. I hate living in a dump. I guess you can leave your room the way you want it, but if it's trashed, I'd appreciate it if you'd at least keep your door closed so I don't have to look at your mess. Messes tend to make me irritable." He shrugged again. "That's just one of my quirks."

"I'm pretty neat myself," Alma retorted dryly. "I don't know if I'm a freak, but I squeeze the toothpaste from the bottom of the tube, and the only place I squirt it is on my toothbrush. My aim's pretty good. I'll probably leave my bedroom door closed, but not because my room's trashed. I clean up after myself. That's something Mom taught me."

6

When Porter awoke the next morning, Alma was already gone. Porter had heard him leave around five thirty. An hour and a half later, Porter rolled out of bed and spent thirty minutes on his stationary bike and another fifteen minutes lifting weights. He showered and shaved and then wandered down to the kitchen for a light breakfast. He was just closing the refrigerator when the front door opened and Alma entered, wearing a sweaty T-shirt, basketball shorts, and running shoes. He was panting, and his brow and the sides of his face glistened with beads of perspiration.

"What'd you do, run a marathon?" Porter questioned curiously.

Alma brushed his forearm across his brow. "Just checked out the town."

"You didn't have to run. You could have taken the car."

Alma shook his head. "I wanted the exercise."

"How much of the town did you see?"

Alma smiled smugly. "It's not a very big town. I think I saw all of it."

Porter held up a chocolate protein drink. "Breakfast?"

"I'm hungry enough to eat." He studied the protein drink and shook his head. "But I prefer to chew my breakfast, not gulp it from a can."

Porter opened the cupboard, revealing several different cold cereals, a variety of flavored instant oatmeal packets, three boxes of granola bars, and a dozen cans of different flavored protein drinks. "There's juice, milk, and fruit in the fridge, along with a few yogurts," he added. "There might be bread or bagels in the drawer."

Without another word, Alma poured himself a bowl of cereal and grabbed a yogurt and an apple. The two sat at the table, eating in silence. After his conversational experience the day before, Porter was hesitant to say much, fearing it'd turn uncomfortably personal.

"Are you going to work today?" Alma asked after a while.

"I don't have to go far. Just across the hall. I do my work here at home."

Alma glanced at the clock on the wall. It was almost nine. "Are you a nine-to-five kind of guy?"

Porter smiled. "I'm whatever kind of guy I want to be. Usually I don't start working until a little after nine. Some days I knock off at two or three in the afternoon. Other days, depending on what I have going, I might work till midnight. That's one of the benefits of working for yourself."

Alma looked around. "You must make pretty good money."

"I don't go to bed hungry, and most of what I've got is paid for—except the house."

Alma nodded. "We didn't go to bed hungry, and most of what we had was paid for too. There just wasn't much of it. Besides, it wouldn't have fit in our little trailer."

Porter let the remark pass without comment.

* * *

In the evening, they shopped at the local Bashas' supermarket. At first, Alma was reluctant to get anything, making remarks about his mother and him not being able to afford this or that. "Look," Porter finally countered in exasperation, "maybe you couldn't get some of these things before, but we can afford them now. You don't have to feel guilty. If you want something, grab it." After that, Alma loaded the shopping cart to overflowing, tacitly testing Porter to see if there were any limitations. There didn't seem to be any.

For the next five days Porter and Alma lived in the same house but seemed engrossed in their individual activities and interests without very much interaction. Porter immersed himself in his work, staying in his office until late and trying to catch up on some of the sales he had neglected while in Panguitch. Alma spent time in his room, arranging it to his liking. He wandered around the town, hiked the hills closest to the house, watched a little TV, listened to music, and tinkered on the truck. They attended church together Sunday morning, but they spent the rest of the day apart.

It wasn't long before Alma became rather bored, especially in the afternoons, and it was then that he longed for the old life in Panguitch that was filled with farm work from early morning until evening. He didn't know anyone in Eagar, and he wasn't interested in establishing any friendships just yet.

Wednesday evening, almost a week after arriving in Eagar, Alma was making himself a dinner of fried potatoes mixed with scrambled eggs, an old favorite of his, when there was a series of gentle taps on the front door. Snatching a dishcloth to wipe his hands, he threw open the door.

A woman in her late twenties stood on the front step. She was six inches shorter than Alma and very slender. Her short, brown hair barely reached her earlobes. She was pretty, with a wide, infectious smile that seemed to fill her whole face. In one hand she carried a small gray tool case, the kind one might buy at a discount store. "Oh . . . I didn't . . ." she stammered. "I wasn't expecting . . ."

"Hi, I'm Alma," Alma said, hurriedly wiping his hands on the dishcloth before holding his right hand out to her. "I'm staying with Porter for a while," he explained.

The woman flashed her disarming smile and shook Alma's hand. "Nice to meet you, Alma," she said. "Is Porter around?"

Alma's brow furrowed as he glanced up and down the road. "I'm not sure where he is," he answered slowly. "He said something about going out for a walk, but he didn't say where." Alma looked back at the woman. Her dark, sparkling eyes and her warm, engaging personality put him at ease. "You can wait for him." He blushed apologetically and grinned. "I don't know how long you'd have to wait, though."

She hefted the tool case in front of her. "I was just returning his tools."

Alma's jaw dropped as he scratched his head in amusement. "I didn't know he even owned a screwdriver, much less a whole tool case—even a cheap one. Are you sure you borrowed tools from Porter Huggins?"

The woman let the tool case drop to her side. "I took them a couple of weeks ago to fix a dresser drawer. Then I left town."

Alma grinned. "I doubt he missed them. He sure hasn't asked for them. He's probably hoping you'll keep them."

The woman laughed. "Well, to be perfectly honest, I don't think he had ever used these particular tools. They were still in the original package, covered with cellophane wrap. You can tell him that I appreciated his generosity." Before Alma could take the tool case, the woman raised her eyebrows slightly and added, "Have we met?"

Alma smiled sheepishly. "Not unless you've been to Panguitch, Utah."

She smiled. "I know where it is. Does that count?"

"It counts for something." He shook the dishcloth out and folded it into a neat square. "Most people have never heard of Panguitch. What made you find out about it?" He chuckled and lifted the tool case from her grasp.

"I had a roommate who had an uncle in Panguitch. We were going to go horseback riding there." She shook her head. "But her car engine blew up, so we never went." She pointed to the tool case and grinned. "If Porter wants any pointers on how to use those, tell him Darbie will give him some lessons."

"Darbie?" Alma asked, taken aback. "Darbie Montgomery?"

"How did you know my name? Are you sure we haven't met?" She cocked her head to one side and scrutinized Alma, who blushed a bright red.

"Porter mentioned you. Oh," he moaned, setting the tool case just inside the door, snapping his fingers and backing up, "I left the potatoes on the stove. Come in." He disappeared, leaving Darbie on the front step. She looked up and down the road. "Come in," Alma hollered from the kitchen. Gingerly, she stepped through the open front door and crept to the kitchen.

Alma stood in front of the stove, hovering over a pan of sizzling, steaming potatoes as he worked them around the pan with a plastic spatula. "You hungry?" he called over his shoulder when he saw her step into the kitchen and look around. "I always make more than I can eat," he explained. "I was hungry as a horse, so I peeled this huge pile of potatoes." He laughed. "But I won't finish half of them. I'm going to scramble some eggs and mix them in with the potatoes. I put in ham, too. It doesn't look all that hot, but it's pretty good. Especially if you're hungry."

Darbie strolled across the floor and peered down into the frying pan. "I just drove into town, and I am hungry. But what you're fixing sounds like breakfast."

Alma laughed. "I never worry about what time of day it is." He glanced behind him at the table across the room. "Do you mind grabbing the salt and pepper?" She retrieved the two shakers and handed them to Alma, who liberally sprinkled salt and pepper over the potatoes. "It's time for the eggs," he announced.

Darbie spotted a carton of eggs on the counter by the fridge and grabbed them without being asked. "How many?" she inquired helpfully, taking out an egg and getting ready to crack it on the edge of the frying pan.

Alma paused and gave her a sly grin. "Have you decided to accept my dinner invitation?"

Darbie turned the corners of her mouth down into a thoughtful expression and then shrugged. "I don't have anything cooking at home, and my stomach's starting to growl. So yes, I'll be adventuresome and try this concoction." She broke the egg and dumped the contents over the potatoes. "Is it habit-forming?"

Alma laughed. "I'm hooked. Put in six eggs," he instructed.

Darbie laughed too. "Whoa, now. I said I'd try it. I'm not planning to pork out or anything."

"Hey, after you try this, you just might want me to scramble up another batch." While Darbie put the eggs in, Alma stirred the pan with his spatula. "So you're Darbie Montgomery?"

"Is that good or bad?"

Alma shrugged. "I thought you were out of town for another two or three weeks. I didn't expect you to show up packing Porter's tools."

"I'm curious. What did Porter tell you about me?"

Alma smiled and shrugged. "Sometimes it's tough to get a straight answer out of him." He shrugged and kept stirring the eggs and potatoes. "He says he's gone to church with you. I think he's shaken your hand a few times," Alma added with a teasing grin. "At arm's length, of course."

"Of course! Always the epitome of propriety." Darbie laughed and shook her head. "Is that all he told you?"

Alma glanced over at her. "Don't tell me he's your home teacher too." He burst out laughing. "Now that would be serious. And that would also mean you'd probably get home taught more than just once at the end of the month."

She grinned. "He's not my home teacher, but we've done a few things together."

"A few things? More than just church?"

Darbie paused, her eyes narrowing. "Yes," she answered.

"Hey, there are some ham bits in a bowl over on the counter where the eggs were. Do you want to snag those for me? This will be ready in just a second."

Darbie handed the bowl to Alma. "I'll set the table," she offered, stepping to the cupboard and taking out two plates and two tall glasses. After putting the plates and glasses on the table, she searched through the drawers until she found the utensils. Alma turned off the stove and set the frying pan on the table. "I'll get the chocolate milk," he said, wiping his hands on his pants. "You can't eat this without cold chocolate milk."

"What about toast?" Darbie inquired.

"Toast sounds good. There's strawberry jam in the fridge."

A moment later the two were sitting across the table from each other, and Alma began dishing up his potato, egg, and ham mixture. After he dropped a heaping scoop onto Darbie's plate, she held up her hands. "Whoa," she protested, "I was thinking along the lines of a sample, not an entire feast."

He grinned. "Give it a try. You said you were hungry."

Waiting with his forearms on the table and a fork clutched in his right hand, Alma watched Darbie take her first bite and waited for her verdict. She chewed slowly, swallowed, and then nodded slightly. She took another forkful. "You're quite the chef."

For the next couple of minutes, the two of them ate, concentrating on their food rather than conversation. Darbie was the first to speak as she thoughtfully stirred her potatoes and egg with her fork. "So your name's Alma, huh?" she remarked. "That's a good Mormon name. I've always liked the name Alma. It has a unique ring to it."

"That was Mom's idea," Alma answered after he had swallowed. "She always liked the name. In fact, in junior high she wrote in her journal that her first son was going to be named Alma. When she got married and was getting ready to have me, she already knew what she was going to call me."

"So what are you to Porter?" Darbie asked, staring across the table at Alma. "You've got to be related. Younger brother?"

Alma stopped chewing as he stared down at his half-eaten pile of food. A smile pulled at the corners of his mouth, and he began to chew again, although more slowly. Finally he swallowed and looked across the table at his guest. "I'm a relative, alright."

Darbie waited for more details.

"I'm his son."

"Oh," she managed slowly, glancing down at her plate and pushing her food with her fork. She took another bite and looked up, studying the young man across the table as she chewed. "Now I see why you look familiar," she said after swallowing.

Alma pushed his chair back and stood. "Hold on." He left the room and returned within thirty seconds. Dropping onto his chair, he handed Darbie a three-by-five photograph.

Darbie studied it, occasionally looking across the table at Alma and then turning back to the picture in her hand.

"What do you think?" he asked, amused.

"Is this you?" she inquired.

He shook his head and pointed at the picture with his fork. "That's Porter his senior year in high school. People who knew him in Panguitch when he was younger tell me we almost look like twins."

Darbie's brows raised and her mouth dropped open. "Porter's from Panguitch?"

"I guess there are a few things he hasn't told you," Alma mused.

"He told me he'd been married and things didn't work out."

"They didn't work out twice," Alma added casually. "Mom was the first one."

"He didn't say anything about . . . children."

Alma grinned across the table at Darbie.

Darbie divided her attention between the photograph and the young man sitting across the table from her. Then she set the photograph to one side of her plate. "So . . . where have you . . . well, where have you been the last little while?"

Alma's grin widened, and he pointed toward the basement. "He usually keeps me downstairs in one of the closets under lock and key, but I busted out today." He suddenly looked around secretively, pretending someone might be spying on them. "You'll have to lock me up before he gets back," he whispered across the table. "Otherwise he'll get suspicious. He really doesn't like me out in public, complicating his life." At the bewildered look on Darbie's face, Alma burst out laughing, enjoying his joke.

"Do you have any brothers and sisters . . . locked up with you down there?"

Still chuckling, Alma shook his head. "No, I'm the Lone Ranger."

"Any brothers and sisters in Panguitch?"

"I'm an only child." He pointed at her unfinished eggs and potatoes. "You better keep eating. Everything's getting cold."

She returned to her food, and they ate in silence until their plates were clean. Then, setting her fork on her plate, Darbie picked up the photograph again and studied it. "So you're Porter's son," she mused. "He said he was going to tell me more about his past." She raised her brows. "When the time was right," she added, almost as an afterthought.

Alma smiled. "Well, I'm a chunk of Porter's Panguitch past."

Darbie smiled. "If the rest of his past is as nice as you are, then I'll be impressed."

Alma shook his head and became serious. "I don't know that I know a heck of a lot more about his past than you do. We haven't been all that close." He pushed his plate to the side. "Part of that's my fault," he admitted. "There were times when he wanted me to visit him and I really didn't want to. I made sure I had other things going on."

Darbie set her elbows on the table, clasped her hands together, and rested her chin on the backs of her intertwined fingers. "Where's your mother? In Panguitch?"

"That's where she's buried," Alma answered softly. "She was killed in an accident a while back. A month or so ago, actually. That's why I'm here."

"I'm sorry." An awkward silence ensued, then Darbie picked up her plate and held it out. "This stuff really *is* habit-forming. I'll have another little bit."

Alma smiled and took the spatula. "I'll split it with you." He divided the remainder of the potatoes and eggs and put half on Darbie's plate and the other half on his own. "How long have you two been, uh, 'going to church together'?"

"Well, we've been going to church together since I moved here a year ago. We're in the same ward. This past year was my first year in Eagar, just like your Dad."

"How long have you been serious with each other—you know, swapping tools, shaking hands at church, and special things like that?"

Darbie pretended to glower across the table at him, narrowing her eyes and pursing her lips. Her attempts at anger were thwarted by the laughter in her eyes. "Sister Reynolds—an older lady who's my visiting teacher—had been trying to set us up ever since I moved here. She's about as subtle as a major train wreck. A while back, the ward had a special dinner. Porter, being the recluse he is, hadn't planned to go, but that didn't deter intrepid Sister Reynolds, who, unbeknownst to me, sent half the ward to invite Porter. He politely declined each invitation. The evening of the dinner, Sister Reynolds coerced her poor husband into picking Porter up for dinner. Brother Reynolds refused to take no for an answer. I guess he didn't dare face his wife without Porter in tow. And, of course, when Porter reluctantly arrived, Sister Reynolds made certain the two of us sat at the same table. Neither one of us knew that she was finagling the whole thing until she escorted Porter to the place next to mine. By then I was so embarrassed I practically crawled under the table."

"And after that you started sitting next to each other in church," Alma mused.

"Something like that."

"So, do you like him?" Before she could respond, he quickly added, "I mean, do you ever go on real dates with each other? Not just to church. Maybe dinner at Dairy Queen or McDonald's? Are you like his girlfriend?"

Darbie smiled, and her cheeks colored slightly. "I'm a friend. And I am a girl. I don't know if that qualifies as 'girlfriend,' according to your definition."

"That's an evasive answer. You sound like him."

"Would it worry you if I was his girlfriend?"

"I haven't thought too much about him having a girlfriend. But I've thought about having a stepmom." Alma pressed his lips together. "That doesn't exactly appeal to me. It's nothing personal," he quickly clarified. "I just don't want a stepmom."

Darbie smiled. "Well, just so you know, being a stepmom hasn't ever been one of my secret ambitions."

He shook his head. "You don't seem like his type."

"Oh? And what's Porter's type?"

The question caught Alma off guard. He blushed and looked down at the table. "I really don't know, because I don't know him all that well. Maybe it's just an impression I have of him. You're different from that impression."

"So I'm not like your mom?"

He quickly shook his head. "Actually, you're a lot like my mom. Maybe that's why I didn't think you were his type. I can picture Mom borrowing a set of tools and fixing her own dresser. She also liked my potato and egg concoction." He smiled wanly and nodded at the frying pan. "We used to have supper together, kind of like this," he said softly. He cleared his throat without looking at her. "You do remind me a lot of her." He swallowed and added quietly, "I suspect that people around here like you too. Everybody in Panguitch liked Mom." He was silent for a moment and then pressed his lips together and asked, "How well do you know Porter?"

She took in a slow, deep breath. "Apparently not quite as well as I thought." She pondered a moment. "Porter has always been a little withdrawn. Oh, he's opened up more recently, but he seems a bit cautious when it comes to discussing his past."

"You mean about discussing me, the kid he's got stashed in the basement?" Alma teased with a smile.

She returned his smile. "And apparently other things." Before she finished eating her second helping, she set her fork down and leaned back in her chair. "So . . . if you and your mom lived in Panguitch . . ." She bit down on the corner of her bottom lip. "I mean, if . . ." She shook her head. "I guess I shouldn't pry."

"You want to know why they split up?"

Darbie reflected on that and then nodded. "Well, that wasn't exactly what I was going to ask, but yes, I guess I'm curious about that, too."

"Actually, I don't know everything that happened. Mom wouldn't go into a lot of detail, and I was young when it happened. I don't remember much. He got married again, and that lasted a couple of years. He moved out of state, so visiting regularly was pretty tough. He finally ended up here. He'd call every couple of months or so, but what do you talk about when you're both living in different worlds?"

"Now, how could somebody not be close to a great kid like you?"

Alma smiled wanly. "I always wondered about that."

"Well, Alma, thanks for . . ." She hesitated. "Was this breakfast or dinner?" she asked, pretending to be puzzled. "Thanks for whatever it was. I might even be hooked on it. Next time I get a craving, you'll have to fix me some."

He smiled. "Thanks for eating with a stranger." He started gathering the plates.

"Hey, I'll help with the dishes really quick," she offered. "Will you be staying in Eagar long?"

"It looks that way."

"Then I might have you in my English class. In fact, I'll insist that I get you."

He grinned at her. "You don't seem like an English teacher."

"Do I detect a hint of prejudice, Alma Huggins? You expect all English teachers to wear pointy black hats, ride brooms, and use blood-red marking pens for wands?"

Alma smiled awkwardly. "There were three English teachers in Panguitch—Mr. Farnsworth, Mrs. Sevy, and Miss Addison—and you're not like them. But that's good."

"And what does Alma Huggins want to do five or ten years from now?"

"I'd like to be a dentist." He pondered and added, "I also like being a mechanic—getting my hands dirty, grabbing a wrench, and pounding on an engine."

"I know a few dentists like that. When they work, I wonder if they're trying to grind out an engine block instead of my tooth."

Alma looked at her for a moment, then said, "Let me show you something." He tossed the dishtowel onto the countertop and started for the door. "I've got a truck. You probably saw it when you came in."

A few minutes later the two of them were in front of the truck, its hood gaping open while they examined the greasy, black engine inside. "It still needs lots of work, but when I'm finished, this will be a hot item on the road."

"You're ambitious," she remarked.

Before Alma could answer, they spotted Porter strolling up the street. He seemed surprised when he saw Darbie and Alma together.

"Hello, Darbie," he greeted her cautiously. "I wasn't expecting you till the end of next week or later."

"I came back early. To return your tools." She nodded at Alma. "Alma was shocked that you owned a set of tools." She laughed. "Actually, I came back to teach summer school. Tricia Cardwell was supposed to teach this summer session, but she's having an unexpected gallbladder surgery in the morning. Mr. Harris called me yesterday and asked if I'd fill in. So here I am. Lucky for you, because I was able to return your tools." She gave him a thumbs-up sign. "And I've been introduced to that past you said you had." She smiled in a teasing fashion and patted Alma on the shoulder. "He even fixed me dinner and showed me his truck. Now that you have your tools back, you'll be able to help him out."

Porter's cheeks colored. "The truck is Alma's project."

"I suspect that Alma can teach you a few things about fixing cars and trucks." She turned to Alma and held out her hand, and he shook it. "Thanks for dinner, Alma. It's been great talking to you. And I'll see if the office can put you on one of my class rolls." She waved at Porter and started down the road.

"Aren't you going to stay for a while?" Porter called after her.

"I've stayed for a long while," she called over her shoulder. "You just weren't here. But Alma was a great host." She turned and faced him.

"He told me tons of interesting stuff." She frowned. "A few things I thought you probably should have told me." She shook her head, looked at Alma, and remarked, "It really was nice meeting you, Alma." Without saying anything else to Porter, she started for the street.

Porter watched Darbie walk briskly down the street toward her home until she turned the corner and headed up Crosby Street, and then he confronted Alma. "What did you two talk about?"

"Stuff," Alma answered simply, reaching up and grabbing the hood and pulling it down with a resounding crash. "She's nice." He glanced in the direction Darbie had gone. "She said you've done more than just go to church together. I was shocked."

"I didn't say going to church was all we'd done," Porter countered defensively. "We're good friends."

Alma smiled. "I got that impression. You hadn't ever told her about me."

"What did *you* tell her about you?"

"I didn't have to tell her much. I was right here." He enjoyed observing Porter's discomfort.

"You liked exposing my past," Porter accused, trying to remain calm.

The amused smile disappeared from Alma's lips. "What was I supposed to do, hide in the basement?" he asked. "I just answered the door. There she was. I didn't know she was coming."

"And you had to invite her for dinner? Were you trying to embarrass me?"

Alma faced Porter. "You said you didn't care what anybody in Eagar thought."

"So you figured you'd prove it?"

"I wasn't trying to prove anything." There was a mixture of hurt and anger on Alma's face. "Look, I wasn't trying to do anything to you. That's the truth. If anybody was dishonest, it wasn't me." He pushed past Porter and headed for the house.

* * *

As Porter watched his son disappear, he glanced down the street in the direction Darbie had gone. Disgustedly, he shook his head, realizing that within a few short minutes, he had managed to offend both Alma and Darbie.

7

"You didn't stay and talk much yesterday," Porter remarked as Darbie invited him into her house. He had stewed all day about visiting her and finally built up his courage to drive the two and a half blocks to her place. Behind an inscrutable smile, she motioned for him to follow her into the kitchen, where she was fixing dinner.

"I stayed a long time," she answered lightly. "I had a great visit with . . ." She ostentatiously cleared her throat and cocked her head to one side. "Your past," she finished with her back to him while she worked. "Alma's a great kid. Why hide him?"

Porter dropped uneasily into a chair and clasped his hands tightly in front of him on the kitchen table. "I planned to tell you about him. He had planned to spend a few weeks here this summer. That was before his mother's accident." He knit his brow in somber concentration. "I've been meaning to tell you a lot of things. I just haven't known how."

She faced him wonderingly. "Alma said he was your only child."

"He's my only child, but there's more to my past."

"Well, if the rest of your past is like Alma . . ."

"It's not."

She turned back to her work. "So that's why you haven't shared very much with me. You don't go around sharing those things with just anybody."

"You're not just anybody."

"What I meant is that one doesn't go around sharing those things with someone else unless there's a closeness between them."

"Darbie, I've felt that closeness, so I should've told you about Alma."

"Only about Alma?" Darbie continued to stir the contents of a bowl without turning around. "Alma has a mother. I mean, he did before the accident."

After a long, uneasy pause, Porter said huskily, "I told you I'd been married."

"You didn't say you'd been married twice."

"What do you want to know?"

"Probably nothing. I suppose I know more now than I want to know. But I would like to get to know Alma better. I'd like to think of him as the nice kid down the street who makes a terrific pan of fried potatoes, eggs, and ham bits." She chuckled. "I was tempted to ask him to whip up another batch for my supper tonight." She stopped working. "I'd like to think of both of you as great neighbors. And that's where it ends," she said somberly.

"I thought we knew each other better than that."

"So did I. I guess we were both wrong."

A long, tense silence ensued before Porter ventured another comment. "So the fact that I have a sixteen-year-old son changes everything between us?"

Darbie turned the stove on, set a pot on the burner, and turned around. For a moment she studied Porter, but soon she looked away and folded her arms while she leaned against the stove. "Porter, I've been doing a lot of thinking since yesterday evening. I finally admitted a lot of things to myself. I realized that I probably haven't been completely fair to you. There are things you don't know about me."

"Don't tell me you've got a sixteen-year-old daughter someplace," Porter remarked, making a weak attempt at humor. "No, you're too young. What is she, five?"

Darbie heaved a sigh without smiling. "Since meeting Alma yesterday," she began softly, "I've done some serious thinking. I'm glad I finally met him. Alma isn't what threw me; it's that there *is* an Alma." She held up her hands when Porter tried to speak. "No, Porter," she warned, "hear me out."

She pulled out the chair opposite Porter and dropped down onto it, but she kept the chair back from the table. Crossing one leg over the other, she folded her arms and continued. "I really should have expected Alma, or someone like him. I should have suspected a lot of things. I mean, here you are, a thirty-eight-year-old guy, educated, well-established financially. You're nice looking and friendly, in a reserved kind of way. You're athletic, in shape, active at Church. You have your own house, a nice car, and—"

"Hey, you're making me sound pretty good," Porter cut in, joking.

Darbie smiled plaintively. "And you're single."

"That's not good? You wanted to date a married guy?"

She ignored his attempt at humor. "I guess I pushed that little fact to the back of my mind. Of course, you indicated that you had some things in your past. All this was pretty early in our friendship. And to begin with, that's all it was—a friendship. You were a nice guy, a fun neighbor, someone that dear old Sister Reynolds manipulated into my path." She studied her fingernails for a moment. "Back then you were pretty reserved, and I decided to pull you out of your shell, help you discover something besides a dull life in front of a computer monitor. That was my personal challenge. Unfortunately, I mistakenly thought I could do all of that without getting too . . . personally attached."

She nodded with a sardonic smile. "You took me out to dinner. We went to a couple of baseball games, but we were still just friends. I was cautious. I had my guard up, because, after all, I didn't want this friendship to go anywhere. That's why I didn't want to know about your past. I preferred it that way. It made it easier for me."

Darbie breathed deeply and brushed at a spot on her pants. "But things were gradually changing, in spite of what I kept telling myself. I guess I didn't want to admit that I was liking you. I'm generally not naïve. I'll admit that I was curious about your past. When I called my mother and told her about you, I was selective about the details I shared with her. You see, I generously gave you a pass, a nice benefit of the doubt. I speculated. You could have married when you were older and become a widower, and the death of your wife had left you devastated for a long time, and you were just emerging from your grief. You could have married a real weirdo and been forced to end the marriage or had it annulled. That experience had wounded you, and you were finally breaking from your past. I was very creative as I searched for all the possibilities. I liked to think I was helping you get back on your feet. Wasn't that magnanimous of me?"

She threw her arms out wide and then let them drop to her side. "Back to my mother. I didn't mention to her that you were thirty-eight and single, because she's very astute, and those two facts tell a whole lot about you—more than I wanted Mom to know right then. Because, after all, I had everything under control."

"I take it you don't like older men?"

"Porter Huggins, I'm not exactly a 'young chick.' Maybe that's part of the reason I wanted to bury the important details that you were thirty-eight and single. I mean, nobody's asking me to the junior prom anymore. No twenty-one-year-old guy fresh off his mission is taking a second look at me. I'm old, relatively speaking."

"It sounds to me like we're a good fit."

Darbie sighed. "I'm going to be really honest—honest with you and very honest with me. Someday I'd like to get married."

"Hey, I didn't come over here to make any proposals. Or to accept any," Porter returned with a devious grin. "Can you give me a few weeks, or is this something we need to do this evening?"

"Let me finish."

Porter nodded.

"I've always wanted to get married. And when I've contemplated marriage, I've projected myself into a brand new relationship—new for both of us."

"With no baggage."

"Right. No son, no ex-wife, much less ex-*wives*."

Porter's cheeks colored, and he looked down at the table so he wouldn't have to look into Darbie's probing eyes.

"Now, I'm not entirely naïve. At twenty-eight, my options are fewer and fewer. But I'm not desperate, willing to take the first man who walks into my life and shows me a modicum of interest. I used to think I'd marry someone two or three years older than I was." She shook her head. "I realize now that I might marry someone two or three years younger."

"There are advantages to being with an older guy. I can give you a dozen right off the top of my head. I have them memorized."

"What I'm saying is that I'm not ready to give up on my dream of marrying someone and having it be the first marriage for both of us." She closed her eyes and shook her head. When she finally opened her eyes, she looked directly across the table at Porter. "This is my fault," she said gently. "I should have known most of this about you without your having to go into the gory details. I can see now that I did know. I just didn't *want* to know. I still think you're a great guy."

"But you'd just as soon that I stepped off your boat before you push out to sea?"

"My head's been in a bit of a whirlwind since yesterday. I have to admit that I still have some pretty strong feelings for you. But I don't see this relationship going anywhere or getting serious. We'll be friends—good neighbors—but we need to move on."

"My past might not be quite as bad as you think," Porter injected jovially. "Maybe I'm still a candidate."

She smiled ruefully and shook her head. "I'm trying not to be judgmental, but there's a certain way I want things, and . . ." She paused, seeming unsure how to conclude.

"And I'm not the way you want things," Porter finished for her.

She smiled sadly and nodded.

"You said you really like Alma. We're a package deal, you know."

"He doesn't want a stepmom." She breathed deeply. "And I'm not cut out to be a stepmom, even to a nice kid like Alma."

Silence prevailed once more. Porter knew he should leave, but he lingered.

"What *did* happen between you and Alma's mom?" Darbie asked, just above a whisper.

"Her name was Allyson."

Darbie shook her head and stood up. "I don't believe I wanted to know that," she said, stopping him. She kept shaking her head. "I'm not sure I want to know any of it, even though I am curious." She hugged herself as she paced the kitchen floor. "You left her, didn't you?" Porter didn't answer immediately, so Darbie filled in for him. "That's the only way it could have been, isn't it?"

"I've learned a lot over these past few years, Darbie. I'm a lot smarter now than I was back then—but I'm not making excuses for anything I did."

"You don't have to tell me anything," Darbie offered gently. "I really don't have a right to know, because we're just going to be good neighbors, and those are personal things—things that good neighbors don't necessarily share with each other." She returned to the stove and pretended to work there, but Porter knew she was merely occupying her hands so she wouldn't have to face him.

After a while, Porter stood and pushed his hands into his pockets while staring down at the tabletop. "Well, I guess this good neighbor will be moving on," he said slowly. Then he turned and left the house.

* * *

"That was pretty short," Alma commented when Porter walked into the family room. He watched Porter. "Things didn't go well?"

Porter smiled ruefully. "Things won't be going anywhere from now on."

"Because of me?"

"Because of *me*. In fact, she likes you. It must be that concoction you fed her. I should have tried that instead of taking her out to dinner those times."

"She wouldn't make a good stepmom."

Surprised, Porter turned to Alma with a puzzled look on his face.

Alma shrugged. "Being a stepmom would ruin her," he explained simply. "I mean, she's cool now. If she were a stepmom . . ." He shook his head. "Well, that wouldn't be so cool."

Porter studied his son for a brief moment, then turned and retreated to his office.

* * *

Trying to keep his mind off his conversation with Darbie, Porter immersed himself in a computer sale he'd been working on and soon lost track of time. Then suddenly Alma spoke from the door behind him. Apparently he had been watching from the doorway for several minutes. "So this is where you work?" he asked, leaning against the doorjamb, a glass of water in his hand.

Holding a yellow legal pad in one hand and a pen in the other, Porter swiveled around in his high-back office chair, pleasantly surprised. This was the first time Alma had actually ventured to this part of the house. Previously, he had confined himself to the kitchen, the family room, and his bedroom below, acting as though this level of the house were off-limits.

Alma glanced down at his watch. "You've hardly left that computer all day."

Porter tossed the pen and legal pad onto the desk beside him and gently rubbed his eyes with his fingertips. "I was just finishing up some things," he moaned. He dropped his hands into his lap and smiled. "I'm about ready to close this deal." He turned halfway around so he could see his computer screen. "Assuming nothing goes wrong, I should make eight or nine thousand on this little project."

Alma's eyebrows furrowed in thought. "Not to be snoopy or anything," he began, "but exactly what kind of work do you do? I mean, you just park yourself in front of that computer all day. You hardly leave the house."

Porter scratched his head and sucked in a breath of air. "Actually, I travel all over the world. Most of the time, though, I do it from this desk."

"Doing what?"

"I buy and sell computers and software. A lot of the computers I deal with are used and refurbished or are upgraded lower-end machines. They're still good machines, just not on the cutting edge of technology. I deal in new machines, too. I know places that can do the upgrades inexpensively. I find companies, usually small ones, who need ten, twenty, maybe fifty computers, and I provide them."

"So how do you make your money?"

"Take Albert Benton, Inc.," Porter said, jabbing a finger at his monitor, "the company I'm working with right now. I'm furnishing fifty-five machines. They had planned to order thirty-five, even though they really needed more. I figured out that with the money they had set aside to purchase thirty-five computers from a major retailer, I could set them up with fifty-five machines and still make eight thousand in the process."

"Where do you put the computers when they get here? Out in the old shed behind the house?"

Porter shook his head. "I usually never see the computers. I just arrange things."

"You sell fifty-five computers that you never actually see?"

Porter smiled. "Hey, Alma, I don't have this magic touch that says if I see those fifty-five computers they're better than they are without my seeing them. I trust the original suppliers, and I trust the people who do the upgrades. My job is to know where everything is and where and how to move it around."

"It seems too easy."

Porter stood up and pointed to his chair. "Try it. See how much you can make."

"I don't know where the stuff is," Alma muttered.

"Neither does Albert Benton, Inc." He raised a portentous finger. "But I do. And what I know," he went on, dropping back into his office chair, "is worth money."

Alma thought a moment. "Is this legal?"

Porter laughed out loud. "Alma, I know you think I'm a rather unsavory character, but I'm not working for the Mafia or some drug cartel. I'm not trading stolen goods, marketing human cargo, or doing anything else illegal. This is all aboveboard."

"Does this Albert Benton, Inc., know how much money you make off them?"

"Alma, the only thing Albert Benton, Inc., cares about is that I just got them fifty-five computers when they thought they could only afford thirty-five, and they can still afford to pay me my commission. The next time they need a computer, who do you think they're going to call? Who would you call if I just swung a deal like that for you?"

"But it seems a little . . ." He wet his lips and searched for the right word.

"Crooked?" Porter helped him.

"Yeah, crooked describes it pretty well." He shook his head. "You're buying and selling and never seeing anything and still collecting all this money."

"I provide a service—a good service. I used to do this kind of thing for a big company in Denver. I started doing some of my own business on the side; now I do it full time. I also do some investing, some buying and trading." He smiled at his skeptical son. "Not to brag, Alma, but I'm good at what I do. I can't help you fix your truck, but I can do this."

"And you're sure it's legal?"

Porter laughed as he tipped back in his chair and stared up at the ceiling. "I assure you that no SWAT team is going to kick down the doors and charge in here with loaded guns trying to break up my business. In fact, a couple of months ago I provided eight computers to a little police department in Kansas." He smiled. "Are you satisfied?"

"I don't know how satisfied I am. I'm a little hungry."

"Good, so am I. I'll take you out to dinner."

"You really are used to eating out a lot, aren't you?" It was more accusation than question. "Mom and I hardly ever ate out. Except on special occasions. I'd feel guilty eating out all the time."

"I can't afford not to eat out. I'd starve to death if I didn't eat out. I'm a lousy cook. For me, eating out isn't a luxury; it's a matter of survival."

Alma grinned. "You finish squeezing your eight thousand dollars out of Albert Benton, Inc., and I'll fix something to eat. You won't starve, and I won't feel guilty."

* * *

A few minutes later Alma had made grilled cheese sandwiches, warmed up a pan of vegetable beef soup from a can, and set a jug of milk on the table. Porter came into the kitchen and washed his hands in the sink while Alma set the soup on the table. "Hey, do you want to grab some spoons from the drawer?" Alma said.

Porter looked over his shoulder as he grabbed a towel to dry his hands. "You talking to me?" he asked with an amused grin.

Alma glanced at him as though he wasn't exactly sure what Porter was asking. Finally he nodded.

"I've got a name." Porter went on as he opened the utensil drawer, extracted two soup spoons, and set them on the table as he sat down. Alma sat across from him, looking down at his soup. "I've had the distinct impression that you haven't decided what to call me." Alma began stirring his soup. "You can call me whatever you're comfortable with."

"That's just it," Alma muttered, reaching for one of the grilled cheese sandwiches. "I'm not comfortable with anything."

"What did you call me when you were in Panguitch?"

"I didn't need to call you anything. You weren't around."

"But when you needed to think about me and had to hang a name on me, what was it?"

With his head down, Alma smiled slightly without answering.

"Oh," Porter mused, nodding his head and suspecting the worst. "So you used a lot of four-letter words when you were hanging names on me, is that it?"

"Mom didn't let me use those, so if she was around, I was really careful about what I said, whether I was talking about you or someone else."

"So you just *thought* the bad names?"

In spite of himself, Alma smiled more broadly. He took a spoonful of soup. "Nothing I used there seems to fit here."

Porter took a huge bite and began chewing and talking at the same time. "You could call me Porter. Walter and Calvin call me Port. Toni probably calls me Dirty Mangy Dog." He grinned. "You could call me Pops, Dad, Pappy, Daddy, Father." He smiled as he ticked off the names. "What's your pleasure?"

"I don't feel like using any of the 'father' forms," he answered honestly, keeping his eyes on his bowl. "I don't figure we've got that kind of relationship."

"That's fair," Porter conceded. "So just call me Porter."

Alma shook his head. "Calling you by your first name doesn't show respect."

"Oh," Porter mused, nodding. "How about calling me Mr. Huggins?"

"I don't think so."

Porter shrugged. "Well, you ought to call me something. I don't want you stammering around trying to get my attention." Porter finished his first sandwich and swallowed. "Oh well, when you think of something, let me know."

* * *

The next morning as Alma was finishing a four-mile jog, he made a wide loop through the neighborhood just south of Porter's place. As he was heading back toward School Bus Road, he spotted Darbie pacing tiredly in front of a white-framed house. Although he knew she lived in this area, he hadn't known where until then.

"So you're a jogger too?" Alma questioned as he slowed to a walk.

Darbie wiped the back of her hand across her perspiring forehead, took a couple of quick gulps of air, and smiled, nodding. "An old habit." She wet her lips. "You too?"

Alma shrugged. "I didn't run much in Panguitch. Sometimes I'd go with my mom. She was quite a runner. Over the years she ran in a few 10Ks. She was actually pretty good. She tried to convince me to be her jogging partner." He smiled affectionately and shook his head. "But back in Panguitch I put in a lot of hours working. I didn't figure I needed to jog for exercise." He shrugged. "But there's not a lot of physical activity around here, so I started to jog. I'm getting so I like it, and I get a look at the country around here."

"I was a sprinter in high school," Darbie explained, putting her hands on her hips and strolling over to where he stood. She shook her head. "I didn't think I was cut out for distance. But while I was going to college, I started jogging to stay in shape. I got hooked. I've been pretty consistent ever since, except while I was in Spain on my mission." She grinned. "None of my companions were willing to run with me." She bent over a few times to stretch out her legs. "Jogging's good therapy. I run three or four miles a day."

Alma pondered a moment. "Do you want a bodyguard?" He laughed. "I think that's why Mom wanted me to run with her. I didn't think she needed protection in Panguitch, Utah." He studied Darbie. "I'll run with you if you don't mind the company."

Darbie considered the offer without accepting.

Alma laughed and held up his hands. "I'm safe. Honest. I'm not like Porter—now, you might not feel safe around him." He laughed and winked at her. "I don't blame you. Just think of me as the kid you never had, the one who's there to protect you. Of course, you probably don't need protection in Eagar any more than Mom needed it in Panguitch."

Darbie grinned. "I feel pretty safe here in Eagar. And for the record, I'd feel safe running with your dad, but he doesn't like to jog. I've already asked him. You up to being my bodyguard?"

"To be honest I might not be much of a bodyguard if somebody jumps you." He smiled playfully. "I'm not exactly the warrior type." He laughed. "But if nothing else, I'll be an eyewitness." He filled his lungs with air and exhaled. "I'll be here tomorrow at 5:30."

"Sounds like a plan." Darbie dropped down on her front lawn and sat with her legs crossed. "Now that you've had a chance to see Eagar up close, what do you think of it?"

"It's bigger than Panguitch."

"From what I've heard, most places are bigger than Panguitch. Have you found much to do here?"

"Well, I haven't been to the mall yet." He cleared his throat ostentatiously. "Actually, I haven't *found* the mall yet."

Darbie laughed. "There's the supermarket, the pharmacy, and the variety store all in one center. There's that Chinese food place, too. That's Eagar's version of a mall. Do you like to read?"

"If the book's decent."

"I've got some books I think you'd like." She pushed up from the grass. "I'll bring some over. Or you can stop by later today after my summer school classes get out. I'll let you look through my collection. There are a lot of things I don't have, but I have plenty of books."

"Shakespeare?" Alma asked dubiously.

"I've got some Shakespeare," Darbie returned dryly. "But my interests go beyond Shakespeare." She started moving away. "Trust me. I'll find something you like. And it won't be a bunch of mushy poetry that will offend your delicate macho sensitivities." She shook a finger at him. "Remember, five thirty in the morning. Bring your running shoes, because I'm serious about my daily jog." She smiled deviously.

8

The following Sunday, Alma was up early and eating a light breakfast before his church meetings. Porter finally clomped downstairs, tying his tie and shaking the residue of slumber from his brain. The two didn't speak much until they walked outside and Porter headed for his car.

"You're not driving again, are you?" Alma asked, surprised, even a little annoyed. "On a morning like this?"

Porter turned to him. "The chapel's a ways down the road."

"Yeah, I jog past it every morning," Alma returned. "It's less than a mile away."

"Is there some kind of rule that says you can't drive a mile to church? If there is, I've been breaking that rule for a long time. And I plan to break it again this morning."

Alma shook his head. "Mom always figured that you shouldn't drive anywhere that was closer than a mile. It's a waste. I'll walk."

"You can still ride with me and keep a clear conscience. I'll be the guilty one."

"I'd rather walk," Alma said over his shoulder as he started for the road.

Porter stared at his car keys and then glanced down the straight road to the church that seemed so far away. Slowly, he stuffed the keys into his pocket. "Wait up. I'll be virtuous this morning and walk." Shaking his head in frustration, he muttered, "If riding to church each Sunday was my worst sin, I'd apply right now for sainthood."

"Nobody said it was a sin to drive," Alma returned. "Don't you prefer being out in the fresh air? There are tons of advantages to walking."

"I can make an impressive list of reasons why driving is the preferred option."

As soon as they reached the corner of Crosby Street and School Bus Road, which was about a hundred yards from Porter's house, they met Darbie, who was walking to church too. "Good morning," she greeted cheerily as she joined them.

"That's good timing," Porter joked, brightening as the three of them continued down the road, Alma ending up between the two adults.

"Don't believe him," Alma cut in, trying not to smile. "He's been waiting in the bushes, watching for you. I'm glad you finally came. It was getting embarrassing." Alma laughed, and Porter's cheeks colored as Darbie chuckled.

"I believe it," Darbie returned, nudging Alma with an elbow. "I've never seen Porter walk to church. He doesn't walk anywhere. If he has to cross the street, he gets in his car and drives. It's pathetic. But I didn't know he knew I was walking today."

"Oh, yeah, he's been excited all weekend about his weekly date," Alma teased. "And I know why he likes these Sunday dates. Church doesn't cost anything, and there's always a chance you'll invite him to Sunday dinner."

"Now aren't you on one this morning?" Porter grumbled, fighting to keep the smile from his lips. "I should have driven so you two wouldn't take potshots at me all the way to the chapel."

"I'm sorry about Sunday dinner, though," Darbie playfully chided Porter. "Sister Reynolds invited me to eat with them today. I could ask if there's room for two more."

"No thanks," Porter returned hastily. "Alma will throw something together."

* * *

That evening as Alma and Porter ate an evening meal of macaroni and cheese, Porter asked casually, "How long do you figure you'll leave the truck on the street?" He tried to sound indifferent, but Alma sensed he had been stewing about the truck ever since it had been parked in front of his house.

"I guess till I get it fixed."

"That could take a while."

Alma poked at his macaroni. "I've got some serious work to do on it."

"I don't know if we should leave something like that out on the street."

"Yeah, it kind of clashes with the Mercedes, doesn't it?"

Porter coughed. "It doesn't have anything to do with the Mercedes. I just don't think other people around here want an old truck parked out on the street like that."

"Other people?" Alma questioned dubiously. "Or you in particular?"

"Well, I'm not crazy about my place looking like a wrecking yard."

"It's one truck." Alma studied Porter, who kept eating without looking up.

"Why don't you put it somewhere besides out there?"

"On the driveway next to the Mercedes? That would get it off the street. Then the people in the neighborhood wouldn't complain," Alma said, knowing very well that wouldn't appease Porter.

For several minutes the two ate in silence, avoiding each other's eyes. Alma finally spoke. "So what you're really saying," he began slowly, deliberately, "is that it was all right to bring the truck here but not to keep it here."

"I didn't say that," Porter replied evenly. "I just don't like it parked out front. I told you that I'm a bit fanatical about things being neat and orderly."

Alma put his fork down and stood to take his plate to the sink. "You don't like that truck, do you?"

Porter chewed slowly. After a long pause, he swallowed, set his fork down, and leaned forward. "I'm not crazy about it."

Alma began rinsing off his plate. "Can I put it out back?" he asked.

"On the lawn?" Porter sounded incredulous. "Dripping oil all over the place?"

Alma put his plate in the dishwasher. "I'll think of something," he muttered.

"Hey, I've got an idea," Porter offered. "Mel Franklin has a mechanic shop not far from here. His place is fenced, so no one would bother the truck. I can talk to him."

Alma leaned against the doorjamb. "So if I wanted to work on it late in the afternoon or in the evening, that probably wouldn't work," he stated knowingly. "The place will be locked up."

"Well, you'd have to work on it when Mel was there."

Alma turned and started for the stairs. "I'll come up with something."

* * *

The next day Alma left the house early and disappeared. At noon he returned for a bite to eat, and then he was gone again, not returning until early evening. "That old shed out back, is it just a place where you dump your junk?" he asked Porter, who was watching TV.

"Oh, I've got some stuff stored out there. I need to organize it a little better."

"If I straightened things up, maybe I could work on the truck in there. Then no one would complain about me messing up the neighborhood. You don't seem to care if you've got a bunch a junk out there."

"That shed's not all that big, and there's a ton of stuff out there. I don't have it organized right now, but it's not junk. It's stuff I want to keep."

"Do you need all that stuff, or is it that you just haven't decided what to keep and what to throw away?"

"I might be able to get rid of some of it, but I'd have to go through it and see what there is. I don't have time right now. I mean, I'm still trying to catch up on a lot of stuff."

Alma nodded and glanced knowingly toward the baseball game Porter was watching on TV.

"But I know that old truck wouldn't fit in that shed. If you crammed it in there, there wouldn't be a place for my things."

"What if everything would fit?"

Porter shrugged and shifted uneasily in his chair. "I guess we'd have to see then."

The following day Alma disappeared again. Several times Porter went to the window to see if he could spot him, but he was never there. Lunchtime came and went, and Alma never appeared. It was after four when he finally showed up. "The truck fits fine in the shed," he announced, standing stiffly in Porter's office doorway. "I measured it."

Porter turned from his computer monitor and glanced at Alma, who stood there, dusty and tired, with sweat dripping down the sides of his face and damp splotches under his arms.

"The truck fits in the shed fine. And I took care of your stuff."

"What?" Porter questioned worriedly, his brow knitting sternly.

"Come take a look. You might like the improvement."

Porter followed Alma out the front door and around the right corner of the house to the old shed. Porter noticed that the truck was still parked on the street. When Alma threw the shed's double doors open, Porter gazed into what appeared to be an empty interior with the exception of tools, hoses, lawn furniture, and a few other items hanging on the walls. Along the back wall there was a series of shelves, which had been empty but were now stacked neatly with boxes, a weed-eater, and three red six-gallon plastic gas containers. Surprised, Porter glanced upward. Several boards and pieces of plywood had been laid across the open rafters, and additional boxes were stacked neatly up there, leaving the entire floor empty.

"I figured I could put the truck in here," Alma explained, stepping into the middle of the concrete floor and looking around. "There will still be three feet on either side so I can move around and work. It'll be hidden from all those pesky neighbors who have been pitching such a fuss, because I'll close the doors so nobody can even see the truck."

Dazed, Porter entered the shed and looked around, amazed by the transformation that had taken place. The last time he had opened the shed doors, there had been boxes, tools, hoses, lawn furniture, and sundry other articles strewn everywhere. Now everything was neat and tidy, and the floor had even been swept clean. "So this is where you've been yesterday and today," Porter mused, running his tongue along his upper lip. "How will I find anything?"

Alma shrugged. "How did you find anything before? I mean, could you have found anything the way it was? For a guy who's a fanatic about having things clean and orderly, this place was a junk heap. I figured that's why you kept the doors closed all the time. It wasn't that you thought someone might steal or bother this stuff— you just didn't want to look at it."

"I was the one who put all this stuff in here, so I knew more or less where to find things."

"Did you happen to know where your old college books were?"

"In boxes," Porter sputtered. "I don't know exactly which ones," he snapped testily. "But I had a general idea. I could have found them. What do I do now?"

Alma pointed to the back shelf. "Bottom row, third box to your left." He stepped to the back shelf and picked up a spiral notebook and held it up. "I wrote it all down. I guess I'm a bit of an organization freak too. You can find everything now—and you don't have to wade through a bunch of junk to get to it."

"If you pull that old truck in here and start tearing it apart, won't you be getting oil and grease all over the floor?"

"Is that worse than all the dirt and junk that was here before I cleaned it?"

"You can sweep dirt up."

"I'll put down some cardboard. That will catch the grease and oil."

"Except what soaks through and what spills where you don't have the cardboard."

For a moment Alma gazed around the inside of the shed, appraising the work he had done over the past two days. "So the shed's still a big no?" He slapped at the dust on his pant leg. "Well, at least your shed's clean," he said flatly.

"I appreciate that," Porter mumbled, choking on his words of coerced gratitude.

"I was sure you would." There was no mistaking Alma's sarcasm.

"Look, I didn't ask you to clean it. And if you were thinking of working on the truck in here, you should have mentioned something to me."

"I did mention it to you."

"I didn't give you permission to do all this."

Alma nodded. "I knew if I asked, you'd say no," he said quietly. "I thought if I cleaned the place up, you might change your mind." He shook his head. "I was wrong. Again."

"I just wish you would have discussed it with me first," Porter responded lamely.

"Yeah, that would have been a good discussion. I'm sorry I missed that one."

"Alma, you're the one who struck out on this project without consulting me."

Alma chuckled humorlessly. "You really don't want me to work on my truck, do you?" He didn't wait for a response. "I don't get it. I'm not asking you to help me. I'm not asking you to pay for anything. Back in Panguitch you said you'd cough up big bucks to buy me a new truck. Now you act like you'd choke if you had to pay three cents for an oil filter." He shook his head. "You don't want to have anything to do with the truck, and you don't want me to have anything to do with it either."

"I just want you to find the right place to do it."

"There is no right place for you, and you know it." He tossed the spiral notebook back on the shelf. "Well, there's your shed, cleaned and organized. At least you got something out of it." He stalked from the shed, brushing past Porter. Suddenly he stopped, his back stiff, his hands clenched at his sides. Slowly he turned. "Why'd you want me here in the first place?" His chest rose and fell as his breath came in tight, angry gulps. "Just so Uncle Walter or someone else couldn't have me?"

The question was so sudden, so unexpected, that Porter didn't know how to respond. He found himself staring, openmouthed, as Alma stormed away and disappeared into the house.

Porter stood in the middle of the shed floor, his shoulders sagging as he dug his hands into his pockets. He looked around, taking in the huge chore Alma had undertaken. Alma's stinging last words echoed in his mind, and he found himself squirming under the onslaught of the harsh, pointed criticism. He tried to rationalize it away, coming up with all kinds of reasons for doing what he had done, but his arguments were hollow.

He glanced out toward the street and studied the old Ford pickup. He wasn't sure why he was so averse to the truck or to Alma working on it. He had to admit that he didn't want it around. But the elusive *why* was baffling. Perhaps it was jealousy, knowing that as long as Alma concentrated his efforts on the truck, his attention was away from Porter. Porter had hoped that by bringing Alma to Eagar, there would be a fresh start for both of them. He had harbored high hopes for the rebuilding effort with his son, but Alma hadn't responded the way Porter had anticipated.

Porter admitted that the truck made him nervous. It reminded him of his obvious deficiencies. He didn't understand it, didn't know how to fix it, didn't know how to help Alma fix it. It was a reminder of his broken past, a past he wanted to forget, a past that caused nagging, painful guilt.

Porter didn't know how to explain any of that to Alma. He was barely coming to understand it himself, but in the meantime he was losing his son, and he felt desperate to keep him. Watching Alma walk away that afternoon, Porter sensed that Alma was walking away from him—not just for a few minutes but for good.

Frustrated, Porter wandered out to the truck and opened its door. He slid onto the seat and gripped the steering wheel—smooth, worn, and polished from hundreds of hands gripping it over the years. Finally, he pumped the gas pedal and turned the key. The engine moaned a protest but then rumbled into action. Putting the truck in gear, Porter backed it toward the shed. Just as Alma had insisted, the truck fit nicely.

It was several minutes before Porter mustered enough resolve to rap lightly on Alma's closed bedroom door. There was no answer. He stood at the door with his head bowed, listening and wondering. Finally, he cleared his throat, knocked a second time, and spoke. "I parked the truck in the shed." There was no response. "You can work on it there." Still no sound from within. "Don't worry about oil and grease on the floor."

He would have appreciated even a grumbled "thank you" from Alma, but there was nothing. He returned to his office.

* * *

Three hours later, when Porter finally pushed away from his monitor, he stepped to his window, which was on the back side of the house, and glanced toward the shed. The double doors of the shed were open, and although he couldn't see Alma, he spotted his open toolbox on the floor.

Porter wasn't a great cook, but he had a few specialties. This particular evening he decided to make waffles topped with frozen strawberries and whipped cream. When he wandered out to the shed to invite Alma in to eat, he found him resting his forearms on the truck bed, staring blankly at the opposite wall. He didn't notice Porter's approach.

"I'm fixing waffles," Porter announced.

Alma jumped slightly and turned to face him.

"I know it sounds a little like breakfast, but I was in the mood. I prefer mine with strawberries and whipped cream. I'm ready to put the first waffle in."

"Waffles sound good." Alma rubbed his stomach and grinned sheepishly.

Porter nodded toward the truck. "What will you do first?" he asked.

Alma pressed his lips together and reached out and ran his hand along the side of the truck, as though he were caressing it. He shrugged weakly. "I need a few parts."

"Do you need help?" Porter ventured, knowing the answer but wanting to offer anyway. Any repairs were far beyond his limited mechanical abilities.

"No, I like working on the truck. I don't have anything else to do."

Porter nodded. "Well, I'll have the first waffles on your plate in five minutes."

When the waffles were ready, the two men ate in silence. Alma did comment on how good the waffles, strawberries, and whipped cream combination tasted. The rest of their talk was simple requests for one thing or another on the table. When they had both finished eating, Alma stood and started gathering the place settings.

"I'll clean up," Porter insisted. "You go work on the truck."

Alma hesitated, almost as though he were going to protest; then he reconsidered and started for the back door. After opening the door, he stood in the doorway for a moment with his back to Porter. "Thanks for the shed," he finally quickly said before slipping outside and closing the door behind him.

Porter finished the dishes and then walked out to the shed. Alma was gathering a few tools he had lying on the floor. Seeing Porter, he straightened up and asked, "Do you know anybody around here that could use a little help? It could be anything—grunt work, dirty work, anything that would earn me a few bucks."

Porter pulled the corners of his mouth down. "I could pay you for cleaning up the shed. You did good work here."

Alma shook his head and returned to his tools. "No, I did that so I could use this place. I wasn't expecting pay for it."

"I could find you work around here in the yard, cleaning up or whatever."

"I'm not looking for a handout. I want real work."

"There's real work around here that needs to be done."

"Then I'll do it. But that's part of my job for living here." He closed the toolbox and set it in the bed of the truck.

"What exactly do you need right now for the truck?" Porter asked.

"The basic stuff—oil filter, oil, air filter, spark plugs, fuel filter. I'd like to replace the water pump and flush the radiator. Those are the basics. There will probably be other things later, but those things would get me started. So if I could find a job around here, some yard work or something like that, in a few afternoons I'd have enough to buy some of that stuff."

* * *

The next afternoon when Alma came into the kitchen, he found the kitchen table stacked with NAPA boxes. "What are these?" he called up the stairs.

"They're for the truck," Porter called back, trying to sound casual. A moment later he came down the stairs, smiling with satisfaction. Alma was examining the boxes, reading the labels. "I think that's everything you said you needed."

Alma pinched the bridge of his nose and then pursed his lips. "I didn't ask you to buy this stuff," he stated indifferently.

"You didn't ask me if you could clean the shed. You just did it. I wanted to do something without being asked. Now you can fix the truck. It won't be out there just gathering dust."

"And getting in your way?" Alma muttered.

"It's not in my way. Not now. I want you to fix it. I thought that was what you wanted." Some of Porter's previous aplomb dissipated. "If it gets fixed, what difference does it make how or why it gets fixed?"

"It makes a lot of difference to me. The truck means something to me. It doesn't mean anything to you. To you it's an annoyance. You'd just as soon take it to the junkyard."

Porter was silent for a moment. "Help me understand this," he said incredulously, throwing his hands in the air and then letting them drop to his sides. "You've been pacing the floor for days, wondering how you were going to fix the truck, because you didn't have the parts. Now you've got the parts, and you're complaining because you've got the parts and you can now fix the truck. I don't get any of this."

"That's right, you don't get it." Alma swallowed and picked up the oil filter. "The truck means something. To me. I've always loved the truck. I remember driving all over the farm in the truck. We used to drive into town or go camping in the truck. I figured the truck could go anywhere, do anything. I didn't care that it had a few rust spots or that the paint was faded or the windshield was chipped. It was the truck. That was just the way it was. It wasn't perfect, but it was the truck, and that was all that mattered. I used to beg Grandpa to let me have it. He'd laugh and tell me that by the time I was old enough to drive, I wouldn't care anything about the truck. I'd want something new, something fancy, something showy."

Alma gnawed on his lower lip. "When Grandpa and Grandma got their mission call to Nigeria, Grandpa told me the truck was mine if I still wanted it. Back then it was parked under the elm tree by the barn, just filled with junk and covered with dust and bird droppings. It hadn't been driven for . . ." He shrugged. "For forever."

With a far-off look in his eyes, he continued. "It wasn't until after Mom's accident . . . that I got serious about it. Working on the truck helped me get my mind off everything else. I got rid of all the junk packed inside the cab and piled in the bed. I cleaned it up some, scrounged up an old battery, and finally got the engine to actually turn over a few days before you showed up."

Alma swallowed. He set the oil filter back on the table. Heaving a sigh, he shook his head. "Now the truck's mine." He pointed in the direction of the shed. "My truck. It needs some fixing up. And I want to be the one to fix it up." Turning to Porter, he jabbed a stiff thumb against his own chest. "*I* want to fix it. *I* want to be the one. Not you! *Me!* I want to prove to myself that I can actually make the truck run, that it's not just a pile of junk, that it's as good as I always imagined it to be."

"Great. And there's the stuff you need. Does it matter that I help you buy the parts?" Porter asked, hurt and confused.

"I guess maybe it does. The truck's my project."

Porter stared at Alma. "So how do you plan to do it? You won't accept the parts, because I bought them. You won't work for me so you can buy the parts yourself. Are you going to go downtown, put a tin can on the curb, and sing and dance, hoping for public donations?"

"I'll work to earn the money."

Porter rolled his eyes. "You are stubborn. You won't give an inch." He shook his head. "You don't want to me to do one thing that might be construed as helping you."

"I didn't know that helping me out was a high priority for you."

"I'll never win in your eyes, will I? You'll make sure of that." Porter stared at the items on the kitchen table. "Well, it's good that I kept the receipt." He started gathering the boxes while Alma watched. Getting a flash of inspiration, he stopped. "I don't suppose you'd consider buying these things from me? I could keep them, and when you earn your money—from someone besides me—you could buy what you need. I've got the receipt, so you could check to make sure I wasn't giving you a special deal."

Alma shook his head.

"Well, it was a thought," Porter muttered.

"Do you want me to take these out to the car?" Alma offered timidly.

"No thanks," Porter muttered. "I brought them in here. I can haul them out. I don't want you to do anything that will compromise your lofty commitments."

"Thanks for buying them."

Porter froze in the midst of filling his arms with boxes.

"But I really want to do this my way." Alma turned and walked to his room.

* * *

Later that evening, Porter came down from his office, rubbing his eyes and the back of his neck. He saw Alma fixing something at the kitchen counter. "I thought we'd eat out tonight," Porter announced, hoping that eating out would be good news.

Alma glanced at Porter standing on the bottom step just outside the kitchen. "I figured I'd throw together a quick bite," he offered helpfully, turning back to his dinner preparations. "I want to work on the truck before it gets too late."

"Eating out won't take all night," Porter pointed out. "There will still be time to work on the truck." He shrugged. "You know, we haven't eaten out since you got here. I used to eat out all the time. There are some good eating places around here." He shrugged. "And it would give us a chance to talk."

"Talk about what? What's on your mind?"

Porter breathed deeply and exhaled slowly. "Does something in particular have to be on my mind? Shoot, we've hardly talked about anything. I mean really talked—you know, gotten to know each other."

Alma kept working without responding.

Pushing his hands into his pockets, Porter jingled his keys and fidgeted, wanting desperately to close the gap between himself and his son and willing to try anything to build some kind of bridge. "There's a nice Mexican restaurant on the other side of Springerville called Los Dos Molinos. They've got good food." Porter shrugged, smiling uneasily, the uncertainty in his eyes obvious. "Look, I'm inviting you out to dinner. Most people jump at a chance to eat out. Of course," he added nervously, "if you don't like Mexican food we could go to the Safire or Booga Red's and get a steak or something."

"Dinner's almost ready," Alma returned, pointing down at the sandwiches on the counter. "Nothing fancy, but it's cheaper than eating out. I've fixed enough for both of us."

"The sandwiches will keep. We can have them for lunch tomorrow."

"No need to waste money eating out when we've got stuff right here. I make a pretty decent ham-and-cheese sandwich. It won't be like eating a steak, but it'll be good."

"What if I'd prefer to eat out?"

Alma hesitated and then shrugged. "I guess you can still go out. Have the sandwiches tomorrow. They'll be a little soggy, though."

The pleading look and the nervous smile slowly vanished from Porter's face. A shadow of frustration colored his cheeks. "Why is it that every time I try to do something for you, you push me away? I offer to take you to dinner, and you throw it in my face."

Alma paused, the butcher knife poised over one of the sandwiches. It remained there for a moment, and then he quickly sliced the sandwich into two halves. "I thought you'd like eating here," he said quietly. "I wanted to surprise you by fixing dinner and having everything ready before you came down from your office. Mom used to love it when I made dinner for her. So that was my idea. Apparently you don't think it was all that good of an idea. So I don't know what good it will do to talk, because we can't even decide what to do for dinner."

"We could if you gave me a chance."

Alma shook his head. "I don't think that's the problem," he muttered. "We don't talk the same language. Maybe we don't have anything in common."

"Bull!" Porter flared. "You're my son. That gives us something in common."

"Biology doesn't necessarily give us a lot in common," Alma grumbled, keeping his eyes focused on the sandwiches and the counter as anger flickered across his face. "At least in the important things," he muttered quietly. "The last ten years proved that pretty well."

Porter glared at the floor. "Are you going to beat me over the head with the past ten years every time I turn around? I'd like to prove I'm better than that part of my life."

"That's easy for you." Alma turned and began setting the sandwiches on the table and arranging two place settings while he talked. "You figure because you finally want things patched up, everybody should jump in line. It doesn't always work that way."

"And I guess holding a grudge forever is the perfect solution?"

"Maybe you can give me ten years to think things over," Alma snapped. There was a long, cold silence while Alma got milk from the fridge and glasses from the cupboard and set them on the table. "Dinner's ready," he announced indifferently.

"You won't give even a little, will you?" Porter steamed.

Alma stood behind his kitchen chair and studied his dad for a moment. Finally, he allowed his own anger to push to the surface. "Look, you feel guilty about the last few years, so you want to make . . ." He gulped, groping for the right words. "A restitution," he finally managed. "You want to do something to clear up your own guilty conscience. That's where I come in. I guess I'm not ready to be your special project."

"What do you mean 'special project'?"

Alma considered the question for a moment and finally responded slowly, "I'm the work you've got to do. You patch things up with me, and then you've done your duty, taken care of your responsibility. Then your conscience is conveniently clear, and you can go on with the rest of your life." He shook his head and sat down. "No thanks."

"Is that how your mother wanted you to look at things?"

Alma held up his hands defensively and shook his head. "Let's not drag her into this. This doesn't have anything to do with Mom. She's gone."

"I know Allyson well enough to know that she wouldn't want you packing a grudge for the rest of your life. She taught you better than that," Porter added ruefully.

"And did she teach you anything?" Alma shot back.

"As a matter of fact, she did," Porter returned, suddenly feeling defeated. "The difference between you and me," he rejoined quietly, "is that it didn't stick with me. I take all the blame for that. But it did stick with you."

"What's that supposed to mean?"

"It means . . ." He swallowed and shook his head. "It means you're like her. You've got her heart. It's not in your nature to be mean and rude and angry. You have to work at those things."

Alma stared back at Porter without denying anything.

"I can see it in your face. I can see how you are with other people. And if it weren't for the fact that you were trying so hard to despise me, you and I would get along fine. I'm just asking you to give me a chance. Stop trying so hard to hate me." He looked down. "It's not in your nature," he finished softly.

When Alma didn't respond, Porter stepped to the table and pulled out the chair opposite Alma without making a move to sit down. "I know that during the last ten years," he started gently, gripping the back of the chair, "I've been a miserable excuse for a dad. I can't change that. I wish I could. The only thing I can do is go on from where I am. I haven't had much practice being a dad, and what practice I did have was a long ways from being perfect. But I'd like to learn." He paused, waiting for Alma to reply, but he didn't. "I just have this deep-gut feeling that maybe you'd like to give me a chance. I think your mom, in spite of everything I did or didn't do, would want you to give me a chance too. Not for me. For you. She knew even better than I do that hate and grudges don't fit you very well. I hope they never will." Porter pushed the chair back under the table and left the kitchen.

Alma watched him tromp up the stairs and disappear. He heard the office door open and close and then silence. Alma stared down at the simple meal he had prepared for the two of them. Despondently, he reached for a sandwich and began to eat, but he soon discovered that he had no appetite. He ended up eating only half a sandwich and drinking a glass of milk. He wrapped the remaining sandwiches in plastic bags and put them in the refrigerator. Then he retreated to the shed, but he ended up sitting on an upturned plastic five-gallon bucket, his forearms on his knees, while he stared straight ahead at the side of the truck, sifting through memories of hurt, disappointment, and anger, and trying to make some sense of it all, wondering who was to blame and whether things would ever change.

9

"I found a job," Alma announced to Porter two days later. Porter looked up, interested and curious. "It's a guy down the road here. Marshall Harrison. Know him?"

Porter thought for a moment. "By sight. He's an older guy, a bit crusty around the edges. He lives in the big place a couple miles down School Bus Road, right?"

Alma nodded. "I start Monday morning. It's grunt work—chopping weeds, clearing brush, raking trash, stuff like that. He wants me to clean a big lot behind his house. If he likes my work, he might use me for some other stuff."

* * *

Monday, after his morning jog and breakfast, Alma disappeared and didn't return until late afternoon. When he did return, he was covered with dirt and dry sweat, his face haggard and showing signs of exhaustion, but his eyes were bright with satisfied determination.

"Did you finish?" Porter asked, looking him up and down.

Alma shook his head. "There's lots more, but I'm finally doing something besides sitting around. I like hard work."

"Does Harrison like your work?"

Alma grinned. "He's a little crusty like you said, but he hasn't fired me yet."

"He probably hasn't paid you either," Porter responded doubtfully.

* * *

Midmorning the following day, Porter appeared at Harrison's place with a pair of new leather gloves in his back pocket and a rake and shovel over his shoulder. Alma stopped raking when he first spotted him.

Porter stopped ten feet from Alma and made a quick inspection of the work still to be done. "Where do I start?" he asked pleasantly.

Alma looked him up and down before following his gaze about the Harrison lot. He spit and wiped his mouth with the back of his hand. "What do you mean?" he questioned, confused.

"I came to work," Porter announced. "Where do I start?"

Alma ran his tongue over his dry lips and shook his head. "Mr. Harrison gave me the job," he explained slowly, trying to conquer his puzzlement with patience.

"So I figured I'd help you." Porter let the shovel and rake clatter to the ground. He reached back and pulled the leather gloves from his pocket. They still had the tags holding them together. He ripped the tags off the gloves and, squinting against the glare of the sun, pulled them on. "The sooner you finish, the sooner you have money to buy your parts and finish work on the truck."

"Mr. Harrison didn't hire you," Alma exclaimed, still trying to be patient but experiencing frustration in the process.

"Harrison wants a job done," Porter countered. "He doesn't care who does it."

"But if you do part of the work, then there's less for me to do, which means I earn less money, so how does that help me out?"

"Count my time as yours. If I work an hour, it's yours. That's not complicated."

Alma pulled his hat off, wiped his brow with the back of his arm, and looked up at the sun for a split second before staring down at the ground, shaking his head incredulously. "Look," he stated slowly, as though explaining something complex to a youngster, "this is my project. I want to do it. The truck's mine. I want to do that too. I want it all to be something I do. Can you understand that?" He cleared his throat. "Besides, this isn't your kind of work. You'll die out here in this sun. I'm used to it. You're not."

"Look, I'm just trying to help you out. Maybe be a part of your life in the process."

Alma wet his dry lips. "I can do it alone."

Porter began to chuckle sardonically, tugging at his gloves as though trying to pull them on even farther than he presently had them. "Alma, I'm not questioning whether you can do any of this. You're plenty capable." He reached down and snatched up the rake. "You don't need me. Believe me, you've made that clear." He chewed on his lower lip, pondering. "But has the thought ever occurred to you that maybe I'd *like* to help out, be part of this too? I sure don't know how to help you fix up that old truck—that's beyond my skill level—but I can rake up a few rocks and hack down some weeds."

"You've got other stuff to do—your sales and your investments. That's your work, not this. You're a desk and computer kind of guy. Sweating out here in the sun for six fifty an hour will just give you a headache or a stroke. This isn't your brand of work."

"It is if you're here," Porter fired back. "I'm not doing it because I have this great love for dirt and sweat. Besides, you're the one that's telling me—or at least hinting pretty strongly—that I worry too much about making money. Well, I'm not going to worry about making any more money for a while. I'm going to be out here in the heat of the day, slaving alongside you and getting another perspective. Is that too much to ask?"

"I'd really planned to do all of this myself. I prefer working alone."

"And you can't make a slight adjustment in your precious plans?"

"I'd rather not," Alma muttered, disgruntled and terse.

Porter leaned on the rake for a moment and squinted out across the lot. "Your mother did a good job teaching you, didn't she?"

"Huh?"

"I mean, she taught you all the virtues of good living—patience, kindness, charity, hard work, diligence, honesty, cleanliness, and the list goes on." Porter glanced at Alma, who was staring at him as though he'd lost his mental faculties and was rambling incoherently. "She taught you all those virtues, or at least most of them."

"Yeah," Alma grumbled suspiciously, not sure where Porter was going with this.

"While she was teaching you all of these wonderful virtues, did she warn you about some of the vices lurking in this hard, cruel world?" Alma's eyes narrowed, confusion written on his face. "I mean, surely she warned you about tobacco, alcohol, and drugs, and about wild, conniving women . . ." He paused. "And, of course, the horrible vices of pride, stubbornness, pigheadedness, obstinacy, and so on and so forth. Did she ever warn you about some of those vices?"

Alma looked away without answering.

"You seem to have picked up the virtues fine. You've even managed to avoid a lot of the vices, but I'll be darned if stubbornness and pride aren't ingrained in your system so strong that it'll take a team of mules to drag them out of you." Porter hammered a hole in the ground with the heel of his boot. "You don't give an inch, absolutely not one."

The two men stared at each other, neither wanting to be the one to flinch and look away. Alma was the first to speak, but even when he spoke, he didn't avert his gaze. "All right, stay. But if Mr. Harrison comes out here wondering what you're doing, you explain this whole arrangement to him. You explain that your hours are part of my time. And if he doesn't like it, you leave. Agreed?"

"What isn't there for him to like?"

"If he doesn't like it," Alma repeated slowly, "you leave. You agree to that?"

"You're a hardnose, Alma, do you know that?" Porter looked away, giving his son the satisfaction of winning the glaring contest. "Shoot, if I can convince you, I won't have any trouble convincing Harrison. Harrison's a little mama's boy compared to you."

Once the two arrived at an understanding, Alma explained what needed to be done, and they went to work, although on opposite sides of the lot. Alma didn't explain his reasoning to Porter, but he wanted to make sure that if Mr. Harrison came out, he wouldn't confuse Alma's work with Porter's.

* * *

It was afternoon when Porter finally waved to Alma and told him it was time for lunch. Alma had already determined that he would work indefinitely, just to see how long Porter could endure the work in the hot, relentless sun before requesting a break.

"Don't you ever take a rest?" Porter demanded when he had shuffled tiredly over to Alma. "Your prideful, stubborn streak runs mighty deep. Clear to the bone, I'd suspect."

"I'm trying to get the work done."

Porter sighed, his exhaustion obvious. "Let's go have lunch."

"You should have worn a hat," Alma commented, observing Porter's red, sunburned face, smudged with dust and streaked with trickles of sweat.

"I figured I needed a tan," Porter retorted lightheartedly.

"You'll just end up with a red face today and gobs of peeling skin tomorrow."

"I'm not worried nearly so much about my sunburned face as I am about these hands," he complained, wincing as he gingerly pulled one of his gloves off. "I thought these gloves would keep me from getting blisters." He peeled the second glove off and dropped both gloves on the ground. Holding his hands out with the palms up, he muttered, "Look at those. Blisters on both of them. Lousy gloves. I ought to take them back for a refund. Do you have blisters?" he demanded of Alma.

Alma shook his head and smiled, stripping his gloves and holding up his hands for Porter's examination. "First of all," he explained, "you bought the wrong kind of gloves, especially since you were going to be using a shovel and a rake."

"I thought gloves were gloves. These cost me fifteen bucks."

Alma grinned broadly. "Price doesn't mean anything. When you use a shovel or a rake, a pair of two-dollar cotton gloves would be better than leather ones."

Porter glowered at Alma. "Who made you a glove expert?"

Alma chuckled and shrugged his shoulders. "Experience."

"Why didn't you share all these pearls of wisdom with me before we started?"

"I didn't figure you were in the mood to take advice from me." He pointed at Porter's hands. "But the gloves are only part of the problem."

"And what's the other part of the problem?" Porter grumbled.

"You've got spongy computer hands. You're not used to doing work like this. Your hands need to be toughened up some or you'll still get blisters, whether you're wearing gloves or not. You better quit before you get blisters on top of your blisters. You work out here much longer, and you won't even be able to use your computer."

"I don't plan to use it for a while." Porter spit into the dirt and then swallowed. "I'm a working man now. Let's get some lunch. You do eat lunch, don't you, working man?"

Alma nodded, smiling.

"And we're eating out today," Porter charged emphatically. "After working here, I don't plan to go home and fix my own lunch. I'll pay someone else to do it for me."

"I can fix something," Alma offered, mainly to goad Porter. "It'll save money."

"I'm not interested in saving money. Right now I'm grouchy and sore, and I want to eat. And don't give me a lecture about what your mom would think about eating out when it's not a special occasion. I consider this a special occasion."

"So we work all morning to earn a little money; then we turn around and blow it on lunch?" Alma fought back a grin.

"Young man, why don't you choke down your stinkin' pride and come with me."

As they were walking toward the car, Mr. Harrison came from his house and called to them. Marshall Harrison was in his early sixties, a hard, grizzled, physically fit man with thick, bushy, prematurely white hair, rough gray stubble along his jaw and chin, and permanent frown lines around his eyes and mouth. "What're you doing here?" he demanded gruffly of Porter, his cool, blue eyes drilling him.

"Alma's my son," Porter returned jocularly. "I've been lending him a hand."

"You expecting to get paid?"

Porter shook his head. "I figured you could take my hours and stick them on Alma's account, pay him for the work I do."

"I'm paying him six fifty an hour."

"That sounds fair to me."

With his narrowed eyes still on Porter, Mr. Harrison pointed a gnarled finger in Alma's direction. "That boy's a hard worker.

Somebody's taught him what it means to put in a full day's work for a full day's pay. I don't figure you was his teacher. He's worth every penny of that six fifty an hour, but I'm not sayin' the same for you." He hitched up his pants. "I don't make it a habit to go around hiring grown men to do this kind of work." He nodded toward the lot. "They expect higher wages."

"Six fifty suits me fine," Porter said, his good nature waning under the accusatory attack of Marshall Harrison.

Mr. Harrison shook his head. "You don't work as hard as the boy here. Every few minutes you're gazing around, pulling your gloves off to check your hands, taking a breather. On his worst day, this boy here would run you into the ground."

All traces of a smile were gone from Porter's face. "Well, how much would you say my work is worth?" He tried to keep his voice steady and devoid of emotion.

"Four fifty, maybe four seventy-five. Even that might be pushing it."

"Then I guess I'm working for four fifty an hour. Does that meet your approval, Mr. Harrison?" The muscles along Porter's jaw tightened while Alma ducked his head and struggled to hide the smile threatening to spread over his face.

"I'll hire you for four fifty. And the money goes on your boy's account."

Porter nodded. "You've hired yourself another man."

Mr. Harrison spit and wiped his mouth with the back of his hand. "I've hired another hand. Whether the hand's a man or not is still to be determined." Turning, he stomped back to the house.

Porter glowered after him. "When I told you that Harrison was a bit crusty around the edges," he said, shaking his head, "I was wrong; he's crusty all the way through." He spat into the dirt. "Is this the best job you could find in Eagar? Maybe McDonald's or Dairy Queen is hiring."

"You can't always be picky," Alma remarked, suddenly chuckling. "Besides, this is my kind of work. I'd make a lousy hamburger flipper."

"You thought that was funny, didn't you?" Porter grumbled, pointing toward Mr. Harrison's house.

Alma answered with a wide grin.

"Standing around!" Porter sputtered. "I might have checked my hands twice. Four lousy bucks an hour."

"Four fifty," Alma corrected him. "But you don't have to take it," he pointed out. "I mean, you can go back to your computer and—"

"I'm taking it," Porter snapped. "Get in the car."

As they drove down the street, Alma remarked, "There was this old guy in Panguitch who used to hire me to buck hay for him. He paid four fifty an hour. Everybody else paid at least seven fifty for bucking bales."

"So why'd you do it?"

"Uncle Walter told me that four fifty an hour was more money than I'd make just sitting home or working for him." He smiled over at Porter, still amused by what had just happened between Mr. Harrison and him.

"Well four fifty an hour isn't more money than I can make sitting at home. The old buzzard. On a bad day I can make four hundred and fifty dollars sitting at home."

"So you'll be at your computer after lunch?" Alma inquired, biting back a laugh.

"No," Porter snapped, "I'll be working for Marshall 'the Buzzard' Harrison, and I'll earn every lousy cent of that four fifty an hour or I'll die in the sun trying."

"If you'd like, I'll give you some pointers . . ." Alma began, intent on needling Porter as much as he could.

"No, I don't need any pointers from you," Porter growled.

"Well, I was just thinking," he said, snickering as he spoke, "Mr. Harrison seemed pretty pleased with the way I was doing things. I just thought—"

"And I definitely don't need any pointers from Marshall 'the Buzzard' Harrison."

After eating lunch, Porter and Alma returned to Mr. Harrison's lot. This time Porter put on a hat he found stuffed in the trunk of his car. While he worked, he refused to pause for short rests, even to straighten and massage his back, just in case Mr. Harrison was spying on him. Although Porter became thirsty, he refrained from drinking unless Alma drank first. He worked doggedly throughout the afternoon and into the evening. The blisters on his hands broke and burned, but he refused to nurse or pamper them.

It was nearly seven thirty when Alma finally gathered his tools and shouted to Porter, "Are you going to work all night?"

Porter straightened up and felt a stab of shocking pain shoot through the small of his back and between his shoulder blades. He ran his tongue along his dried, chapped lips and swallowed against the dryness in his mouth and throat. "Don't tell me you're going to quit so early," Porter mocked as Alma approached, carrying his rake and shovel. "I mean, there's still daylight, man."

Alma grinned. "Actually, I wanted to see how long you'd work before you started to whine."

"Who's whining?"

Alma nodded knowingly. "I decided to call it quits. I don't have anything to prove. And I didn't want to stay out here till midnight and have you pass out on me. Then I'd have to pack you home. Just more work for me."

"That's a likely story. You were the one ready to pass out, and that would slay you to have something like that happen with me standing there to witness it."

Alma didn't comment on the challenge. He turned back to the lot and surveyed it. "I figure we should finish by the middle of the afternoon tomorrow." He glanced at Porter. "Can you make it another day, or are you going to recuperate tomorrow?"

"Do you hear any whining?"

Alma grinned and shook his head.

Both men took long showers. When Porter finally emerged from his room, Alma was in the kitchen making his famous fried potatoes. As Porter dropped onto a kitchen chair, Alma stepped over to him and said, "Let me see your hands."

Porter was reluctant to show them, but he finally held them up.

Alma winced. "You should have told me. You could have quit."

"I could have quit when the first one popped up. This was my idea. I didn't need your permission to stay or go." He dropped his hands in his lap.

"Maybe you'd better work at your computer tomorrow."

"Are you planning to stay home and catch up on your rest?" Porter challenged.

Alma shook his head and returned to the frying pan. "Another day at Mr. Harrison's place, and your hands will be worse than hamburger. You won't be able to use your computer for a week. What about your business?"

"You let me worry about that."

Alma and Porter were at Mr. Harrison's lot first thing the next morning. Porter had made certain that they had plenty of water and a few snacks besides, explaining that he planned to stay until the job was complete.

It was three thirty when the last piles of trash were either burned or loaded up to be hauled away. Porter hadn't realized that he could hurt in so many different places and have such a variety of pains, but he gritted his teeth against the very thought of complaining. He kept anything even remotely resembling a whine to himself.

Mr. Harrison must have been watching their progress, because as soon as they began gathering their tools, he strolled from the house with his checkbook in hand. "How many hours?" he demanded gruffly of Alma.

"Ten on Monday, twelve yesterday, and eight today."

"That's $195," Mr. Harrison announced after about five seconds of mental calculation. "I'll make it an even $200." He spit and scratched his stomach, then turned his glare on Porter. "And yours?"

"Nine yesterday and eight today."

Mr. Harrison's nose and mouth twitched as he did his quick calculation without taking his eyes off Porter. "That'll be $110.50. I'll make it an even $115."

Porter shook his head, his eyes narrowing defiantly. "Four fifty times seventeen is seventy-six fifty."

Mr. Harrison hiked up is pants and looked down at his checkbook. "I've been watching you work, mister. You gave the boy here a run for his money. You kept up to him. I'll pay you the six fifty just like him."

Porter shook his head. "We agreed on four fifty. That's what I'll take."

Mr. Harrison looked between Alma and Porter and then took in a long, hard breath of air. "I was in a bit of a foul mood yesterday and went to shooting off my mouth. You earned the six fifty, fair and square."

"I'll take the four fifty," Porter insisted. "Include it in Alma's check."

Grumbling and scowling, Mr. Harrison made out the check and handed it to Alma. "Your old man's a little crusty around the edges, isn't he?" he muttered.

Alma grinned. "Sometimes, like today, he gets crusty all the way through."

Mr. Harrison pinched the bridge of his nose and cleared his throat. "I've got some other jobs if you're interested," he offered Alma. "It's tough finding good help."

Alma grinned. "I'll take you up on that, Mr. Harrison."

Porter gathered all the tools and put them in the trunk. As soon as he and Alma were in the car, Alma remarked, his mouth twitching against the urge to smile, "Now who did you say was a bit crusty around the edges?"

"Don't even go there," Porter grumbled.

"All those years you knew Mom," Alma went on, "did she ever bother to warn you about any vices? You know, tobacco, alcohol, drugs, pride, stubbornness, bullheadedness, pigheadedness, orneriness . . ." He coughed and then snickered.

"No, she didn't ever warn me about any of that junk," Porter muttered, staring straight ahead as he drove. "I guess she never saw the need."

"It wouldn't have killed you to take the six fifty." He smiled.

The faint traces of a smile pulled at Porter's lips. "Oh, I don't know. Have you ever tried to swallow a hunk of pride about the size of a big fist? It's tough getting it down. Shoot, you should know. You choke on yours right regularly."

10

Even before washing up after finishing at Harrison's place, Alma made a quick trip to NAPA and picked up the parts for the truck. He spent the next several hours in the shed working. Porter tried to do some work in his office, but he was tired and his heart wasn't in it, because he wanted to be with Alma. Instead he wandered around the house, periodically peering from the window toward the shed.

The phone rang, startling Porter to the point that he jumped and whipped around as though an intruder had burst into the house. He let the phone ring five times before finally picking it up. "Port, I was starting to wonder if you were home."

"Calvin," Porter responded with a weak laugh. "What's the occasion? Is Panguitch looking for a lynching victim? I'm not interested."

Calvin chuckled. "I was thinking about you and Alma. How are things going?"

"I suppose that depends on which one of us you ask. And when you ask."

"Well, I'm asking you right now."

Porter shook his head. "I don't know if I did the right thing bringing him here," he answered tiredly.

"I don't know if you did either," Calvin returned with sympathetic honesty, "but you did."

"Calvin, he doesn't give me a chance. Sometimes I think he's opening up to me, and then bang, it's like the door slams closed."

"He's just trying to figure out if you're genuine, Port, if you really care. Do you?"

"I'm his dad. I'm all he's got," Porter returned in frustration.

Calvin grunted. "That's not enough. What guarantee does a sixteen-year-old kid have that you're not going to ship him back to Walter and walk out of his life again?"

"Do *you* think I'm going to do that?"

There was a long pause on the other end of the line.

"Oh, come on, Calvin," Porter burst out, "give me more credit than that!"

"I didn't think you were going to dump Allyson."

"Look, I made mistakes with Allyson."

"No, you made mistakes with both of them. Right now, if I had to bet a hundred dollars on you sticking with Alma, I'd take the bet and feel safe. But Alma isn't betting a hundred dollars on you. He has to bet his heart. His hopes are on the line here. If someone was forcing me to bet all of that on you . . ." There was a long pause on the other end of the line. "Well, I might not be so quick to lay down the bet. You've got to show him you're for real. Not for a few weeks. This is for the rest of his life."

"But he pushes me away, like he doesn't want me to get close to him."

"He pushes you away to see if you'll come back. That's the only way he can know if you're for real. He might not know he's doing that or why he's doing it, but that's what's happening. You've only been with him three weeks. What do you expect?"

"I expect him to pay more attention to me than he does to that old beat-up truck."

Calvin chuckled. "That truck's something he can hold on to. It might not run very good, but it's always there. He needs it." Calvin hesitated and then added softly, "And whether you know it or not, you need that old truck too."

"Not me," Porter muttered. "Every day I wish that old pile of junk would have rolled off Walter's trailer between here and Panguitch. That would have spared us all a whole lot of grief."

"That's where you're wrong, Port. If you want to get close to Alma, you'll do it when you've got a wrench in one hand and grease up to your elbows."

"I don't know the first thing about fixing cars. You know that better than anybody."

"Then let Alma teach you something about it," Calvin growled.

"It's not that simple, and you know it."

"You're right. And if you think you're going to go out there one night and tighten a few bolts and have everything change, you're mistaken. When he sends you back to the house, don't go. Stick with him."

"You're a lot of help," Porter grumbled.

But after Porter hung up the phone, he visited the shed. Alma, who was holding a light on the end of an extension cord in one hand while he worked on the engine with the other, glanced momentarily in Porter's direction when he stepped through the shed door. "Do you need any help?" Porter asked awkwardly.

Alma smiled. "Do you think you can help me?" he questioned skeptically.

Porter shrugged honestly. "If it's not too complicated. What do you need?"

"I don't want you fainting the first time you see a pool of oil on the floor. I know you have a weak stomach when it comes to that sort of thing."

Porter forced out a smile. "So you don't want my help?"

Alma strained to reach something in the engine cavity while still holding the light. He was having a difficult time doing both. "I don't know that there's anything you can do," he grunted. "I really doubt there's anything you *want* to do."

Porter watched Alma struggle a while longer. "Are you saying that *I* don't want to do anything or that *you* don't want me to do anything?" Porter inquired pointedly. "Maybe I'd like to learn."

"What for?"

Porter pondered a moment. "Maybe I just want to hang out with you a little bit."

"Then tomorrow you'll let me help you with one of your sales projects. Is that it?"

Porter hesitated. "Probably not," he admitted.

"Why? That way we can hang out a little more."

"First of all, because you're just trying to make a point."

"Actually, you don't want me working on your sales projects because you don't think I have a clue what I'm doing, and you're right."

"Calvin called," Porter confessed. "He thought it might be a good idea for you to show me a few things. He thought it might be good for both of us."

"Kind of a warm, fuzzy, little family-bonding exercise." Alma nodded while he worked. "I see. That sounds kind of sweet." He smirked. "So you've suddenly got this burning desire to learn a few things about the truck? You sure you don't want to just go buy me a hamburger and fries like you did for Calvin?"

Porter simmered for a moment, regretting that he had tried to follow Calvin's obviously ridiculous advice. "Tell me, why is it that every time I offer you something, you have to make it as difficult as possible for me?"

Alma thought a moment and then shrugged, but he didn't answer.

Porter studied him. "What's been eating you since you came here?"

Alma stepped back from the engine, a wrench in one hand and the light in the other. He shook his head. "For your information, it didn't start when I got to Eagar. Things have been eating me for a long time. You just weren't there to notice."

"So now I'm around. Tell me what's eating you."

For a long moment, Alma considered the request. "Maybe it's pointless to tell you," he replied quietly. "You'd just make it into your neat little family-bonding thing."

"Can't you understand that I care?"

"That you really care, or that you figure you should care and don't? There's a big difference between those two things."

"So we're just a couple of confused guys who will never figure things out?"

"Something like that." Alma dropped down on his haunches and stared into his tool chest, but he didn't take anything out. Porter observed him in silence. The silence ticked away a second at a time, eventually stretching to a full minute.

"I've made mistakes," Porter finally conceded softly. "I'm not denying that."

"You won't get any argument from me there." Alma heaved a sigh. "See, we're already agreeing about something."

"I'd like to fix a few of those mistakes."

"Some things can't be fixed. They just stay broken."

"You seem to want to keep them broken."

"And you seem to think they can be fixed with the snap of your fingers. You like things all neat and orderly, so you figure that since you want things fixed right now, they should be fixed just like that." Alma shook his head. "It's not that easy." He stood up and returned to the engine.

"Well," Porter replied plaintively, "if you need some help sometime, I'll help." He turned to leave and then stopped. "It's getting late, and if you're going to get up early to help Mr. Harrison, you'd better close down here pretty soon."

Alma looked away and asked unexpectedly, "Can you hand me that crescent wrench before you go?"

Porter paused and looked down at the tarp in front of the truck covered with a variety of tools. He studied them for a moment, uncertain which one Alma wanted. Finally he made a guess, bent over, selected one of the tools, and handed it to Alma.

Alma reached for it and then saw what tool it was. For a moment he stared at the tool, and then he looked at Porter. "I need a crescent wrench," he muttered.

"This isn't a crescent wrench?"

"You don't know what a crescent wrench is?"

Porter studied the tool in his hand. "Well, if this isn't a crescent wrench, I guess I don't." He dropped the tool onto the tarp. "Which one's the crescent wrench?"

"Never mind." Alma sighed impatiently. "I'll get it." He pushed away from the truck, stepped to the tarp, and snatched up the crescent wrench.

"I told you I didn't know much about cars and trucks and engines and things."

"I just wanted you to grab a tool, not rebuild the engine for me."

"I didn't ever learn much about the tools either," Porter retorted, embarrassed.

"It's no big deal. I can get my own tools."

"I was trying to help. Just the other day you were complaining because I didn't care about this truck, that I just wanted to get it out of the way."

"Isn't that what you want?"

Ignoring the question, Porter pressed on. "You said that the only thing I ever do is sit in front of my computer and make money." He fought to keep his anger and frustration in check. "So I come out here and try to show some interest, and what do you do? Try to make me feel like an idiot. All right, that's not too tough to do with me out here. But I can take you inside and drop you in front of my monitor—and I know you don't care about making money—and in a few minutes, I could make you feel like a fool too. And what would that accomplish? What do you want, Alma? You can't have everything both ways. What do you want?"

Alma reflected for a moment without working. He heaved a sigh. "I guess if I could choose, I'd like to be working on this truck in Panguitch, where someone who knows what a crescent wrench is could lend a hand."

"You're not going back to Panguitch," Porter muttered tiredly. "We live here now. Both of us. I'm sorry about everything that's happened. And I mean everything. Not just your mom's accident. Everything! Everything in the past, everything that got us to where we are right now. But I can't change that, Alma. You got dealt a lousy hand. I know that. And I'm the one that dealt most of it to you, and I'm sorry. But this is what we're stuck with. So we've got to buck up and face it and make the most of it."

With his jaw clamped tight, Alma returned to his work without responding to Porter's words.

Porter turned his back to Alma and stared stiffly out into the blackness beyond the glow of dull yellow light from the open shed doors. Gradually, he lowered his head and gently massaged the back of his neck. His shoulders slumped slightly. "Look," he muttered, "I wish I was like Calvin and could tell you what needs to be done." He shook his head. "I can't." He took a deep breath and exhaled slowly. "I hate to admit this to you. I hate to admit it to anybody, because people just assume that if you're a guy, you know about trucks and cars and engines and tools and a whole bunch of other stuff. I don't know what I was doing when Calvin and Walter were learning those things. Probably out playing baseball or basketball or going on a hot date. Shoot, Calvin and

Walter had been working on engines since they were out of diapers. They grew up on farms. That stuff was second nature to them. It's second nature to you. But I didn't do any of that stuff. The fact of the matter is, I was scared of the whole thing. Just being around a truck or car with its hood up made me nervous. And if somebody started talking about engines and pistons and crankshafts and wheel bearings, then I'd get panicky and want to change the subject to basketball or something safe. There was a reason why I was the one who left Calvin under the hood and went off to buy the soda pop and the hamburgers. In fact, I'll probably have to have some intensive therapy just to recover from these few minutes out here while you worked on the truck. I'll have to bust out a video of the last Super Bowl and watch it from start to finish two or three times just to purge all this mechanical stuff out of my system. I'm a lousy wreck is what I am."

Alma rested his forearms on the fender without working. He leaned there studying Porter's back.

"Well, good night," Porter mumbled. "Take your time. When you're finished with what you're doing, come in. I won't bother you anymore." Stuffing his hands into his pockets, he trudged from the shed into the night, heading for the house.

Alma watched him disappear and then called out, "Hey."

There was no answer.

He pushed away from the truck. "Hey . . . Dad, I just . . ." He shook his head and his shoulders hunched a little as he stared down at the ground. Heaving a long sigh, he kicked at the ground and tossed the crescent wrench onto the tarp. Dejectedly, he dropped to his haunches in front of the tarp and stared down vacantly at the tools scattered there.

"What did you call me?"

Startled, Alma looked up. Porter stood in the doorway. "It just kind of slipped out," he muttered as an apology, obviously embarrassed. "It won't happen again."

Porter shrugged and shook his head. "It's all right." He smiled. "I've been called worse things in my life. You know, a lot of four-letter words. *Dad's* a nice change. *Dad* is an all right name to be called. I can live with it."

Alma sat on his haunches looking down, his neck and ears blushing red.

"Don't make it a habit or anything, but when you get really frustrated or desperate, you can cut loose with a *Dad* or *Pop* or something similar." He chuckled. "Good night, Alma." He started to turn back toward the house.

"Dad," Alma said softly.

Porter stopped, facing in the direction of the house.

Alma reached down and held up a tool. "This is a socket wrench. This is what you gave me."

Slowly, Porter turned.

Alma popped off the socket and held it up. "There are different sizes of sockets that fit on this wrench. You flip this little switch on the back of the wrench, and that changes the direction of the torque, depending on whether you're tightening a nut or loosening it." Dropping the socket wrench, he picked up another tool. "This is a crescent wrench. This is what I asked for." Pointing to some other tools on the tarp, he said, "Those are pliers. That over there is a Phillips screwdriver." He grinned.

"I recognize the screwdriver." Porter smiled appreciatively. "I even know what a hammer is. I've used one a time or two. Usually to bust something up that was frustrating me really bad."

"I could use a little help to finish up here."

"You want me to hand you the crescent wrench?"

Alma smiled and shook his head. "Actually, I'm going to use the socket wrench now." He picked it up.

"See," Porter joked, "I knew what you wanted before you did. I was just a couple of steps ahead of you. You should have let me hand it to you."

"Can you hold the light? I'm trying to get the last three spark plugs out. It's tough while I'm holding the light too."

"I can hold a light. I'm a good light-holder." Porter smiled sardonically. "With my college degree and extensive business experience and background, I think I can manage to hold a light for you. Just don't spill any oil. I don't want to faint."

For several minutes, Alma struggled with the last three spark plugs, which were frozen tight. He needed both hands cranking on the socket wrench before he finally managed to get them to budge. He would have never done it had he still been holding the light. "Those three definitely need changing." Alma panted as he scrutinized the spark plugs. He pointed to the gap. "See that buildup? The engine's not getting much spark."

"Do you have to get new plugs, or can you fix those?"

"I can sand these down and make them better, but the best thing is just to get new plugs. They're not all that expensive. I probably ought to change the cables, too."

"Do you know how to do that?"

"It's a little like plugging in a toaster." He grinned. "Just a different outlet."

"Oh," Porter remarked, embarrassed.

Alma dropped his wrench into the toolbox. "Thanks for helping," he said, almost as an afterthought.

"No problem. I learned something tonight."

When the tools were gathered and put in the truck bed, Alma opened the cab door to see if he had left anything inside, but he was stalling. He had something else on his mind, and finally he decided to ask it. "When did you stop loving Mom?"

There was a long pause. "What did your mom tell you?"

"That she didn't know what went on in your head."

"She must have had some theories."

Alma closed the truck door. "Hey, if you don't want to talk about it, that's fine."

"Mine was a fair question too."

"I didn't ask about Mom. What she thought doesn't have anything to do with you. Mom didn't walk out. That was your act." There was bitterness in his tone.

Porter held up his hands in surrender, not wanting to return to their previous antagonism. "It's hard to explain." He shifted his weight and glanced at his watch.

"Look, if you don't want to talk about it, just say so."

"I didn't say I wouldn't talk about it. Don't put words in my mouth."

"I won't put words in your mouth, but it would be nice if you'd put some of your own words in your mouth. And I don't want the canned answers, just some truth."

"Sometimes two people discover that they can't—"

"Please!" Alma groaned. "Let's just go in. I don't want to hear that sometimes two people find out they're not meant for each other or something really stupid like that. I get sick of junk like that. I just asked a simple question. When did you stop loving Mom? I don't expect the day or the minute. A month or year is close enough."

Porter pondered a moment. "There are some things you might not understand."

"So it's really too complicated," Alma growled sarcastically.

"Not all that complicated if you have a basic understanding of the situation."

"I have a pretty good grasp of the basics—you and Mom got married, you had me, you were together for a while, and then you left. What basics don't I understand?"

"I don't know if *I* understand everything that happened."

"That's an easy way out."

There was a long pause. Finally, Porter stepped to the truck and put his hand on the hood. "Maybe it's like this truck. When it breaks, I know it's broken, but I don't know why. I don't necessarily know what caused it."

"That's a great analogy. Now all I'm asking is when did your and Mom's truck die on you? I'm curious."

Porter became sullenly silent. "Sometimes you can drive a truck quite a while after it's broken. It's still—"

"In other words, the truck analogy is totally bogus. That was just to get me to mind my own business. All right, I'm sorry I brought this whole thing up."

Porter heaved a sigh. "It's not just the facts, Alma. There are some things that are personal."

"And, of course, Mom wouldn't want me to know those personal things about her. So you're being a real noble guy and protecting Mom's privacy?"

"No, I'm protecting my own privacy."

"Well, that's different. I sure don't want to embarrass you or make you uncomfortable. Because you're probably the only one who's been uncomfortable or embarrassed these last ten years. Shoot, it was a piece of cake for Mom and me. Mom loved telling people she was divorced. Especially at church. Being divorced is only a couple of steps below being a leper in a place like Panguitch. And I loved telling everybody that I didn't have a dad, that he just walked out on us. It made me feel pretty special, because Judy Holmes and Stu Bentz and I were the only ones in my whole class who could say our parents were divorced."

"You twist everything I say."

"No, I'm just asking a simple question. I'm just trying to understand when you stopped loving Mom. I don't expect a long, drawn out explanation. You could say, 'I got tired of her about ten years ago and decided I didn't love her. A couple months later I packed up and left.' An answer like that is pretty short and simple, not too painful."

Porter's face turned a darker shade of red as he endured Alma's insistent onslaught. Every answer he gave, Alma shredded it with his sharp knife of reasoning. "I didn't always know how much I loved her." He shook his head. "Sometimes you lose your focus. And then when you get your focus back, it's too late."

"Losing your focus is a nicer way of saying you stopped loving Mom," Alma remarked sarcastically. "Nicer for you. You like to paint things so you come out looking pretty good." Alma's words bordered on jeers. "So when did you lose your focus?"

"This is really going nowhere. You've already made up your mind what you're going to think of me, and nothing I say is going to change your mind."

Alma glowered at Porter and nodded slowly. "Maybe you're right." He kicked at the truck tire and glared at the floor. "I've had a long time to think about all of this. You know, I used to even argue for you. I used to be the one who tried to explain why you left Mom and me. I used to be on your side. A few years ago, what you're telling me now might have made sense to me." He shook his head. "But I'm past that now. Maybe you should get past it too."

Another long pause followed. "I'll admit I screwed up," Porter said softly, most of his defense washed away. "I did something stupid. Sometimes when you do a stupid thing, you don't always know why. Or you make a mistake and you don't want to admit it. Then you run from anything good that reminds you of your mistake. I ran from you and Allyson. The next thing you do is immerse yourself even more in your mistake, or similar mistakes. I did both those things."

Alma turned away, reaching out and running his hand across the truck's hood. "I'm sorry I brought it up in the first place." His tone had softened, and he seemed to feel bad about being so pushy and rude. "Just forget it. I've gone this long without knowing. It isn't going to kill me now."

Porter turned his back on Alma and pushed his hands into his pockets. "I left your mom for someone else." It was as though he were talking to the wall instead of to Alma. "I've gone back a thousand times to figure out why. I always come up with a blank. I just don't know. Back then I thought I'd found something better. I thought your mom and I had come to a dead end, that there was nothing there, that the lights were out, and I was entitled to another chance with someone else."

"You didn't stay with the other one very long," Alma pointed out.

He shook his head. "No, no I didn't."

"Why?"

Porter turned and faced Alma. "You might think I'm being evasive, but I just don't know. Over the years I came up with some pretty good explanations for why I did what I did. When I heard about Allyson's accident and went to pick you up, you asked some pretty hard questions. Even now I don't know that I've come up with the answers. Maybe I never will. I guess I just messed up."

"Your fault, not hers?"

Porter considered that for a moment. "If you're looking for some-place to cast the blame, I've got to be the one you pin it on."

"Maybe that's all I need to know for now," Alma muttered. "Thanks for holding the light for me. It made things a lot easier."

11

"You know, I've done a lot of thinking about what you asked me last night in the shed," Porter remarked to Alma as they were finishing dinner. Alma continued to eat, keeping his head down. "You asked me when I stopped loving your mom."

"Forget it," Alma mumbled, stirring his food with his fork. "It's no big deal. I should stop beating a dead horse. I just got myself in a lousy mood last night. That happens sometimes when I start thinking of Mom. I get to thinking that someone's to blame and that I need to find out who. It was nothing personal."

"No, it was personal, but it was also a good question." Porter smiled sheepishly. "And I'm still working on the answer." He bit down on his lower lip and narrowed his eyes thoughtfully. "But your question also got me to thinking that maybe you asked the wrong question."

Alma looked up, and Porter pushed back his plate.

"Maybe you should've asked when I *started* loving your mom. I know the answer to that question." Porter stared at the opposite wall and smiled. "My dad was a regional supervisor in the Forest Service, and he got transferred to southern Utah. We moved to Panguitch just before my sophomore year of high school. Your uncle Walter and I became best friends, along with Calvin Crosby—the terrible threesome." He shook his head, remembering. "Of course, I saw Allyson all the time, because I was always over at Walter's place, but she was just my friend's kid sister. I really didn't pay much attention to her. She was a bit awkward and shy and hadn't found herself, and I figured

I was a pretty hot item. There were even junior and senior girls showing serious interest in me."

Alma looked dubious, and Porter's cheeks colored. "I'm not bragging. That's just the way it was." He cleared his throat. "I didn't ever think of dating Allyson, not back then. Besides, she was too young.

"My first date ever was when I was a sophomore. I asked Tanya Sevy to some big school dance. She was a senior and one of the cheerleaders. I told Walter and Calvin that I was going to ask the hottest girl in town, and I figured that was Tanya. I didn't care that she was older than I was. Walter and Calvin told me she'd turn me down flat, but she didn't. I even started dating her. I did a lot of dating through high school, probably more than anybody in Panguitch."

"Mom said you always found the best-looking girls, the popular ones."

Porter nodded sheepishly. "I guess I was a bit of a knothead even back then." He leaned back in his chair and folded his arms across his chest. "My junior year I asked Bridget Hancock to the prom. She was a freshman at Snow College, so I thought I was uptown. Walter and his date doubled with us. Well, I stopped to pick Walter up, and when I got there, Allyson's date was there to pick up Allyson. It was her first date, and she was nervous and flustered. I'd never paid much attention to her until that night. It was weird, because the rest of the night I'd see Allyson, and it was like I was seeing her for the first time. I kept thinking about her. She got into my brain, and I couldn't get her out. I didn't want to get her out."

Porter pursed his lips as he reflected. "I said I didn't have much to do with Allyson, but that's not exactly true. Often she'd hang around or tag along when I was at Walter's place." He smiled, remembering. "I loved to scare your mom. She'd go out to do her farm chores, and I'd hide around a corner or behind a door or by the haystack, and she'd come by, and I'd jump out. She'd scream and practically have a heart attack. She was always threatening to beat me with a board. She probably would have if I hadn't been a faster runner than she was. She got so she was paranoid to go outside if she knew I was around.

"Your mom liked to take walks along the river, and she liked to talk to herself. Sometimes I'd hide in the bushes and listen. If she ever caught me, she'd get mad and threaten to choke me if I ever repeated a single word she'd said. Of course, I'd have to tease her that I was going to tell everybody in town. She'd work herself up till she was on the verge of tears. The only way I could calm her down was to promise, practically on pain of certain death, that I wouldn't blab."

Porter laughed. "But from time to time she got her revenge. One time I hid behind a clump of willows by the river. I didn't know it, but she had seen me sneak down there, so she started talking, making up all kinds of things about who she liked and what she was going to say to them. I was hanging on every word, trying hard not to bust out laughing. She got real close to that clump of willows, and when I wasn't expecting it, she gave me one hard shove and knocked me sprawling into the river. Then she sprinted for the house. I took off after her, but I was soaked and dripping and couldn't run worth a darn. She beat me to the house and taunted me from the steps as I sloshed into the yard."

Alma grinned as Porter told the story.

"Another time I scared her out in the corral. She jumped about ten feet high, and I couldn't stop laughing. She charged at me and knocked me over the feed manger. I landed on my back in six inches of thick, soupy manure. I was covered. It was Allyson's turn to laugh. I had to leave my car at her place, and she drove me home in the back of the truck. It was a week before I got that stink off me."

Alma almost laughed out loud.

"We used to drive the truck around the farm, checking on the irrigation or going down to the pasture to drive the cattle up to the corrals. She was fun to tease, but she was never afraid to tell me what she thought. If she figured I was doing something stupid, she didn't hesitate to tell me. I got so I'd run things past her just to see what she thought. She was always honest, and she took time to figure every-thing out. I appreciated that."

Porter puffed out his cheeks and blew slowly, pensively. "After the prom my junior year, I started paying more attention to Allyson, not as my friend's kid sister but as a girl. I realized that she'd grown up and turned into a lady. The more I saw of her after that, the more I was interested. Calvin and I talked about doubling, and I found out he planned to ask Allyson. Well, I told him I wanted to take her too. We ended up flipping a coin to see which one got her. I ended up taking her.

"I think I knew then that I was going to marry her. We dated off and on after that. Of course, I took other girls out, but Allyson stayed on my mind. Before I left on my mission, I told her I wanted her to wait for me because I was going to marry her." He shook his head. "She just laughed and said I'd find some gorgeous babe and marry her instead."

"She really wasn't your type, was she?" Alma interjected softly.

"Why do you say that?"

"That's what Mom said," he answered simply. "She wasn't a gorgeous babe, wasn't the type you usually asked out."

"Your mom was beautiful," Porter insisted. "She had a beauty that kind of grows on you, the kind that makes you feel content. She had so many other qualities that she didn't have to be drop-dead gorgeous. She wasn't stuck on herself. She was genuine. And I was in love with her. Once, your mom told me that she fell in love with me when I first moved to Panguitch. I thought that was strange, but the more I've thought about that, especially lately, I've wondered if I fell in love with her then, too. I just didn't realize it. She was always more perceptive than I was. Maybe that was my problem; I didn't ever see things as clearly as she did."

They were both quiet for a moment. Finally, Porter stood up. "I just thought you'd like to know when I first fell in love with her." He wet his lips. "And, Alma, in spite of everything else you might think, I did love your mom."

"As much as she loved you?"

Porter ran the tips of his fingers across the tabletop. "Knowing Allyson," he began slowly, "and knowing me, I'd have to say . . ." He hesitated, then shook his head as a pained looked pinched his face. "Allyson was a better person than I was. She loved deeper than I did. I was too selfish, too self-centered, to love as deeply as she did. Had I loved like she did, had I seen things through her eyes, I suppose things would have been different."

"So why did you choose Mom when she really wasn't your type?"

"She was good for me."

Alma shook his head. "But she would've been good for anyone. Not everyone was good for her. Were you good for her?" he asked pointedly.

"Not always," Porter admitted guiltily, shaking his head. "I should have been." He knit his brow and stared intently at the floor as though trying to discover something there. "I used to think I did Allyson a favor by marrying her. I guess I was a bit conceited."

"That sounds a whole lot conceited," Alma said.

The two of them were quiet for a several moments, and then Alma remarked hoarsely, "I don't think she ever stopped loving you. Even at the end. That's why everything hurt her so much." He swallowed. "And I guess that's why I wanted to hate you a lot of times. You still held onto a piece of Mom's heart, and she couldn't let it go."

Porter grimaced. "Just before I found out about her . . . accident, I considered some things. I wondered if she would take me back."

Alma stared across the table at Porter, his eyes narrowing some in disbelief.

A rueful smile tugged at Porter's lips. "The thought staggered me," he whispered. "It was like standing at the foot of a tall mountain and contemplating climbing to the top." He shook his head. "There was so far to go, and I didn't have a clue whether I was up to the climb or whether Allyson would even want me to try. But I wanted to."

Porter sat down again and leaned forward with his elbows on the table and put his head in his hands. "When I found out about her accident, I . . ." He pressed his hands against his head and closed his eyes tightly. "It was like a door closed on me. I had been wanting to call her but didn't have the courage. And since you've been here, I've wished with all my heart that she was still here, even for a short while, so I could go back and ask her to forgive me and see if there was some way to repair the damage."

For a long time neither of them spoke. Alma was the first to break the silence. "I used to hate you sometimes," he rasped, shrugging. "I think there's still a part of me that wants to hate you. Actually, it's kind of ironic. I'd start hating you because of what you'd done to

Mom, but she was the one who stood in my way. I don't know how many times she told me not to go down that road. I tried to sneak down it without her knowing it, but she always seemed to know, and she'd talk me back."

"She was pretty close to perfect, wasn't she?"

Alma laughed sadly. "Close, but she had her moments. Sometimes she'd get on me. Nobody else, but on me. She didn't want me messing up, and if she thought I was even getting close to the line, she'd kind of flip out. Then she'd apologize later. I always knew if she ever got on my case and yelled at me, it would only be a little while before she'd come back bawling with her apology. I used to think it was kind of funny. As I got older I'd joke with her and tell her there was no point in yelling at me, because she'd just have to apologize later. That really made her mad, but she knew it was true."

"She didn't want you turning out like me. That was enough to scare anybody." Porter wet his lips, reluctant to say more but impelled. "What was she like?" He shook his head. "What was she like when she went back to Panguitch?" He grinned guiltily. "The way people talked, she was Panguitch's patron saint."

Alma got a far-off look in his eyes. "Everybody loved Mom. She was good to everybody. I think people expected her to be sad and bitter. The first few months were hard. I don't remember them, though. I mainly remember her being happy, always smiling." He paused and reconsidered. "Oh, there were times at home when she got down, and I knew she was hurting, but with other people she was always happy and positive. She had a good word for everybody. She did a lot of little things for people, mostly on the sly, but everybody knew it was her.

"She started working at the high school the year after we moved to Panguitch. At first she was just an aide, but then they made her the secretary. The kids liked her a lot, and she knew all of them. She'd walk down the halls and everybody would say, 'Hi, Mrs. Huggins,' and she'd say hi back and call them by name. If she figured someone was down in the dumps, she'd help them out. If a girl didn't have a date to a dance, she'd line something up for her. She helped get girls dresses and helped the boys pick out flowers for their dates."

Porter smiled as Alma talked. "She could get the kids to do about anything. Last year Troy Miller and Arney Dodds got in a fight. Mr. Carson, the principal, was gone, and Troy and Arney were about to have a knock-down-drag-out right in front of the school." Alma laughed. "Mom marched out there and stood between them. If it had been anybody else, those two would have probably decked whoever was butting in, but not Mom. She backed them both up and even made them shake hands."

Alma grinned. "There was one time she almost got herself fired for whacking a kid upside the head with a broom."

"Allyson?" Porter gasped, shocked.

"It was a couple years ago. Reg Houston was a big bully, and he was always harassing this Mexican kid, Mateo Zapata. Well, one day Reg spilled his soda in the hall and told Mateo to clean it up. Mateo wouldn't, so Reg grabbed him and was going to use him as a mop. They were wrestling around when Mom walked down the hall. She told Reg to stop, but he didn't. He got Mateo in a full nelson and was getting ready to push him to the floor right in his spilled soda. The janitor's closet was open across the hall, so Mom grabbed a broom, and before Reg could get Mateo down on the floor, she smacked Reg. She said she was aiming at his back, but she caught him in the head. Hammered him good. His nose was bleeding, and he was pretty mad. He went home and bawled to his dad. Even before his dad came in to talk to Mr. Carson, Reg had blabbed around town that he was going to have 'the maniac lady in the office' fired."

Alma took a deep breath. "Nobody's exactly sure what happened, just rumors, but I think about half the guys in the school had a long talk with Reg. They must have told him that if anything happened to Mom, nobody would have anything to do with him, and every other weekend he'd end up in a ditch with a lump on his head."

"So what happened?" Porter asked.

"Mr. Houston showed up at school in his Sunday suit like he was making a case before the Supreme Court. He strutted in, muttering about how he was going to turn the whole school upside down. Mr. Carson called Reg in. He went into the office and claimed that he'd been confused about the whole thing."

Porter chuckled. "And what did Mr. Houston say?"

"He went through the roof, but Reg wouldn't back down. Mom even went in and admitted hitting Reg on accident, but Reg told her that she must be mistaken. Mr. Houston sputtered and blew for a while, but he finally gave up."

"And what happened to this Reg kid?"

"Mom made sure everybody left him alone. Reg and Mom became good friends." Alma smiled mischievously. "You know how the freshmen usually get harassed by the juniors and seniors? Nobody harassed me."

"Because you were Allyson's son?"

Alma shook his head. "Because of Reg. He made it clear that nobody was to bother me." Alma became solemn. "Reg bawled his eyes out at Mom's funeral."

For a long time, both men were quiet. Then Porter started gathering up the plates and utensils. "I'll clean up here," he volunteered. "You get out to the shed and see what damage you can do to that old truck."

Alma stood up and started for the door. He paused with his hand on the doorknob. "Thanks for telling me about you and Mom," he said quietly. Then he pulled the door open and disappeared.

12

One evening several days later as Porter finished up some work in his office, Alma rapped loudly on his half-open door. Porter turned around.

"I think it runs all right," Alma remarked casually. He shrugged. "It might not make it on a long trip or anything like that, but with the new plugs in and a new air filter, it's sounding pretty good. I cleaned out the carburetor." He took a deep breath. "I figure we ought to celebrate, go out to dinner or something. Of course, you'll have to buy, because I blew all my money on parts."

"You think getting that old truck to run is special enough to get Alma Huggins to actually go out to dinner and celebrate?" Porter teased. "You won't need guilt therapy after we're finished, will you?"

"This is pretty special. In fact, it's downright amazing. I guess I can pay my own way if you're turning into a tightwad all of a sudden."

Pushing up from his desk, Porter shook his head. "If you're feeling festive enough to eat out, I'll break down and pay. It's about time we went out to dinner."

Alma held up the truck key. "Do you want to drive?"

Porter studied the key for a moment. "You trust me with the truck?"

Alma nodded.

"You *are* in a festive mood. This calls for something more than McDonald's."

A few minutes later as Porter started the engine, Alma remarked casually, "Let's see if Darbie wants to go with us."

Porter was about to shift into first gear, but he stopped and stared inquiringly at his son. "Where'd that come from?"

"Maybe she wants to celebrate too. After all, there's free food. I'll pay her way."

Taking his hand from the gearshift, Porter put both hands on the steering wheel and stared straight ahead. "She won't come," he said simply. "Not with me."

"I thought you were friends."

"The key word is *were*." Porter rubbed his nose and puffed out his cheeks. "Look, I already told you that whatever happened between Darbie and me is over."

"She still wants to be a good neighbor and friend," Alma cut in. "Neighbors go out to dinner with neighbors. I figure we can at least invite her. No commitments. Your problem is that you want to twist everything into something serious."

"Well," Porter grumbled, putting the truck into gear and pulling onto the street, "just take my word for it. She won't go with us."

"I'll ask her." Alma smiled slyly. "I told her I'd give her a ride in the truck when I got it running. Dinner's an added bonus. After all, she's my jogging partner."

Porter slowed the truck to a stop. "Jogging partner?" he questioned, his eyes narrowing some. "When did that happen?"

Alma grinned. "I jog every morning."

"I thought you jogged alone."

Alma continued to grin and shook his head. "Darbie needed a bodyguard. She was willing to overlook the fact that I'm your son, and I was willing to overlook the fact that she's your old girlfriend. Darbie and I are good at working things out between us."

"She was never my girlfriend," Porter countered. "We were friends."

Alma shrugged. "Whatever. Now Darbie and I are pretty good friends."

Porter began driving slowly. "She won't go," he insisted. "And she'll think I put you up to this whole thing."

Porter pulled the truck in front of Darbie's white frame house and stared over the hood with his hands gripping the steering wheel.

"She'll be cool," Alma commented, lifting up on the door handle. "If she doesn't want to go with us, she can say so."

Porter glanced at his watch. "I figure that once she sees I'm in the truck, it will take about fifteen seconds, thirty at the most, for her to tell you to go chase yourself."

Alma grinned over at Porter. "So if you were a betting man . . ."

"I'd flat bet against you, yes."

Alma shrugged. "I hate taking money from family, but . . ." He cleared his throat. "I'll make an exception just for you. Besides, I'm broke right now. How does twenty bucks sound?"

"You mean you'd actually stoop to taking money from me?"

"I'll make an exception this one time. It's an easy way to pick up twenty bucks."

Porter stuck out his hand, and Alma shook it. "Sounds like you're going to be twenty bucks poorer," Porter said confidently. "You'll have to put in three hours at Harrison's to pay for this indiscreet little wager."

Alma sauntered to the door and rang the bell. At first Darbie didn't answer, so Alma rang again. There was another long wait. When Alma rang a third time, Porter smiled smugly. Alma was about to turn around and join Porter in the truck, when Darbie opened the door.

"Hello, Alma," she greeted him, out of breath, glancing first at Alma and then over his shoulder toward Porter, who sat in the truck, looking in the opposite direction, pretending to study something across the street. She stood in bare feet, wearing a pair of faded denim jeans with frayed cuffs and a slightly fitted tee. Her hair was wet, almost dripping, and her face was washed clean of all traces of makeup. "Don't tell me your truck is running!" she called out cheerily.

"I even had a little bit of help from my dad," Alma replied. He cleared his throat and added just above a whisper, "He held the light for me a few times while I put the last spark plugs in. We're going out to dinner to celebrate. Do you want to come? You've never taken a drive in the truck."

Darbie studied Alma warily. "I don't know if . . ." she started, groping for the best words to decline. "I don't know if that would be such a good idea."

Sensing an impending rejection, Alma quickly cut in. "It was my idea. I thought it would be fun to have some lively company. Even on his best days, Dad's pretty dull."

Darbie couldn't help laughing. "Did he put you up to this? Don't lie to me, Alma." She shook a finger under his nose. "I want the truth."

"Actually, he's working up a heart attack. The guy's a nervous wreck." He cocked his head to one side and stared at Darbie's bare feet. "He's really sensitive to rejection." Alma looked up and grinned bashfully. "He was pretty sure you'd turn me down flat. He even bet twenty bucks against you."

"Do you trust him to pay up?" she asked, raising one brow.

"Sure. I'll even split it with you. You haven't eaten, have you?"

"I just got out of the shower. That's why I look like a drowned rat." She looked herself up and down. "I'm really not ready to go out in public."

"Heck, is there anywhere in Eagar so fancy you can't go with wet hair?" Alma, who was wearing a baseball cap, whipped it off. "You can wear this."

Declining the proffered cap, Darbie searched for another excuse. "I don't have my makeup on. I even scare myself when I look like this."

"It's probably better that you look a little scary. That way my dad won't get any romantic ideas." Alma grinned teasingly. "Come on," he begged, "just this once. I want to see his face when you walk out there with me." He pushed his hands into his pockets. "I'm just being neighborly."

"So I'm your weekly neighborhood project?"

"Something like that. Of course, some service projects are more fun than others."

Darbie's eyes narrowed as she studied Alma. "You're not trying to pull one on me are you, Alma Huggins?"

Alma held up his hands. "Honest. This is all aboveboard."

"I'll do it. For you. Let me get my shoes."

Darbie closed the door, and Alma ambled back to the car.

"Well, it took her longer to turn you down than I thought it would," Porter remarked. He held out his hand. "I'll take my twenty bucks any time now."

Alma grinned just as Darbie's front door opened and she emerged carrying a pair of leather sandals. Porter's mouth sagged open momentarily, and then he moved to get out of the truck and open Darbie's door for her.

Alma touched his arm and shook his head. "I'll help her. I think she's suspicious of you." He stepped out of the truck to let Darbie in.

Darbie shook her head and pointed to the seat. "I'll ride shotgun."

Alma nodded and slid across the seat next to his dad.

"Hello, Porter," Darbie greeted as she climbed into the truck and slammed the door. "Thanks for the invitation."

Porter's face burned a bright red. He gulped and tried to say something, but nothing came out. "I wasn't going to bother you," he finally stammered.

Darbie laughed. "Alma already told me you didn't want me tagging along," she teased with a straight face, "but I was hungry and couldn't pass up a steak. We are having steak, aren't we? I didn't get all dressed up for a hamburger."

"Sure, we're having steaks," Porter quickly affirmed. "Anything you want. But I didn't say I didn't want you."

"You bet twenty dollars against me. Same thing."

Porter cast a quick glance in Alma's direction while his blush deepened. He cleared his throat and prepared to explain, but Darbie anticipated his feeble argument. "Don't worry, Porter, I know you were just thinking how much this would cost you."

"I wasn't worried about the money," Porter fumbled frantically.

"I appreciate Alma thinking of me. He's a great neighbor."

They ended up at the Safire in Springerville. As they found a booth and sat down, Porter was awkward and ill at ease. Both Alma and Darbie seemed to enjoy witnessing Porter sweat through the whole experience.

"So how long has this jogging arrangement been going on?" Porter finally asked, trying to think of something to say.

"A while," Darbie answered, smiling. "Do you want to join us?"

Porter shook his head. "I'll pass." He thought a moment and then probed further. "You two act like you do more than jog."

"Darbie has let me hang out a little bit at her place. She's given me a few books to read. We talk."

"Yeah," Darbie cut in. "You spend so much time in front of that computer of yours that Alma doesn't have a chance to talk to you, so he comes over to my place. I'm not so busy." Alma and Darbie both laughed.

"If he doesn't have a chance to talk, it's because his head's always under the hood of that truck out there," Porter muttered, nodding toward the parking lot.

"Hey, tell me what you did to your truck," Darbie said to Alma, changing the subject.

"Well, I'm not taking it to the races any time soon. I still have work to do. I plan to change out the water pump and fuel filter. Several of the hoses need to be replaced. The brake pads should be changed, and I ought to bleed the brake lines and replace the fluid. Those are just the starters. I might need to repack the bearings on the front driver's-side wheel. It'd probably be a good idea if I did all of them. I'm hoping that I don't have to do anything major like a valve job or something."

"Do you know how to do all of that?" Darbie asked, sounding duly impressed.

"Most of it. Not a valve job. I'd need some help and more equipment for that."

"You're ambitious."

As she smiled, Alma reacted bashfully to her obvious praise, smiling but ducking his head and reaching for his glass of water. He was reminded how his mother had been so liberal with her praise of him. "It's just something I've wanted to do for a long time," he added after taking a sip.

"And I hear you've started using those tools I broke in for you," she said unexpectedly to Porter.

Porter glanced at Alma, who smiled knowingly. "The truck's Alma's project."

"He said you helped him."

Porter glowered in Alma's direction, but Alma just held up his hands. "I held the light for him and handed him a few tools," Porter explained sheepishly. "That in itself taxed my mechanical abilities. From now on Alma will have to do everything on his own."

"Don't you want to learn to be a mechanic?" Darbie pressed, her eyes teasing him.

"Alma wants to fix his truck, not teach me to be a mechanic."

During dinner, Porter found himself defending himself from Darbie's playful jabs. She obviously enjoyed watching him squirm. Alma relished the prankish exchange too.

After dropping Darbie off, Alma casually observed, "I think your neighbor still likes you—and not just as a neighbor."

Porter shook his head. "Is that why she harassed me all night while you sat by and grinned encouragement to her?"

Alma chuckled. "It seemed the right thing to do at the time."

* * *

"Where are you headed?" Porter asked Alma late the next afternoon as Alma came up the stairs from his room and headed for the front door, buttoning his shirt and tucking in the tails. Thirty minutes earlier Alma had returned from working at Marshall Harrison's. Although he hadn't mentioned anything to Alma, Porter had considered taking him to a movie at the tiny theater in Springerville.

"Darbie's cleaning up that big backyard of hers. I told her this morning that I'd lend her a hand."

"We've got yard work around here," Porter replied sourly.

Alma considered that. "Yeah, but then you wouldn't have anything to do." He smiled. "After sitting in front of that computer all day, you should go outside and get your hands dirty, maybe sprout some new blisters."

"I had enough dirt and blisters over at Harrison's place," Porter grumbled.

Alma opened the front door and stood there for a moment. "If you get overwhelmed, I'll come back and lend a hand." He waved. "Catch you later."

For thirty minutes, an agitated and restless Porter puttered around the house. Finally, he grabbed a rake and shovel, fully intending to work in his own yard. As soon as he surveyed his place, however, he lost interest. He was about to put the tools away when he admitted to himself that he didn't want to do yard work by himself; he wanted to do it with Alma and Darbie. Shouldering his garden tools, he marched down the street.

As Porter stepped into Darbie's front yard, he heard Darbie and Alma before he actually saw them. He recognized Darbie's laugh and Alma's teasing. Reaching the corner of the house, he almost lost his nerve, but forging ahead before he could chicken out, he marched stiffly into the backyard. Darbie was on her hands and knees, pulling weeds from a flower garden while Alma was a few feet away raking leaves and twigs from around the trunk of a ball willow tree. Both of them were laughing.

"It doesn't sound much like work around here," Porter remarked to announce his arrival. Darbie and Alma stopped laughing and faced him. "From the street it sounded more like goofing around. I figured you needed somebody to keep you on task."

Darbie turned to Alma and spoke as though Porter wasn't standing there. "Great! Now we've got to put up with a taskmaster." Dusting her hands off, she remarked to Porter, "Look, this isn't some state road project where we need a quota of guys standing around leaning on their shovels. We are accepting a few highly qualified volunteers with a minimum of thirty minutes raking and shoveling experience. Packing the rake and shovel over here from your place doesn't qualify as bona fide experience. That's merely related work experience. Also, we prefer at least two personal references."

Alma spoke up. "He used a rake over at Marshall Harrison's place, he worked there for more than thirty minutes, unless you subtract the time he spent whining."

"Whining doesn't count as work experience. Whining is just whining."

Porter let the shovel and rake slide from his shoulder onto the ground. "Cute. Very cute. What do you want me to do?" he asked dryly.

Darbie turned to Alma. She pretended to whisper but spoke loud enough for Porter to hear. "He'll probably just get in the way, but we'd better let him stay. Besides, his rake is better than mine." Darbie looked around her yard. The front thirty feet of the backyard was lawn with shrubs and narrow flower gardens along the back of the house and a half dozen fruit trees growing along the property line. The very back of the yard, which extended another forty feet beyond the edge of the lawn, was a choked jungle of weeds, brush, and trees that had never seen serious trimming, pruning, or weeding. "We planned to mow the lawn and weed the flower beds." She cringed and nodded toward the tangled growth at the back of her lot. "If we built up enough courage, we were going to tackle that mess back there. How's your courage, Porter?"

He cleared his throat and dropped his tools. "I'll need something besides a shovel and rake."

Alma pointed to a pruning saw and a pair of heavy-duty shears. "Those are your weapons."

"So I get the dirty work?" Porter complained.

"He hasn't even started to work, and already he's whining," Darbie said to Alma. "Mr. Huggins," she stated pompously, turning to Porter, "I'm not impressed with your attitude or shallow qualifications. We'll have to ask you to vacate the premises."

"And if I refuse?"

"You'll be severely punished—forced to get the lawn mower and mow the lawn, both front and back."

"Is there gas in the mower?"

"I wouldn't trust him to put gas in the mower," Alma interjected. "When it comes to engines and motors, he's helpless. He'll end up putting gas in the crankcase. And the sight of grease or oil makes him hyperventilate."

Porter waved the two away and grabbed the mower. As he started on the lawn, Darbie disappeared into the house. A moment later she returned with a plate in her hand. She pushed a gas grill onto her small patio and proceeded to grill some steaks.

By the time the steaks were finished cooking, Darbie had set up a small round card table on the patio and had it loaded with a tossed green salad, soda pop, chips, potato salad, hard rolls, and steaks. She called to Alma and Porter and handed them a bar of soap, pointing as she did to the garden hose at the corner of the house.

"We can't wash up in the sink?" Porter complained playfully.

"You can—" Darbie smiled back—"if you wash in *your* sink. Just because you clean up my yard doesn't mean you can dirty up my house. I am feeding you," she pointed out pleasantly. "In fact, I'll be gracious and give you a choice. You can have dinner with me out here, or you can wash your hands in my sink."

Porter thought a moment as he glanced at the steaks on the table. After quick deliberation, he shrugged and remarked, "I guess I'll use your hose."

* * *

"I stopped by the school this morning," Darbie said as the three of them ate. "I ran into the football coach. I told him he had a new football prospect." Porter and Alma both stopped eating and looked across the table at Darbie. "He was very interested. I told him that Alma jogs with me every morning and that he seems fast." She set her fork down and looked at Alma. "He'll probably look you up."

Alma chewed slowly, thoughtfully. Swallowing, he shook his head. "I've never played football, except in the backyard. I'll be a junior. Everybody around here has probably played since junior high."

"It's not all that complicated," Darbie observed. "You just run around the field with a funny-shaped ball. If you're fast, you're good. Porter could probably even play—if he stopped whining." She grinned and winked at Alma.

"For your information," Porter defended himself, "I used to be quite an athlete."

Darbie heaved a sigh and rolled her eyes. "Now I really asked for it." Speaking to Alma from the corner of her mouth, she added, "He'll probably spend the next three hours bragging about his glory days. You know, thirty or forty years ago when he was on his high school junior varsity ping-pong team. I don't want to get him started. We'll never be able to shut him up."

Alma laughed while Porter protested playfully, "What is this, Hammer Porter Night? You've been taking potshots at me ever since I showed up."

"I just like to tease you, Porter." She stood up. "But I'm not teasing you when I tell you," she quickly added, "that you have clean-up duty. That's part of your punishment for staying after I told you to vacate the premises."

"I figured there was some catch to your hospitality," Porter returned, beginning to gather the plates and utensils.

Darbie quickly pushed his hands away. "I was just kidding," she reprimanded humorously. "That's your problem, Porter, you never know when I'm kidding. You're always so serious. You need to loosen up, like Alma here. I'll clean up." She smiled. "And seriously, thanks for helping me out. Thank you, both of you. We'll have to do this again." She nodded to the tangled jungle that they hadn't started on. "When I tackle that mess, I'm going to need some serious help. You're both invited." She quickly jabbed a finger at Porter. "But next time, you buy the steaks."

"How about tomorrow?" Porter offered.

Turning to Alma, Darbie spoke behind her hand, "Now he's trying to get fresh with me. You can never trust these older men. You try to be nice to them, and they just take advantage of you. Now he'll start coming over every day." Turning back to Porter, she smiled and said, "I can't tomorrow, but we'll do it again."

* * *

When Porter and Alma returned home, Porter asked Alma to wait outside; then he darted into the house and returned with a football. "Let's see what you can do," Porter challenged him, waving him back.

Alma jogged halfheartedly, and Porter tossed the ball. Alma caught it without a problem. For several minutes they tossed the ball back and forth; then Porter told Alma to go deep for a pass. Porter's aim and delivery were good, making it easy for Alma to catch each ball. Then on one running route, Porter zinged the ball in his direction, but it was high and to his left. Hardly interrupting his stride, Alma leaped high into the air with his hands and arms outstretched. The tips of his fingers touched the ball, and he pulled it in, coming down smoothly.

"Dang!" Porter gasped, grinning. "What have you got, glue on those hands? I didn't think there was any way you'd catch that."

Embarrassed by the praise, Alma blushed and shrugged. "Somebody once told me if you could touch it, you should catch it."

"Yeah, but touch it with what? I think the only thing that touched that ball was the tip of your middle finger. That was an unbelievable catch."

Porter continued to throw balls that were either high or to one side or the other. Rarely did Alma miss. Finally, Porter waved him in. "I can't believe your hands," he marveled. "I used to think I was good." He shook his head. "But nothing gets past you."

"Yeah, but nobody's covering me either."

"Go inside and put on your shorts and running shoes. Let's see how fast you run."

"What is this, football tryouts?"

"I'm just curious."

While Alma changed into his running things, Porter took a hundred-foot measuring tape and marked off forty yards and one hundred meters. When Alma returned, Porter took off his wristwatch and adjusted it to the stopwatch setting. "I want you to run a forty first."

Alma did the forty in 4.8 seconds. "You're not trying," Porter told him.

"You mean 4.8 isn't good?"

"I know you're faster than that. Try the hundred meters."

Alma ran the hundred meters in 11.9 seconds. "You're not pushing yourself," Porter complained. "You've got more speed than you're showing."

"So this is how you get back at me?" Darbie called from down the road behind them. Both of them turned and watched her approach carrying a shovel and a rake. "I tease you a little bit," she accused Porter, "and you leave your tools behind so I have to bring them to you."

"He just wanted an excuse to go back and see you," Alma suggested.

Darbie tossed the garden tools at Porter's feet. "Well, he can forget that sneak play." She glanced at Alma's shorts and running shoes and saw the football lying on the lawn. "Is your dad getting you ready for Coach Slade?" She shook her head. "Maybe I shouldn't have opened my mouth. Has he been telling you about his fourth-place finish in the school ping-pong tournament?"

"Very funny," Porter complained, but he liked Darbie's teasing. "He's got speed," he told her, pointing to Alma. "But he won't use it. Tell him to run," he pressed her. Turning to Alma, he added, "Show Darbie what you can do. She's your cheering crowd."

Darbie put her hands on her hips. "Burn up the pavement," she coached.

Obviously embarrassed, but wanting to impress Darbie, Alma jogged to the starting line. This time he burst forward with determined energy, his legs pushing powerfully, his arms pumping at his sides, and his face contorted in a grimace of utter exertion. When he sped past the finish line, Porter snapped the stopwatch and let out a yell. "Now you're running with your heart in it! That was 4.5. Try the hundred."

Once more Alma burst from his starting position with determination and energy. When he raced past the finish line, the clock registered 11.3. "Yes!" Porter burst out. "The coach will be drooling when he hears about you."

"But I don't know that much about football," Alma pointed out.

"There's a ton of guys that can tell you lots of stuff about football. But they can't play the game. They don't have the talent. You can learn that other stuff, but a coach can't teach you speed and quick hands. That's talent."

Darbie smiled and patted Alma on the shoulder while he grinned his shy acknowledgment. "You're fast," she congratulated him. "Take it from an old sprinter who knows." She jabbed a thumb in Porter's direction. "If you're not careful, your dad's going to bust his buttons. He's really pumped."

13

Over the next two weeks, Alma and Porter settled into a more comfortable routine. Most days Alma worked at least a few hours for Marshall Harrison. He often spent part of his later afternoons at Darbie's place, helping her in her yard or just visiting.

One evening Coach Slade stopped by and invited Alma to join the Elk football program. Alma reacted with seeming indifference, but he agreed to at least consider the invitation.

"Give it a shot," Porter encouraged him. "You've got the talent, and I'm convinced that you'll like it."

"Who knows if I'll even be here," was Alma's short reply.

Porter chose not to argue the point, but two days later Alma showed up at the high school football field for an informal practice for an upcoming passing league competition. Alma didn't tell Porter how he did, but two days later the coach stopped by when Porter was mowing his lawn.

"Alma says he might move back to Panguitch this fall," Coach Slade remarked after a few pleasantries. "What will it take to keep him here?"

Porter brushed grass from his pant legs. "I don't know anything about Alma moving back to Panguitch. I'm planning to stay here, and Alma's staying with me."

Coach Slade grinned. "That's good news." He shook his head. "He can really help our program. The kid can catch anything," he reported in amazement, excitement sparkling in his eyes. "If he can touch it, he pulls it in. His vertical leap is amazing. It's like he can fly. We need him, Mr. Huggins, so anything you can do to keep him in

Round Valley will sure be appreciated." He shook his head. "They don't even play football in Panguitch. He'd be wasted there."

The same day that Coach Slade visited with Porter about Alma's football talents, Alma announced, "I think the truck needs a new timing belt, and possibly a valve job."

"And what does that mean?" Porter inquired, wishing to demonstrate interest but not having any idea what a valve job or new timing belt entailed.

"Well, I can't do it here," Alma explained, shaking his head. "I've never done anything like that, and I don't have the equipment." Alma hesitated and then went on. "There's a guy over by the stoplight who has an auto repair shop. Cash Wilkes. Do you know him?"

Porter considered the name and then shook his head.

"I talked to him this afternoon. He said he could help me out, but the cost might be a little high."

Porter nodded and asked hopefully, "Do you need a loan?"

Alma smiled and shook his head. "I'm still doing this on my own."

"I didn't say I'd pay for it. A loan means you'll still pay your own way." Porter grinned. "And if it will soothe your guilty conscience, I'll even charge you interest."

Alma amiably declined. "Cash says I can help him when I'm not working for Mr. Harrison. There are a few jobs I can do around his shop. He'll even show me some stuff. It wouldn't be a real job, but he'd help me after hours."

* * *

That night when Alma came in from the shed, he was shaking his head and seemed discouraged. "Those repairs aren't going to be cheap or easy."

"My offer for a loan is still open."

Alma shook his head. "I'll take the truck to Cash's shop day after tomorrow. It's torn apart some right now, so it'll take me an hour or so to put things back together."

"You tore it apart? Again? I thought you barely got things put back together."

"I did," Alma responded with a sheepish grin. "But that's part of the fun of having an old truck," he explained. "You get to tear it apart and then turn around and put it back together. Then you can tear it apart again."

"And that's supposed to be fun?"

"It is for me. It's like a puzzle. Just because you put a puzzle together once doesn't mean you don't want to do it again."

"I'll take your word for it," Porter muttered. "So right now your truck's scattered all over the shed floor?"

Alma laughed. "It's not that bad. I put everything in the back of the truck, along with my tools. I'll work on it tomorrow after I finish at Mr. Harrison's place."

The following afternoon Porter worked in his office, frustrated at being unable to trace a dozen computers that had been shipped to Mississippi two weeks earlier. While he was working, he smelled smoke, but he didn't think much of it until he took a break and looked out his window. His neighbor behind and to the north was burning off a field of dried weeds and grass, and the smoke was drifting Porter's way. Even though it was warm inside, Porter closed all the windows to keep the smoke out.

An hour later somebody hammered on Porter's door, but thinking he had finally traced the problem of his missing computers, he ignored the knocking and concentrated on his computer search. He heard a few shouts, but he couldn't make out what was being said. Nothing really registered until he heard the wail of a distant siren. Only then did he go to the window again. When he looked out, he felt a sudden knot of panic in the pit of his stomach. Apparently, a gust of wind had come up, and the grass and weed fire that had been in his neighbor's field had suddenly shifted toward Porter's place.

The only thing separating Porter's place from his neighbor's field was a barbed-wire fence that was no match for the wind-driven fire, which had now reached his shed. Along the entire back wall of the shed and down one of its sides was a thick, tangled growth of dried weeds and grass. Several times during the summer, Porter had intended to clear away those weeds and grass, but he had always procrastinated, giving preference to more pressing matters. Now those weeds and grass were in flames.

Racing out the back door of his house, Porter joined several of his neighbors who were struggling frantically to get his garden hose to the shed, but the hose was thirty feet too short, and the fire truck sirens were still distant.

"What's in that shed?" a neighbor yelled, spotting Porter as he bounded from the house. "If there's anything worth something, you'd better get it out."

"My son's truck." Porter raced past the half dozen men in his yard. They yelled at him to wait for the fire truck. "The shed will be gone by then," he shouted back. "And the truck, too."

Porter flung open the double doors, and smoke billowed from the shed's interior. Porter could see fingers of flame licking through the base of the back wall. Pulling his shirt up around his mouth and nose, Porter darted into the shed and jumped behind the wheel. In a panic, he turned the key, but the engine didn't turn over. Only then did he remember that Alma had partially torn the engine apart the night before.

Taking the truck out of gear and releasing the emergency brake, Porter stumbled to the rear of the truck, his eyes burning and smoke clogging his lungs. He pressed his hands against the tailgate and exerted all his energy into pushing the truck from the burning shed. While he choked back smoke in the midst of the scorching heat licking at him from behind, it took a moment for his brain to register that the tailgate was hot. He jerked his hands away and rubbed them vigorously against his sides. Lowering his shoulder, he charged into the tailgate, putting all his weight and power against the rear of the truck. The heat from the fire was intense. He struggled to breathe as the burning smoke and tiny embers swirled around him. He prayed silently, feverishly, that the wheels would move and stay straight so the truck wouldn't veer to one side and lodge against the double doors before he could push it to safety.

Before he finally felt the truck move forward a few inches, his back seemed on fire; then he felt himself getting dizzy from. He was about to charge from the shed to fill his lungs with clean air when the truck seemed to move on its own power, pulling him along as he stumbled after it.

When he finally emerged into the outside air, beyond the choking smoke and the flaming walls of the shed, hands and arms grabbed him on either side, half pulling him, half dragging him, as he stumbled to safety. Only then did he realize that his neighbors had hooked a towrope to the truck's front bumper and helped him get it out of the shed.

Tears from the searing smoke ran down Porter's cheeks, and his lungs and throat ached as he sucked in gulp after gulp of fresh air. Just then the fire truck bounced into the yard. Men in yellow coats and black hats spilled from the cab, dragging hoses and gesturing wildly with their arms while shouting instructions.

"You've got to get back," Porter managed to gasp, waving his hands. "There are three gasoline containers on that back wall. They're going to blow."

As if Porter's frantic warning were a signal, the first gas container exploded, soon followed by the other two. By then the whole shed was a raging ball of orange flame. The intense heat forced everyone backward while the firemen unrolled their hoses and concentrated their efforts on watering down Porter's house to ensure its safety.

It astounded Porter to witness the savage speed with which the flames voraciously devoured the shed, rapidly reducing it to a heap of orange coals and blackened timber. Dazed, he watched the fiery destruction in silent awe. Slowly he sank to his knees from exhaustion and observed the final disintegration of the shed.

"Porter, are you all right?" Darbie's voice sounded almost panicky as she raced up behind him. "What happened? And where's Alma?"

It took Porter a moment to focus on Darbie and actually realize that she was there. She repeated her questions. "Porter, are you all right?" He nodded. "And Alma?"

Porter shook his head. "He's not here," he rasped, choking from the effort.

She knelt beside him and noticed his hands and the freckles of blisters across the back of his neck. Pushing up from the ground, she charged into the house and returned a moment later with three soaking towels. One she draped over his neck and shoulders, and the other two she used to wrap his blistered hands.

"Are you all right?" Darbie demanded again, panic clearly showing on her face and in the tone of her voice.

He nodded, closing his eyes as he relished the cool wetness of the towel on his neck. "I didn't want that lousy shed anyway," he muttered disgustedly. "I should have burned it down myself."

"Ma'am," a burly fireman said, stepping up to them, "your husband probably needs to see a doctor." He nodded toward the ambulance parked on the street with its lights flashing. "The ambulance will take him."

"I'm not going anywhere in an ambulance," Porter growled, coughing and pushing himself to his feet. "I'm fine." He teetered momentarily but quickly steadied himself. "The last thing I need is to be carted around in an ambulance."

"I don't think he's thinking very straight," the fireman gruffly pointed out.

"I'm thinking just fine," Porter barked back. "There's nothing wrong with me. I'll be fine as soon as I catch my breath." He wobbled again.

Darbie gingerly reached out, took Porter's hands, and gently pulled the wet towels back, exposing the redness and a few small, swelling blisters. "It's no big deal," Porter countered. "I had more blisters than this when I worked over at Harrison's. Nobody called an ambulance that day. And I felt worse then than I do now."

The fireman continued to argue, ignoring Porter's macho obstinacy. "I just feel that I need to tell you, ma'am, that your husband ought to be checked." He pointed at Porter's hands. "I don't know what his burns are like, but according to some of the neighbors, he charged into that burning shed like a wild man. I'm sure he's suffering from smoke inhalation. That can be worse than the burns."

"What were you doing in the shed while it was burning?" Darbie demanded aghast, as she turned back to Porter.

"I could see the fire better from in there," he replied flippantly. "I couldn't see anything from out here. Besides, I didn't have anything better to do."

"The neighbors tried to keep him back, ma'am, but he was stubborn. He didn't use a lot of good judgment." It was obvious that the fireman was irritated. "There were three six-gallon containers of gasoline in there, and he charged in there like a bull elk. He could have been killed. That gas blew just a few seconds after he got out."

"Sounds like I timed it just right." Porter rolled his eyes and pressed the wet towels to the palms of his hands. He winced slightly.

"Porter, what were you thinking?"

"I went in for the truck."

Darbie quickly looked around. "Alma's old truck?" She gasped in horror. "Why in the world would you risk your life for that crazy old truck?"

Porter closed his eyes and shook his head. Except for around his eyes and mouth, his face was covered with a thin, black, sooty film. Slowly, a smile crept across his darkened face. "It seemed like the right thing to do at the time." He glanced in the direction of the truck, which was now parked immediately behind the house beyond the reach of the flames. "But that tailgate was definitely warm when I grabbed hold of it." He held up his towel-swathed hands. "That's how I burned these." He peeled one of the towels back and stared down at his exposed palm. "But a few blisters never hurt anybody. And they're sure no excuse for taking a ride in an ambulance."

"You can do what you want, ma'am," the fireman growled, turning away. "But you ought to take your husband to the hospital or at least let a doctor look him over." He shook his head and stomped away.

"Get in the car," Darbie ordered, pointing to her car, which was parked across the road. Porter looked at her oddly. "Get in the car!" she repeated more loudly and more emphatically. "Just try not to be so stubborn. I'm taking you to the emergency room so someone can look at you."

"For a few blisters?" he asked skeptically.

"Get in the car," she ordered again, starting toward her car. Porter didn't move. She stopped and turned on him. "Maybe you are okay." She jabbed a finger at him. "But you won't be if you don't get in that car, because I'll pick up a board and whack you until you're silly. Now move."

"Yes, Mrs. Huggins," he said with a snide smile, knowing full well the response his words would elicit.

She froze momentarily, her back to him. Slowly she turned around. "And if you call me Mrs. Huggins one more time," she threatened, "you won't have any use for the emergency room. You might, however, need a morgue."

Pointing at the fireman, who was standing thirty feet away, Porter defended himself with feigned innocence. "Ma'am, he's the one who put the words in my mouth."

"He didn't know any better. You do."

As they drove for the first several minutes, neither of them spoke. Darbie glanced at Porter, who was slumped down in the seat with the towel draped across his neck and shoulders, his head leaning against the headrest, and his eyes closed. "What made you go back for that old truck?" Darbie asked gently.

He moaned, shifting his weight. "You know, when that gas exploded, I almost lost it. I started to shake and get dizzy. It dawned on me that I could have been in that shed trying to push the truck out. Nobody could have saved me. I'd have been one roasted turkey." He shook his head. "I really do hate that stupid truck."

Darbie turned away and smiled knowingly. "I don't know if you hate that truck as much as you say you do." She pressed her lips together and then opened her mouth to speak, but she didn't say anything. Her mouth closed again. Raising her brows, she commented, "Alma will be relieved."

"Yeah, that he still has the truck. He might be a little disappointed that I didn't get trapped in the burning building after I pushed it out."

"Porter," she said sharply, "don't even joke about that."

Porter smiled wryly. "Who's joking?"

* * *

Twenty minutes after Darbie and Porter drove off, Alma showed up from Marshall Harrison's place. He had spotted the smoke billowing from behind Porter's house when he was still a mile away. He had run frantically, his eyes riveted on the plume of black smoke, until he was close enough to see that the fire had burned down into a heap of black coals and orange embers.

"What happened?" he asked the first fireman he encountered as he charged into the yard. The fireman was about to wave him to the other side of the street when Alma burst out, "I live here. This is my place."

The fireman shook his head. "You've still got to stay back."

"Where's the truck?" Alma pleaded, feeling a horrible sinking in the pit of his stomach as he frantically studied the remains of the fire, dreading the devastating news that the truck was buried under the pile of glowing debris. "Did it get left in there?"

"It should have been," the fireman growled gruffly. "But your old man went in after it and pushed it out. He's worse than crazy. He could have got himself killed. There were three containers of gasoline on the back wall, where the fire started, and they all blew right after your old man stumbled out of that shed. The neighbors around here tried to keep him back, but he charged right past them."

"He went in while the fire was going?"

"Yeah." The fireman shook his head in disgust. "All for a lousy old truck that probably isn't worth five hundred dollars on a really good day. I mean, the thing doesn't even run. He had to push it out."

"It was my fault it wasn't running," Alma explained.

"It doesn't matter whose fault it is. It was stupid for him to go into a burning building for a stinkin' old truck, for crying out loud. Maybe if there'd been a kid trapped in there, but an old truck! The junkyards are full of old trucks. He could have had his pick. Why risk your life for a pile of junk?" the man ranted.

"Where's my dad? Is he okay?" Alma asked, looking around for Porter.

"He's not hurt bad," the fireman reported. "He burned his hands and probably has smoke inhalation. Your mom took him to the emergency room. She had to threaten him, though, because he wasn't going to go."

"My mom took him?" Alma questioned, confused.

"Yeah, she pulled up a few minutes after we showed up with the fire truck."

It was another hour before the firemen drove away, leaving behind a soggy heap of black charcoal where the shed had once stood. Alma stayed in the yard and watched until the last fireman and neighbor were gone. Slowly, he retreated to the house and dropped down on the living room sofa without turning on the lights.

* * *

"Will you be all right?" Darbie asked worriedly as she opened her passenger door and helped Porter from the front seat. His hands were wrapped in white bandages.

Porter nodded. "Thanks for your help," he said with a wry smile. "It was a real neighborly thing to do."

"And what's that supposed to mean?" she asked, feigning annoyance.

Porter chuckled and looked around. "Let's see, you won't whack a guy as banged up as I am, will you?" He backed up and faked a cringe as she glowered at him warningly. "I just meant that it was neighborly of you. Now, if you really were my wife, then it would have been just the natural thing to do, but under the—"

"Don't push your luck, Porter Huggins," she said with a grin, "because if you're well enough to joke, you're well enough to get whacked—and hard! And just because there isn't a stick close by doesn't mean I can't find one."

"Do you want to come in?" Porter invited.

She shook her head. "My neighborly assistance stops here. You'll have to make it into the house on your own. Besides, I'm going home and crashing. You wore me out." She took in a deep breath. "But if you need something—something you absolutely can't do for yourself—feel free to give me a call. That's what neighbors are for." She smiled as she turned away.

After Darbie left, Porter studied the pile of black debris where the shed had stood a few hours earlier. Then he turned and trudged into the house. He flipped on the living room light and had started for the hall when he spotted Alma slumped on the sofa. He stopped. "What's with sitting in the dark?" He grinned. "Saving electricity?"

Alma stared at him for a moment without speaking. When he spoke, his voice was low and husky. "Thanks for saving the truck. You probably should have let it burn."

"That's easy for you to say now," Porter returned lightheartedly, "but if you had come home to a charred truck shell, you'd be telling me a different story. You'd probably accuse me of starting that fire on purpose."

Alma stood and slowly approached Porter. "Did you get hurt bad?"

Porter held up his bandaged hands and stared at them. "These bandages make everything look worse than it really is. Darbie insisted I pay the doctor a few hundred bucks to fuss over me for a few minutes, put a little salve on my palms, and wrap some gauze around my fingers. I could have run down to the drugstore and picked up the same stuff for fifteen bucks, max." He grinned. "Now I'm sounding like you, pinching pennies left and right."

Alma pushed his hands into his pockets. "Thanks again," he said, awkward and embarrassed. "How about something to eat?" he offered hopefully.

"It's late. We can eat out. You drive."

Alma shook his head and started for the kitchen, "I'll fix you an omelet." He grinned. "I make a really good omelet."

"What is it with you and breakfast in the evening?" Porter chided him playfully. "Every time you fix a fancy meal, it's breakfast."

Alma shrugged in the kitchen doorway. "Breakfast is my favorite meal."

Porter shook his head. "All right, I'll try one of your omelets. But," he added, holding up a bandaged hand, "if it's no good, we eat out, even if we just go down to the nearest Circle K and buy a hot dog."

"I'll make it good," Alma promised, backing into the kitchen. "I put in lots of cheese, ham, bell peppers, salsa, a few sunflower seeds, and—"

"Sounds horrible," Porter interrupted.

"I guarantee that you'll love it."

Porter waved him away and started down the hall. "You fix your omelet. I'm going to lie down for a few minutes."

* * *

Thirty minutes later, Alma woke Porter. When Porter entered the kitchen, the table was covered with a white tablecloth. There were two plates of steaming omelets, each with two slices of buttered toast. Behind each plate was a tall glass of milk, and next to the milk was a smaller glass of cold orange juice.

"It smells good enough to eat," Porter admitted as he pulled out a chair and sat down. He stretched, yawned, and awkwardly grabbed his fork with his bandaged right hand. "All right," he announced, "let's see if we're having breakfast here or eating dinner out."

Alma watched Porter clumsily cut a huge piece of omelet and put it in his mouth. He chewed contentedly, smiled, and cut himself another piece while Alma carefully scrutinized his every move and facial expression.

Finally Porter nodded his approval and said with his mouth full, "I guess we'll have breakfast at home tonight." He pointed down at his plate. "This stuff's good enough to get in your mouth." Nodding toward Alma's plate, he said, "You better start eating. When I'm finished here, I might start on yours."

Alma smiled with satisfaction while the two of them ate quietly. As Porter was finishing the final corner of his toast, Alma set his fork down and placed his forearms on the edge of the table. He stared down at his plate as he began to speak. "Thanks again for not letting the truck burn."

Porter let his fork clang onto his plate and shook his head while he chewed. "It was no big deal. If you want to know the truth, I'd left my last issue of *Sports Illustrated* on the front seat, and I was just trying to save it. The truck was secondary." He smiled.

Alma nodded his head. "Why'd you do it?"

Porter heaved a sigh. "I love that truck," he remarked flippantly.

"No you don't."

Porter grinned and leaned back on two legs of his chair. "I have to admit that when I saw that fire lapping at the back of the shed, I thought to myself, 'Finally, I'll get rid of that piece-of-junk truck. Once the gas blows . . .'" He sucked air through his teeth and then pressed his lips together. "But then I pictured you charging home and accusing me of starting the fire or saying that I just sat around and let the place burn down. You'd be moaning and groaning around here with a big long face. I mean, you've been tough enough to live with these past few weeks. What would you have been like with your precious truck reduced to charred scrap metal? I shudder at the very thought."

Alma fought back a grin while Porter rambled through his playful tirade. "Now what's the real reason?" he interrupted.

Porter leaned farther back in his chair and held his bandaged hands up in the air over his head, studying them. He shook his head. "The real reason?" He let the question hang for a moment. "Shoot, I don't have a clue what the real reason is." He let his chair drop to all four legs and stared across the table at Alma. "It just seemed the thing to do at the time." He smiled faintly. "Maybe I have developed a bit of an attachment to that old truck." He cleared his throat. "But honestly, I knew how much it meant to you. I knew how disappointed you'd be if you lost it." He was serious now. "And maybe you'll make a mechanic out of me after all, teach me to do something besides just hold the light. But we'll need that old truck for that."

"You shouldn't have gone in after it." Alma hesitated. "But I'm glad you did. I'm sorry your hands got burned."

"Don't get weepy on me. I couldn't handle that." He looked at the table. "You cooked the food; I'll do the dishes."

Alma laughed. "Yeah, right. With those hands?"

Porter looked down at his bandaged hands as though seeing them for the first time. "That's right," he said pleasantly, "I better not get these all wet just yet." He nodded. "There are some advantages to being a hero and an invalid. I might decide to keep these bandages for a while."

"What about the stuff you had stored in the shed?" Alma asked, concerned.

"I probably won't miss much of it. Most of it was out there because I didn't have the heart to throw it away, but as long as it was locked up in the shed, I didn't have to look at it. The fire probably did me a favor."

"You mean I straightened and cataloged all of that junk for nothing?" Alma asked, cocking his head to one side.

"Pretty much." Porter chuckled and shook his head. "No, I take that back. Your work was worthwhile, because when you stacked everything along that back wall and in the rafters, you made sure that that fire burned fast and hot. If that shed was going to burn, I'm glad it burned all the way to the ground so I don't have to worry about it at all. I might even get a few bucks of insurance out of it."

Grinning and shaking his head, Alma began clearing the table. "Well, I guess now I'll have to find a different place to work on the truck."

"How about out under one of those big cottonwood trees? More fresh air that way. Or we can clear off all that junk on the shed's cement slab and work on it there. I'm not particular."

"So you're going to start working on the truck too?"

"Sure. I already know how to hold the light. After a few more lessons, I should be able to hand you a pair of pliers or a screw-driver—as long as you put little labels on each one." Porter grinned at his son.

14

The next morning Porter and Alma were eating breakfast when there was a knock at the door. Alma answered it.

"How's your dad doing?" Darbie asked him.

Pushing the screen door open, Alma nodded toward the kitchen and said, "He's still alive. Come in and have a look. A shower and a good night's sleep made some pretty impressive improvements. You won't even recognize him."

Darbie stepped cautiously toward the kitchen, where Porter was finishing up a glass of juice, a bowl of cereal, and two slices of toast. She stood in the doorway and studied him critically. "Where are your bandages?" she demanded.

Porter glanced down at his hands. "I couldn't shower with those big bulky bandages strapped to my hands," he explained almost apologetically. "I considered wrapping them in plastic bags." He shook his head and grinned as Darbie glowered disapprovingly at him. "But I figured that there was no sense in running around with all those bandages because of a few little blisters." He held up his hands. "All but two have popped. I'm going to survive."

"You probably popped the blisters yourself. What if your burns get infected?" Darbie demanded.

Porter dropped his hands under the table, out of sight. "I've had blisters before. I always pop my blisters, and they've never gotten infected. I think popped blisters getting infected is an old wives' tale. I'm not worried."

Darbie stepped to the table. "Let me see your hands," she ordered sternly.

"I thought you were my neighbor, not my doctor!" Porter responded cheerily, trying to thaw her somber demeanor but keeping his hands under the table. "I'm doing fine. They're a little tender, but I sure don't plan to lie around for a week waiting for a few blisters to heal."

"I'll bandage them again," she offered, her tone softening. "I have some bandages and ointment in the car. I was pretty sure you'd do something stupid like take all your dressings off."

"Your confidence in me is overwhelming," Porter muttered, shaking his head. "Besides, I can't work with my hands all bandaged up."

Darbie turned to Alma, who was leaning against the counter with his arms folded, watching with an amused look on his face. "He's stubborn, isn't he? He's probably always been stubborn."

Alma grinned, shook his head, and held up his hands in surrender as though to say, "I'm just an innocent bystander. Don't get me involved."

Darbie shook her head and muttered, "You're just like him. Stubborn to the bone."

"You've hit that nail on the head," Porter agreed.

Darbie heaved a sigh and turned back to Porter. She pursed her lips a moment and looked around the kitchen. "Is there anything you need help with?"

"To tell you the truth," Porter answered, nodding at Alma, "Alma's been taking pretty good care of me. For a couple of stubborn bachelors, we do all right for ourselves."

"I'm bringing you dinner tonight," Darbie announced, making it clear that she wasn't asking their permission. "It will be here at six o'clock. I hope gangrene hasn't settled in by then," she murmured under her breath. "Although it would serve you right. And if those hands do get infected," she added spiritedly, "I'm going to be more than a little satisfied to say that I told you so."

Porter laughed. "I'll chop my hands off myself and bury them in the backyard before I'll let you sing your 'I Told You So' song around here."

Sputtering under her breath and shaking her head, Darbie started for the door.

"Darbie," Porter called out to her. She stopped and turned to face him. "Thanks for looking out for me," he offered sincerely. "It means a lot." Then he fought back a grin and shrugged. "It's a very neighborly thing to do."

Darbie glared at him. "Don't give me any more of that neighbor stuff." Rolling her eyes, she left the house.

For a moment, Alma and Porter stared at the door where she had disappeared.

"She still likes you," Alma observed casually. "Not that it makes any difference."

"As a neighbor."

Alma shook his head. "The other neighbors haven't shown up with bandages and ointment." He considered for a moment and then added, "I don't know if she wants to like you, but she does. And I doubt there's any way she'd ever actually tell you." He smiled. "I guess we're not the only stubborn ones in town." He pushed away from the kitchen counter and started gathering the breakfast dishes. "If a guy had to have a stepmom, Darbie would be all right."

"I suggest you not go there," Porter warned. "If she hears you talking like that, we might both be needing bandages."

* * *

True to her word, Darbie showed up that evening at six o'clock sharp with two large pizzas, a bag of chips, a two-liter bottle of soda, and a carton of ice cream. "I planned to cook you something," she apologized as she carted everything through the front door and into the kitchen, "but I was running late, and this was . . ." She heaved a sigh and smiled. "Well, it was just easier to pick up some pizza and drinks."

"I'm not complaining about pizza." Porter laughed as Alma helped Darbie set things on the kitchen table. "In fact, if I could have ordered something, I'd have ordered pizza."

The three of them ate quietly at first, and then Darbie set her slice of pizza down and glanced across the table at Porter. "I'm sorry I've been a little snappy." Her cheeks colored as she looked away. "But you scared me yesterday, you know—the fire and everything and almost getting blown up." She shook her head and smiled sheepishly. "I got to thinking that I must have sounded like a frantic mother protecting her little kid."

"Or a frantic wife trying to . . ." Porter didn't finish before Darbie kicked him soundly under the table.

Alma laughed as Porter groaned dramatically and rubbed his shin. "I was just trying to think of another way of . . ."

"Drop it, Porter," Darbie warned, "or I'll get cranky and irritable again."

Long after the food had been eaten and everything cleaned up, Darbie stayed with Porter and Alma. The three of them visited comfortably like old friends. It was almost ten when Darbie glanced at her watch, saw the time, and bolted to her feet. "I didn't know it was so late. I've got to get home or I'll never get up for school in the morning."

Porter walked her out to her car. As he opened the door, he remarked casually, "Come back again." She dropped into the driver's seat and pulled her seat belt around her. "You don't need a special reason. Just drop by." Without responding, she looked up at him with a smile. "Of course, if you want to bring pizza again, that's fine too."

Darbie laughed and shook her head. "I'll think about it." She pulled the corners of her mouth down and shrugged. "But tonight was fun." She thought a moment and added, "You and Alma are doing better, aren't you?"

Porter considered the question. "Depends on the day." He cleared his throat and nodded once. "But I think maybe things are looking up a little." He closed the car door, Darbie waved, and the car pulled away into the night.

* * *

Two days after the fire, Porter left Eagar early in the morning, drove to Phoenix on business, and didn't return until late that evening. The first thing he noticed when he pulled into the driveway was that the pile of charred timbers and ashes was gone. The cement slab had been swept and sprayed clean, leaving little evidence that the old shed had ever been there.

"What happened?" Porter questioned as Alma stepped out the front door.

"I didn't think you wanted it cluttering up the place. Mr. Harrison had a hole on his ranch that he'd been trying to fill. He said ashes would be good filler."

"What'd you use to haul it in, a bucket and a basket?"

"The truck."

"I didn't think it worked."

"I got it working good enough to haul that stuff off." Alma cleared his throat. "Darbie even came over and lent a hand. She thought it would be a nice surprise for you to come back and have everything cleaned up. She had dirt and soot from the top of her head to the bottoms of her boots. Actually, we had a good time. You missed out."

"I seem to always miss out on the fun times." Porter looked around. The truck was nowhere in sight. "And while you were out there on Harrison's ranch you decided to drive the truck into that same hole to get rid of it? That sounds like a plan. Why didn't we think of that about six weeks ago? Then I wouldn't have had to burn the shed down."

"The truck's down at Cash Wilkes's shop. Monday I'm going down there to help him. I figure with the money I've earned from Mr. Harrison and the work I'll be doing for Cash, I'll be able to replace the timing belt and fix whatever else needs fixing. Or at least I'll get a good start on it."

During the next two weeks, both Alma and Porter were busy. When Alma wasn't working for Marshall Harrison, he was at Cash Wilkes's auto shop. About the only time Porter and Alma saw each other was in the evenings. Even then Alma spent some evenings playing football with a few of Coach Slade's varsity players. Occasionally, Darbie dropped by for a visit. Twice, Porter and Alma went over to her house to take a carton of ice cream to her. They always stayed and helped her finish off the ice cream while they laughed and talked.

Since the fire, the icy wall between Porter and Alma had melted considerably. Alma still exhibited some reticence and caution in his relationship with Porter, but there was a definite softening.

Two weeks after the fire, Alma drove the truck home and parked it on the cement slab where the shed had once stood.

"How does it work?" Porter questioned curiously as Alma stepped back and admired the truck.

"It doesn't look like much from the outside," Alma muttered, shrugging, "but it sure runs a whole lot better." He turned to Porter and tossed him the key. "Do you want to take it for a drive? It's a different machine now."

Porter caught the key, studied it a moment, and then tossed it back. "I'd like to see what it can do. But you drive."

The two of them climbed into the old Ford, Alma behind the wheel. "I still owe Cash Wilkes $150. He said I could work it off," Alma explained as he turned the key and the engine turned over with a strong, steady rumble. "This old beast is working great now. Actually, it was in pretty good shape, not nearly as bad as I first thought."

Alma pulled the truck onto School Bus Road and headed west. "Where to?" he asked, rolling the window down and hanging his arm out.

"Just west of town there's a road that heads to Big Lake. Let's go there and see what this old war wagon can do on a mountain road."

Alma and Porter drove the twenty miles to Big Lake. The truck took every hill with plenty of power. Porter was impressed. "This thing sounds and pulls better than when I used to drive it," he observed as the two of them stepped out of the truck on the shores of Big Lake. He glanced at Alma and noted his son's excitement and pride as he looked the old truck over. "You're kind of attached to this old bucket of bolts, aren't you?" Porter kidded him, dropping the tailgate. He hopped onto it and let his legs dangle.

Alma joined him, running his hand along the truck's warm metal as though caressing a faithful old pet. "I used to dream of this." He grinned.

"Do you mind answering a question?" Porter inquired somberly, staring out at the lake as the descending sun's reflective light cast a shimmering glare across the the rippling surface, making it look like so many shards of broken glass, the tall pines surrounding the lake acting as the perfect backdrop.

"What do you want to know?"

"What started your fascination with this truck? Your grandpa must have junked it a long time ago."

Alma smiled wanly. "He did. At least for a while. Like I told you before, it was parked under the elm tree by the barn, gathering dust and getting pooped on by every bird that made a rest stop in that tree. Grandpa took the battery out because he needed it for his little tractor. After that, if there was something somebody didn't know what to do with, more than likely it got dumped in the back of this truck. It became the farm's junk dumpster."

"So you took compassion on it?"

Alma shook his head and frowned. "When I was just a kid, when Grandpa still used the truck for things around the farm, he told me I could have it when I was big enough to drive it. I think he figured that by the time I was old enough to drive, I wouldn't want the truck or I'd forget he'd promised it to me. But neither one of those things happened."

"It's a genuine piece of junk, you know," Porter pointed out playfully. "You probably should have left it under the elm tree."

Alma shook his head. "Maybe it's junk to you," he said quietly. "Maybe it is to a lot of people. But I didn't ever see the truck as being a piece of junk under the elm tree. I saw it the way it could be." He smiled. "For me the truck was Grandpa's farm. Some of my earliest and best memories of Grandpa's farm—this was before Mom and I ever moved there—were of riding around in the truck. To me, riding around in the truck was what Grandpa's farm was all about."

Alma spoke with a distant look in his eyes. "I remember Grandpa letting me ride in the back when he drove out to check on the irrigation. He'd always tell me to stay in the truck so I wouldn't get all muddy and wet." He smiled and shook his head. "But the irrigation ditch was just too tempting. It seemed that as soon as Grandpa started tromping through the field to check the water, I'd have to get out and play in the ditch—floating grass, weeds, and leaves on the muddy water. I'd start out real careful, but it wouldn't be long before one foot would slip into the ditch, then the other one, and once I got that wet, I didn't figure anything mattered, so I'd just tromp up and down the muddy ditch. By the time Grandpa got back, I'd be a wet, muddy mess, and he'd grumble a little bit and make me ride in the back of the truck, which was where I wanted to be anyway. He'd warn me that Mom was going to be mighty put out with me. That was the life.

"There were other times when we'd head for the hills and take those dirt back roads. I'd sit on the tailgate, hanging on for dear life, and let the dust billow up around my feet. Sometimes Grandpa would head to town for something, and I knew that we would stop for an ice cream or a candy bar or a cold soda pop. Other times we'd go over to Johnson's Feed and Seed and pick up a load of rolled barley. Things were always just fine when I was in the truck.

"When Mom told me that we were heading back to Panguitch, the first thing that popped into my mind was riding around the farm in the truck. The truck's a piece of me, a piece of me that's . . ." He shrugged. "That's special. So you probably wouldn't ever understand how I feel about it."

"I used to take your mom for rides in this truck," Porter remarked. "Even before we were married. Maybe you didn't know that." He chuckled and shook his head. "Walter and Calvin and I used to take this old truck camping. In fact, when I asked your mom to marry me, we were parked down by the river, sitting on the tailgate of this old truck, and watching the sun set. A lot like right now. I remember that."

"So why didn't you like the truck?" Alma inquired pointedly.

After pondering the question for a moment, Porter responded, "Maybe it's that I thought the truck had passed its usefulness. The truck was fine back then, but it wasn't practical anymore. It took more work and effort to get it running again than it was really worth. The memories were fine. Up to a point." He took in a quick breath of air. "But maybe for me the memories had a little more bite to them—a bite that was a bit painful."

"No good memories?"

Porter considered the question. "Most of them are, I suppose," he answered slowly, nodding reflectively. "Yeah, they're good enough memories. I guess it's just . . ." He hesitated. "Sometimes a good memory can still have some sting to it. Sometimes those kinds of memories leave you wondering how things used to be and why they're not that way now. That can be a little painful," he admitted frankly.

Alma grinned and shook his head, basking in his reflective reminiscence. "One of the first things I remember about this old truck was going on a wiener roast. There's this place north of town, maybe ten miles or so, where there's a dirt road off the main highway that cuts down by the river. There was a grassy meadow there with a bunch of brush and stubby trees growing along the bank. Mom and I went there. Walter or Grandpa must have been there too, because there were three of us. We built a little fire next to the river and roasted our wieners and marshmallows. It was so peaceful with the birds singing and the water rippling by and the cattle in the distance. We hunted frogs, snakes, and crawdads. We waded in the creek to catch fish. Mom rolled up her pant legs and got into the water. We trapped a fish in some shallow water, then caught it with our bare hands."

Porter glanced over at Alma. "You would have been about four or five then?"

Alma nodded, staring out across the lake. "Probably. I was pretty young."

"Walter and Grandpa didn't take you," Porter remarked simply, turning away and shielding his eyes with his hand as he gazed out across the lake.

Alma glanced over at him.

"Your mom and I took you. We got chased by that white-faced steer and had to jump into the back of the truck."

Alma's brow furrowed in pensive remembrance, but he nodded slowly, appearing a bit perplexed.

"I liked that place too," Porter went on. "Your mom's the one who took us there. It was a place she had loved as a little girl. She and I used to go there even before we were married." A fine, indiscernible mist momentarily clouded Porter's gaze.

"I always thought those times were with Grandpa and Walter."

"Maybe later they were." Porter swallowed regretfully. "But the first times . . ." He choked on his attempt at reminiscence. "I was with you those first times." He coughed and shook his head slowly. "I'm sorry I wasn't there for the times later on." He fidgeted uncomfortably, looking down at the ground. "We did catch a fish with our bare hands, and we filled the ice chest with water and put that fish inside so we could take it back to the house to show everyone."

Alma's eyes slowly narrowed some as his initial disbelief transformed into a vague recollection of the facts.

"Back in those days," Porter went on, "I don't think we ever visited your grandpa's farm during the summer without driving down to the river for a picnic. You insisted. Allyson too. Just the three of us most of the time. Remember the time when your mom went wading and slipped and fell and drenched herself? I laughed until I was almost sick. Then when I wasn't expecting it, she pushed me into that little pool where there was a bend in the river. I came up sputtering and spitting and gasping for air. It was her turn to laugh. And you were laughing pretty hard yourself."

"I kind of remember that," Alma remarked slowly. "And you pulled me in after that."

Porter nodded.

"We both had to ride home in the back of the truck."

Porter nodded again.

"I guess I'd forgotten that you were there."

"I guess I had too. Till now." Porter pushed himself off the tailgate and ran his hand along the side of the truck bed. "It's kind of funny how the memories come back."

"So aren't you glad the truck's running again?" Alma inquired hopefully. "And we're only getting started. This can be a hot machine."

Porter shook his head. "Fixing up this truck is beyond me."

"But maybe it's not beyond both of us. Not if we work on it together."

"Now that's a case of pure optimism," Porter returned dryly. "It's one thing to remember how the truck used to be. It's a whole different story to actually get it there."

"It already runs pretty good. You saw how it took those hills coming up here."

* * *

The ride back to Eagar from Big Lake was a quiet, solemn one. When Alma parked the truck on the cement slab and shut off the engine, Porter offered gently and sincerely, "Alma, I should have been there more. I'm sorry you had to make so many memories without me." He swallowed hard. "I cheated us both." Before Alma could respond, Porter lifted the door handle and climbed out of the truck, heading for the house.

The next afternoon, Porter was vacuuming out the truck when Alma returned from Marshall Harrison's place. Porter didn't see Alma amble over to where he was working, so it was a while before he finally spotted him. He straightened up and shut the vacuum off. Somewhat embarrassed, he pointed at the interior of the truck and remarked, "It was pretty dirty. I noticed that yesterday when we drove to Big Lake. I doubt it's been cleaned for a while." He grinned. "Maybe since the time we took it for that wiener roast up the river."

Alma studied Porter. "I haven't worried too much about the inside," he remarked. "Not yet. I figured I could do that later. I didn't think the looks would make much difference to anybody unless the engine ran right."

Porter shook his head and looked down at the vacuum hose he gripped in his hand. "Well, I got to figuring. I knew I couldn't do much with your engine. Not with my mechanical inclinations. But I figured I was smart enough to wield a vacuum hose."

"It'll just get dirty again as I keep working on it."

"Then I'll clean it again. It'll give me something to do."

Alma stepped to the front of the truck and leaned against the front fender. "You really don't have to do any of this. I know you don't like this kind of thing. I mean, working on an old truck and all."

Porter smiled wanly. "Oh, you might be surprised." He stepped back and surveyed his work. "I've rather enjoyed it." He shrugged and grinned. "Besides, I think some of this dirt is probably mine. Those bottom layers have been there quite a while. Do you ever remember anybody vacuuming this thing out?"

Alma shook his head.

"That's what I figured." He nodded toward the hood. "You take care of what's under there; I'll take care of what's inside here." He pointed with the vacuum hose to the cab.

When Porter finished vacuuming, he grabbed a roll of paper towels and a spray bottle of window cleaner and started on the windshield and side windows, both inside and outside. After the windows, he scrubbed down the dashboard, using Q-tips to meticulously dig out dirt and grime from every crack and corner.

He moved on to other cracks and crevices. He hadn't intended such a thorough cleaning, but having gotten this far, he found it difficult to stop. He found himself going over parts he'd already cleaned, because once he cleaned one spot more meticulously, he could see that his first attempt was inadequate. Soon his fingers, arms, and shoulders ached from his careful labor. He lost track of time, and dusk found him still cleaning when Alma returned from a football practice.

"You going to stay out here all night?" Alma asked.

Porter was lying on his stomach across the seat and using a Q-tip to get at some dirt along the floor just inside the passenger-side door. He pushed himself up and backed out of the cab, wiping beads of sweat from his forehead with the back of his hand. "I said it before and I'll say it again: it's been a long time since anybody cleaned this truck."

"It's a farm truck," Alma answered indifferently. "That's what happens to them—they get dirty. I'll go fix some supper." He started back toward the house.

"Don't you at least want to see what it looks like?" Porter growled.

Alma turned and studied Porter, who was standing next to the truck with the driver's side door open. Slowly he nodded his head and ambled back. Porter stepped aside so Alma could look inside.

As soon as Alma saw the inside, he froze, staring at the interior. Eventually, a smile tugged at the corners of his mouth. "Wow!" he uttered. "Shoot, I won't dare get in it unless I take my shoes off."

"You sure better *not* climb in unless you take your shoes off," Porter snarled playfully. "You get the inside of this truck dirty, and I'll thump you on the head with the biggest wrench in your toolbox."

Alma couldn't help smiling.

"The seat's clean enough," Porter went on, "but it looks a little ratty, you know with those tears and worn spots, especially on the driver's side. The floor's clean, but it's worn right through the carpet, almost down to the metal floor."

"It's over thirty years old, you know."

"It needs a nice seat cover and some spanking new floor mats. I'll get some."

Alma quickly shook his head and stepped back, slamming the truck door. "I already told you. If the truck needs something cosmetic, I'll buy it."

A few minutes later the two of them were eating the dinner Alma had put together—creamed peas and potatoes. Porter savored the fare, eating heartily. "You're a good cook, Alma," he commented. "I haven't had creamed peas and potatoes in forever." He took another huge bite. "Where'd you learn to make these?" he asked with his mouth stuffed full.

"Mom showed me."

Porter nodded. "You did a lot of cooking, didn't you?"

"Mom used to say that most men are helpless—they can't fend for themselves. They figure someone's got to cook for them, or they've got to eat out or starve. She didn't want me to be helpless like that."

"So that's why you don't like to eat out?"

"Partly."

"You don't want to be helpless, like me?"

Alma smiled and looked down at his plate. "Something like that."

"Well, it's good to have someone around who knows what he's doing in the kitchen." Porter shoveled several bites into his mouth before speaking again. "I knew there was a reason I wanted you here," he kidded.

When the meal was over, Alma began gathering the place settings. "If you cook, I clean," Porter said, stopping him. "I didn't bother you while you were cooking; now don't bother me while I'm cleaning. I don't want to be completely helpless."

Alma grinned and stepped back from the table. "I've never fought anybody to do the dishes." He started to leave.

"Hey, Alma," Porter called to him, picking up both of their dirty plates. "I'm buying the seat covers and the floor mats for the truck." He didn't give Alma time to protest. "You can buy anything you want for that engine, but you haven't done any of the cleaning inside. That's my area. I know you didn't ask me to, but . . ." He shrugged. "It's something I wanted to do. You might say I've got a little investment of my own in that truck now. I can't see doing all that work to clean the truck up and still having it looking like garbage. I just want you to know that." He pondered a moment and then added, "You and I can fight over something else if fighting is what you've got on your mind, but I'm doing this."

Alma watched Porter pack the plates to the sink. A crooked smile tugged at the corners of his mouth. Finally, without saying anything more, he shrugged and left the kitchen.

The next day when Alma returned from work at Mr. Harrison's place, Porter was waiting for him in front of the truck, his arms folded across his chest and a smug, even defiant, look on his face. "Come and see what you think," he invited. He stepped to the driver's side and opened the door as Alma approached. For a prolonged moment, Alma studied the interior with its neat, tight-fitting, red seat covers and heavy black mats that completely covered the worn floor. There was also fabric on the dashboard, covering up the cracked vinyl.

"Red?" Alma wondered aloud after recovering from his initial shock.

"When this truck was new, it was red and white."

"Was it *that* red?"

"It's that red now. And before you get too judgmental, I'm not entirely to blame for the color. I took Darbie with me. She helped pick out this color. She liked it."

"It doesn't match the outside now."

"Nothing matches the outside. I plan to fix that."

Alma glanced quizzically in Porter's direction.

Porter ignored the inquiring stare. "I've decided that we're . . ." He stopped and corrected himself. "That *I'm* going to sand the old paint off, patch up some of the corroded spots, and paint it. It'll be a two-tone, white on red, like the original. This thing's going to look new. When we ride this down Main Street, people will drool. You can't have nice seat covers on the inside and a lousy paint job on the outside." Porter coughed nervously and stuffed his hands into his rear pockets. "Just for your information," he grumbled, "and I didn't ask your permission—I didn't figure I needed it—but I took it down to Ernie's Tire Town and had him put new tires on." Porter quickly held up his hand to ward off Alma's protest. "The old ones were worn. And I had him align the front wheels while I was at it."

Alma stepped back and studied the tires. He kicked the rear one. "How much did all this set you back?" he questioned, returning to the cab and running his hand over the seat cover.

"I don't ask you how much you pay for your engine parts."

"Tires aren't part of the cleaning."

"They're part of the looks." Porter shrugged. "Ernie's also ordering me some chrome rims. Nothing really fancy, just something to spark things up a little."

"I wasn't planning on anything like that."

"Neither was I. It just sort of happened that way. If I'm going to have this old heap parked in front of my place, I want it looking nice. Your job's the engine. You just make sure you get this thing running the way it's supposed to. You don't have to worry about any of the rest. And," he added firmly, daringly, "don't even think about pulling any of this stuff out of here. It all stays. I've still got a few more improvements in mind." He pointed at the rearview mirror. "I think I'll hang some of those oversized, bright-colored, sponge dice that people used to hang in their cars and trucks. I always thought they looked pretty cheesy, but Darbie seemed to think they'd go just fine in this truck. I might even rig some lights around the rear window." He flashed a wide grin.

"I don't think so," Alma retorted, but he smiled as he spoke. "I don't want this looking like a circus truck."

"You don't have to tell me that it looks nice inside," Porter remarked, feigning indifference. "I mean, don't bother telling me that it sure looks better than it did yesterday at this time with about three inches of dirt and grime on the floor." He shook his head while Alma smiled sheepishly. "And I sure don't expect any thanks, because the last thing I want you doing is choking on a tiny bone of gratitude." Porter pointed to the driver's seat. "Get in. See how it feels."

Alma climbed into the truck and sat there for a moment with his hands on the wheel, which had a brand-new black leather cover on it. He looked around, nodding his obvious satisfaction. "I plan to trade out the gearshift," Porter said. "I'm putting one with a crystal ball handle in, something that will have some class. That was also Darbie's suggestion." He folded his arms. "I've got big plans for this truck. When I finish, you'll want to live in it. Shoot, *I'll* want to live in it."

"Actually, all I wanted to do was get it running so I could drive it around. I wasn't planning to live in it. Aren't you getting a little carried away with all this?"

"There's no law against getting carried away."

15

"Where's the truck?" Alma asked as he entered the kitchen after working the afternoon with Marshall Harrison.

Porter was pouring himself a glass of lemonade from a two-quart carton. "The truck? Didn't you take it with you?" he asked casually, turning around.

"I rode your bike. You know I hardly ever take the truck."

Porter stepped to the window over the sink that looked out toward the cement slab where the truck was usually parked. The truck was gone. "It hasn't been there all afternoon." He turned quickly to Alma. "Are you sure you didn't drive it over to Harrison's place and forget about it?"

"I just rode home on the bike. I didn't have the truck."

"So where is it?"

"That's what I'm asking *you!*" Alma sounded exasperated.

Porter shrugged indifferently. "I've been working today. I haven't been watching your truck. Did you leave the key in it?"

"I always leave the key in it," Alma grumbled impatiently.

"So anybody could have taken it. They could have walked onto the place and driven off in it."

"You mean stolen it?"

Porter shook his head. "I don't think anybody in Eagar would steal your truck." He shrugged. "Somebody might borrow it now that it's running."

"You mean somebody would just pull up, see the truck, and drive off in it?" Alma's face showed shock and disbelief. "Without asking permission?"

"It's happened before." Porter took a long drink, set his glass on the table, and stepped to the back door. "Where else could it be?" he said as he opened the door and stepped outside. "Did you let someone borrow it and just forgot?"

"Like who?"

"Like anybody. Darbie, the neighbors . . ."

"No," Alma returned emphatically. "Nobody had permission to take it anywhere."

Porter scratched his head thoughtfully as he stared out at the spot where the truck was usually parked. "That's mighty strange." Suddenly, he shook his head and turned back to the house. "It'll show up. I doubt anybody's stolen it. And if they just borrowed it, they'll bring it back. Or they'll leave it around town someplace. We'll keep our eyes open. You don't have to sweat it."

Alma's mouth dropped open. "You mean we're not going to do *anything?* What if it *has* been stolen?" he demanded, following Porter back into the house. "What if whoever took it has just been waiting till I got it running so they could drive off in it?"

Porter shook his head doubtfully. "That's unlikely. It might run, but it still looks like a piece of junk. This last week I've been sanding most of the paint off it. It looked pretty lousy before that, but lately it's *really* been looking lousy. If you were going to steal a truck, would you pick that one?"

"But we can't just sit here and do nothing!" Alma protested indignantly, his concern for the truck quickly changing to frustration and irritation toward his dad for his obvious indifference. "Shouldn't we call the police?"

Porter turned to his son and studied him curiously. "I guess you can. I doubt they're going to do much. I mean, it's a '71 Ford that looks like it's ready for the dump. They'll just laugh." He heaved a sigh. "Are you sure you didn't let someone take it or leave it over at Harrison's place?"

"Where's a phone book? I'm calling the police," Alma growled, storming into the kitchen where a phone book was lying on top of the refrigerator. Snatching the book from the refrigerator, he began thumbing madly through the pages.

The doorbell rang. Ignoring it, Porter dropped onto a kitchen chair and poured himself some more lemonade.

Alma paused momentarily in his search, glanced at his dad, and then toward the front door. "Aren't you going to get that?" he asked.

Still drinking, Porter shook his head.

Snapping the phone book shut, Alma stomped toward the front door and jerked it open.

"Hello, Alma," Darbie greeted cheerily. "Is your dad here?"

For a moment, Alma just stood in the doorway. Then he stepped aside and nodded toward the kitchen. "Yeah, he's pretty busy, though," he grumbled. "Somebody stole my truck, but he's so busy drinking lemonade that he can't even answer the door."

"Somebody stole your truck?" Darbie questioned with concern as she and Alma walked to the kitchen and Alma started flipping through the phone book again. "They've stolen it since I took it over to the shop?" There was genuine shock in Darbie's voice.

The phone book dropped to Alma's side. "You took it to the shop?"

"Your dad and I took it over this afternoon."

Alma whipped around to face Porter, who grinned back at him, still holding his empty lemonade glass. "I told you somebody probably just borrowed it."

"I was ready to call the police and report a stolen vehicle!"

"You didn't tell him?" Darbie demanded, surprised.

"Tell me what?" Alma broke in, turning to Darbie.

"That we took it over to the body shop."

Alma tossed the phone book onto the table. "You said you didn't take it."

Porter held up his hands. "I didn't take it." He grinned and pointed at Darbie. "She's the one who drove it over there. I just picked her up in my car." He snickered sheepishly. "I didn't exactly say that I didn't know where it was. I just asked you if *you* knew who took it. I even asked you if you thought Darbie had taken it. You said—"

"You let him worry? You didn't even let him know?" Darby had her hands on her hips. "You were going to let him call the police?"

Porter shook his head and chuckled. "I wouldn't have let him call. I would have stopped him before that."

"You know, that's really mean. I mean, that's *mean*," Darbie accused.

Porter laughed, pushing himself up from the table. "I was just seeing if his heart was still working. You know, I wanted to get his blood pumping through his veins."

Darbie and Alma both glowered at Porter, who stood grinning.

"It was just a joke," he offered defensively. "The truck's fine."

"What's it doing in the shop?" Alma inquired suspiciously.

"Getting painted."

"Painted?"

Porter shook his head. "I've been sanding that thing for a week. And in spite of all the work and sweat, I knew that even if I sanded the thing down to the bare metal, I couldn't exactly finish the job with a two-bit brush and a bucket of paint. I don't know a lot about body work, but I know you can't paint your car out under the oak tree in your front yard. So I took it over to Bill's Body Shop."

"I can't pay for that," Alma protested.

Porter shook his head. "You're not supposed to worry about the paint."

"I didn't even care about the paint. You're the one who wanted it painted."

"That's right. The paint's my responsibility. Your job's the engine. Your responsibility is to get the truck running. Mine is to make it look nice. Bill's Body Shop can do that better than I can. It'll be finished in a few days."

* * *

Porter made certain Alma wasn't home when he and Darbie brought the truck home and parked it in its customary place on the cement slab. Both of them watched from the living room window as Alma rode his bike home a little later and spotted the like-new truck off to the side of the house. He laid his bike down on the front lawn and strolled uncertainly around the corner of the house and over to the truck. Porter and Darbie slipped out the back door and crept unnoticed behind him so they could observe his reaction.

The old Ford had been transformed. The faded red-and-white paint, pocked with rust spots, scrapes, and minor dings, had been replaced with a bright, shining, two-toned red and white and decorated with new chrome. The old rims had been replaced with chrome ones. And hanging from the rearview mirror was a set of fuzzy red dice that Porter had found on the Internet.

"What do you think?" Porter asked.

Alma turned around and saw Darbie and Porter for the first time. He studied his dad for a moment without saying anything or giving any outward hint of what he was feeling. He turned back to the truck, still not speaking. He made a careful examination of the truck, walking around it, bending over to study the wheels and rims, glancing inside the cab, and peering into the bed. But he didn't touch it, as if fearful his touch might shatter the dream before him and cause it to disappear.

"I hadn't ever pictured it this way," he finally remarked.

"Is that good or bad?" Porter questioned, not sure what his son was implying.

Suddenly, Alma grinned, and his excitement and enthusiasm exploded across his face. For the first time, he reached out and gently ran his fingers along the truck's smooth, bright side. "I'd never pictured it as being brand-new. I wanted it to run and everything, but . . ." He sucked in a deep breath. "But this is really something. I don't know if I dare drive it anymore."

Porter held up the key. "You can take it for a test drive. I decided not to leave the key in it this time. Maybe nobody would have stolen it before, but I'm not so sure now." He tossed the key to Alma, who caught it. "You've got a real set of wheels now."

Alma laughed and shook his head. "What would people in Panguitch say if I drove this down Main Street? Nobody would recognize it. I wouldn't be even a little embarrassed to take Teddie Dodds in the truck on her first date. She used to tease me that she wouldn't go with me unless I took her in the truck."

"It won't be the same as driving down Main Street in Panguitch," Porter suggested lightly, "but how about taking a loop through Eagar and Springerville? Kind of like a practice run."

Alma gripped the key in his fist for a moment and then stepped to the truck, threw open the driver's side door, and jumped in. When he glanced back and saw Darbie and Porter still standing back, he grinned and waved them over. "Come on. We all have to go. That's half the fun."

With the windows rolled down so the wind could blow over them in the late afternoon heat, and with Darbie sitting between the two men, all three of them started for downtown Eagar. They drove through Eagar and then headed into Springerville, turning right at the light and taking the main highway out of town toward Socorro, New Mexico.

Once they were out of town, Alma floored it. When the odometer registered seventy miles per hour, he let up on the gas, and the truck gradually began to slow down. "I think it could get to eighty-five or ninety, easy," he observed proudly, finding it hard not to grin from ear to ear.

"It was starting to vibrate a little," Porter pointed out. "I think you'd better stick to the speed limit. This might look like a brand-new truck, but it's still thirty-plus years old. You don't want to rattle the old thing into a pile of scrap metal."

Even though Alma usually rode his bike to work, the next day he took the truck. When he returned home in the afternoon, he parked the truck on the cement slab and then sat on the back steps and admired it from a distance. He was still sitting there when Porter stepped out the back door.

"You can't get enough of it, can you?" Porter teased. He grinned at his son. "If it weren't so big, you'd probably take it to bed with you each night."

"It's a sharp-looking truck." Alma pushed up from the steps. "Where you been?"

"I took the car down to the garage to change the oil."

"You did what!" Alma gasped, his mouth dropping open.

"It was time for an oil change."

"And you actually took it to a garage and paid money to have somebody change your oil?" Alma was incredulous.

"And there's a problem with that?" Porter sounded perplexed.

Pointing at himself with his thumb, Alma asked, "I'm here and you take your car someplace and pay good money to have them change your oil? We could have done it here easy."

"I never change my own oil," Porter explained defensively.

"I could have changed it." Alma shook his head. "No," he reconsidered, wagging a finger under Porter's nose, "I could have showed *you* how to change your own oil and saved you twenty bucks." He continued to shake his head. "We've got to get you over this ridiculous phobia of working on engines."

"Actually, I'm rather partial to that particular phobia. It suits me."

Just then they heard a car pull in the driveway. The two of them walked around to the front of the house and saw Darbie climbing out of her car, carrying a plate covered with plastic wrap. "I brought you some zucchini bread," she announced cheerfully. "The zucchini even came from my little garden. Hardly anything else is growing, but I've probably got enough zucchini for the whole town. I considered bringing you over some fresh zucchini, but I figured you two would probably just toss it in the garbage. But I thought you might be courageous and test some fresh zucchini bread."

"Hey, I like zucchini bread," Porter volunteered, taking the plate and peeling back the plastic wrap. He broke off a corner of the loaf. "And you put chocolate chips in it, just the way I like it," he remarked, beaming.

"I wanted to make sure you ate it."

Porter handed the plate to Alma, who broke off his own huge piece and began eating.

"Do you want to know what he just did?" Alma asked Darbie, talking with his mouth full and nodding his head at Porter. "He took his car down to a shop and had them change the oil. I've been changing the oil on tractors, trucks, and cars since I was about two years old, and he doesn't trust me to change his oil."

"Two years old?" Darbie quizzed skeptically. "Did they have special coveralls to go over your diapers?"

Porter and Alma laughed.

"All right, I was a little older than two. But not much. The point is, I know how to change the oil." He took another huge bite of zucchini bread. "The point is," he continued, his words muffled by the zucchini bread, "I could have taught him to change his own oil."

"My oil needs changing. Let your dad change my oil. It will save me a trip to the shop. You can teach him in the process."

"I don't do oil," Porter protested, breaking off another piece of zucchini bread. "But if Darbie wants you to change her oil, I'll stand around and watch—and eat zucchini bread if you've still got some." He held up his bread. "This is good stuff. And I hate zucchini."

"We'll change your oil," Alma declared definitively. He pointed at his dad. "Both of us."

Porter shook his head. "I don't know how."

"It's simple," Alma explained patiently. "All you have to do is unscrew the little plug in the bottom of the crankcase, let the oil drain into a pan, unscrew the filter, screw the plug back in, put on a new filter, and pour four or five quarts of oil into the engine. I know it sounds terribly complicated, but a smart guy like you with a college education should be able to handle it all right."

Darbie looked on and smiled as Alma teased his dad.

"And we'll save Darbie here twenty bucks in the process."

"And with the money I save," Darbie volunteered, "I'll go out and buy some steaks or chicken, and we'll have a cookout in my back-yard." She grinned over at Porter. "I think Alma's going to make a mechanic out of you. Before long you'll be wanting to rebuild that old shed that burned down so you can open your own little backyard mechanic's shop."

"Yeah, right," Porter grumbled, reaching for another chunk of zucchini bread.

The next evening, Porter knocked on Darbie's door. When she opened it, she was barefoot, wearing a pair of white capri pants and a pink knit shirt. She seemed surprised to see Porter standing there. "Did you come over to change the oil?" she teased. "Without Alma? You must be feeling really brave."

Porter cleared his throat. "The oil change will have to wait." He fidgeted a moment and remarked, "Alma's over practicing with some of the football players. Passing league." He coughed nervously. "But I've never watched him play with the other guys. The coach said he's pretty good, but I've never actually seen him out there. I was going to head over that way." He stuffed his hands into his pockets.

Darbie grinned broadly. "Sure, I'd love to go over and watch him. If you'll take me along," she added knowingly. "You don't mind if I tag along, do you?"

Porter blushed and shrugged. "I was planning on asking you. As one neighbor to another." He held up his hands. "Nothing serious. No ulterior motives. I just want some company."

"I'll tag along with you."

When Porter and Darbie arrived, they were the only ones in the bleachers. They were both impressed by how well Alma played. Just as Coach Slade had said, he seemed able to catch anything that touched his fingertips.

"I'm not exactly an expert when it comes to football, but he looks good," Darbie observed.

"He's a natural, especially for someone who's never played. Panguitch is too small to field a football team, but he'll start here for sure."

"You can't tell that you're proud of him," Darbie remarked, staring out at the field and fighting back a grin. "I'm glad you let me come, even though I had to invite myself."

"I was going to invite you," Porter said. "You knew that. You just like giving me a hard time."

Just then three teenage girls climbed the bleachers. When they spotted Darbie and Porter, one of them waved and called out, "Hi, Miss Montgomery."

"Hello, Brandi," Darbie returned, waving.

The three girls ambled over to where Darbie and Porter were sitting. "I didn't know you were a big football fan, Miss Montgomery," Brandi remarked pleasantly.

"There's a lot you don't know about me, Brandi," Darbie kidded. "Actually, Mr. Huggins has a son playing out there. We came to watch him."

Brandi turned to Porter. "You're Alma Huggins's dad?"

Porter was taken aback that this girl would know Alma. He glanced at her and nodded once without speaking.

"He's good," she remarked. "Really good. He's going to really help our team."

The five of them continued to watch the boys play, and after several minutes, Brandi turned to Darbie and said, "Hey, Miss Montgomery, right before school got out you said that if we wanted to get ahead on some of our reading for AP English, you'd help us pick out some books."

Darbie nodded.

"Can we still do that?"

"Of course. I don't have my school keys, or we could go over to my classroom tonight and let you check out some books. I've got a list at home, though. And a few books."

"Maybe we could stop by your house sometime."

"That would work."

Nothing more was said about reading, and the practice ended a few minutes later. Alma strolled over to the bleachers and climbed up to where Porter and Darbie were sitting. He nodded a silent greeting to the three girls, who seemed to have their eyes glued to him, but they didn't speak.

"I wasn't expecting you two here," he stated, straddling the bench in front of Darbie and Porter. "It's just practice. Nothing special."

"Your dad and I wanted to see if you were really as good as everybody has been saying," Darbie said. "You're better than they say. You can catch just about anything."

Alma's neck, cheeks, and ears glowed bright red, and he ducked his head. "Rusty Howard's a good quarterback. A good quarterback can make a receiver look pretty good."

"And a good receiver can also make a quarterback look mighty good," Porter pointed out with a smile.

Embarrassed by the attention, Alma turned to Darbie. "Have you decided when we're changing the oil on your car?"

"How about tomorrow? Change the oil around six, and I'll have dinner ready by six thirty." Nodding her head in Porter's direction, she added, "And don't let him get out of anything. I want to see him with a little oil and grease on his hands."

* * *

The following evening at a little before six, Darbie was in the middle of marinating chicken breasts in barbecue sauce when the doorbell rang. Expecting Porter and Alma, she was surprised to discover Brandi Rogers, Tess Masterson, and Kylee Stuart standing on her front step.

"Hi, Miss Montgomery," Brandi bubbled while the other two seemed to hang back a little, trying to mask their embarrassment. "We were just wondering if you could help us choose those books you promised."

Darbie hesitated, glancing back toward the kitchen, where she was in the middle of her dinner preparations. But pleased by the girls' interest and dedication in getting ahead in their English reading, she cheerfully invited them into her living room, where she had a book-case filled with her favorite literature. Pointing to the two middle shelves, she explained, "Most of the books here you could read." Taking a thick volume from the top of the bookcase, she extracted a two-page list of books and handed it to Brandi. "This is a complete list of our AP reading, so if you don't find something you like in my collection, you can choose a book from the list and check it out at the library. The library will have most of these."

"Is it okay if we just look through what you have here for a minute?" Brandi asked, studiously examining the books on the middle shelves while she handed Darbie's AP list to Kylee.

Both amused and pleased, Darbie shook her head, pointed to the kitchen, and explained, "I'll just be in here. I'm in the middle of fixing dinner."

Five minutes later, the doorbell rang again, but before Darbie could rinse off and dry her hands, Brandi called out, "I'll get that for you, Miss Montgomery." Tess and Kylee both followed Brandi to the door. "Hello," Brandi gushed as she threw open the door, and Darbie knew instinctively from Brandi's tone that Alma was standing there. "Miss Montgomery's in the kitchen. Come in."

A few moments later, after handing Alma her car keys, Darbie stood in her living room with Porter, watching Alma head out to her car with Brandi, Tess, and Kylee trailing behind him. She stood with her arms folded. "I was impressed with those girls' interest in getting a head start in their English reading," she mused wryly. "Of course, I was a little surprised to have them drop by tonight, but I was still impressed by their dedication." She shook her head and glanced over at Porter. "Right now, though, I'm a little skeptical of their motives. Something tells me they're a whole lot more interested in Alma than they are in Hawthorne, Twain, Faulkner, or Hemingway. What's your take, Dad?"

"I thought maybe you were trying to set him up," Porter remarked with a grin.

Darbie shook her head. "No, they showed up on their own. I think Tess and Kylee are pretty harmless, even though they'd love to catch Alma themselves. But Brandi's the bold one. There was nothing accidental about her timing. She must have heard Alma talking yesterday and made sure she was here when the two of you arrived." She cleared her throat while her eyes narrowed a little. "I'm beginning to wonder if Alma might be safer in Panguitch. Of course," she quickly added, "most of the girls there are probably enamored with him too. But I doubt they're quite so conniving. Maybe you'd better go rescue your son."

"He doesn't seem to be in distress."

She thumped Porter lightly on the chest with her finger. "You get out there and change the oil on my car. And keep the she-wolves away from Alma. I recognize that hungry look in Brandi's eyes. She's not interested in my literature or in my car—unless, of course, Alma is within grabbing distance. Believe me, she's ready to pounce. Not that I blame her, but—"

"You're not getting protective, are you?" Porter chided her good-naturedly.

She pointed to the open front door and ordered sternly, "Get out there. He's supposed to be teaching *you,* not them, how to change the oil—although I suspect those girls will volunteer to take his class whenever he offers it."

While the girls hovered around the front of the car, asking questions and feigning deep interest in auto mechanics, Alma nervously coached Porter through the oil change. Porter found he rather enjoyed the experience—not necessarily the mechanical work, but rather watching his son fidget and fumble in front of the feminine audience.

When Porter had poured the last quart of oil into the engine, Darbie sauntered out of the house to announce that the chicken would be ready in a few minutes.

"Dad saved you twenty bucks on that oil change," Alma announced, nodding at Porter and grinning as he wiped his hands on a paper towel.

"How about coming over to my place and helping me save a few dollars on my car?" Brandi volunteered. "I think if you coached me through it once, I could probably do it on my own later on."

Alma blushed and began picking up his socket-wrench set, which was laid out on Darbie's driveway. "You could probably do it alone now after watching my dad."

"I've got the main idea," Brandi came back, "but I'd still need someone to make sure I was doing everything right." She folded her arms. "Save me those few dollars, and I'll grill you up a steak instead of chicken."

Porter laughed. "For a steak," he offered, "I'll show you how to change your oil myself."

Brandi smiled knowingly and shook her head. "I think you need a little more experience. I'd rather have Alma coach me."

"Why don't you two mechanics go in and wash up," Darbie ordered. "We'd better eat while it's hot." She stood on her driveway and watched Alma and Porter retreat to the house while the three girls followed them with their eyes. When the two disappeared inside the house, Darbie turned to the girls and explained, "I think Alma has a girlfriend in Panguitch."

Tess and Kylee blushed noticeably and looked away. Brandi was more brash. She simply smiled and shrugged. "I just want Alma to show me how to change the oil in my car." She bit down on her lower lip. "Where is Panguitch anyway?"

"Southern Utah. About five hundred miles from here, but Alma has known this girl for a long time."

Brandi nodded. "Five hundred miles," she mused thoughtfully. She pointed east. "I live about five blocks that way. Any way you look at it, five blocks beats five hundred miles any day." She laughed. "Hey, thanks for helping us find some summer reading," she said cheerily.

Darbie watched the three girls climb into Brandi's car and drive away. Darbie had never considered herself to be the protective type, and she didn't know anything about Teddie Dodds of Panguitch,

Utah. But right then she found herself preferring Teddie to Brandi Rogers, although she did have to admit she might feel the same about Teddie if the girl pursued Alma with the same calculating determination Brandi did.

While Alma checked the chicken on the grill, Darbie invited Porter into the kitchen to help carry the food to the patio. "Brandi Rogers was throwing herself at your son," she stated stiffly, handing Porter a bowl of potato salad. "Did you notice?"

"Do I detect a hint of worry?" Porter teased as they walked out to the patio.

"I just want you to know what's going on," Darbie hissed back so Alma wouldn't overhear. "Brandi's going to be a senior next year." They returned to the kitchen for another load of food. "She's much more . . . how should I put it . . . world wise than Alma, you know. I don't know that he's prepared for someone as audacious as she is."

Porter smiled over at Darbie. "Brandi trampled all over your nerves, didn't she?" he accused playfully. "I thought she was just interested in mechanics."

Darbie shook a finger at Porter as she whispered back her response. "It's exactly what I told you before. She planned her whole attack. She knew Alma was going to be here tonight, and she showed up to ambush him. She doesn't have an ounce of interest in AP summer reading. If Alma hadn't shown up until seven, she would have browsed through every book in this house until he got here."

"So you figure you were used, kind of set up?"

"Didn't you see what was going on?" Darbie asked, exasperated.

"I'm pretty old," Porter returned with a twinkle in his eyes, "but I can still spot a flirt. She was pretty cunning and subtle, I'll give her that."

"I'll agree with *cunning,* but that wasn't subtle flirting—that was flagrant flirting."

16

"We're taking the truck out for a little ride," Porter called to Darbie as she dug dandelions from her front yard. He and Alma had pulled up in front of her house in the truck with the windows rolled down. "We're going to see if this machine has the muscle to make it to Alpine. Do you think you can leave your yard work long enough to join us?"

Darbie dusted her hands off and surveyed her front lawn. "Taking a ride to anywhere is certainly more tempting than digging dandelions," she mused loud enough for Porter and Alma to hear. She pushed herself to her feet and slapped at the knees of her pants. "I'm a little dirty. And sweaty. Let me run in and at least wash my hands." Leaving her yard tools on the front lawn, she started for the house.

Porter jerked a thumb toward the back of the truck. "No need to clean up," he called after her. "We figured you'd ride in the back so you wouldn't mess up the new seat covers."

Darbie ignored the remark and disappeared into the house. A couple minutes later she reappeared and ambled down her front walk.

"Don't let Dad kid you," Alma called to her, leaning forward so he could look around Porter. "He's the one who has to ride in the back. I told him that he could only ride up front until we picked you up."

Darbie shook her head. "I'll ride in the back," she replied indifferently, heading toward the back of the truck. "I want the wind to blow over me and cool me off." She stepped nimbly onto the rear bumper and then hopped into the bed of the truck, where she plopped down and leaned against the side of the bed. "I'm good to go," she called out, closing her eyes tiredly.

"I was just kidding," Porter called to her. "We'll let you ride up here with the big boys."

She shook her head, keeping her eyes closed. "I'll stay here. I don't like riding with the big boys. Besides, it's been a long time since I rode in the back of a truck."

"We can't have you riding back there," Porter protested. "Everybody in town will think we're a couple of rednecks."

"Aren't you? All you need is a Confederate flag in your rear window. It will match your red-and-white truck."

Porter glanced at Alma, rolled his eyes, shook his head, and then called back over his shoulder, "Darbie, even if we are rednecks, we don't want everybody in Eagar to know it."

"Believe me, it's no secret," Darbie sang out lightly. "Let's hit the road, Alma. I'm starting to sweat. I want the wind blowing over me."

"Look, Darbie," Porter argued, "if you ride back there, one of us will have to join you."

"There's plenty of room."

"You're stubborn."

Darbie laughed. "Swallow your pride, Porter. You're not ashamed of your proper redneck upbringing, are you?" she twanged.

"You just want me back there so you can push me out on my head the first time we come to a sharp turn in the road."

She laughed. "Wrong! I never planned to wait that long."

While Alma laughed, Porter pushed open the truck door and, in one quick, smooth motion, shut the door with a bang and leaped into the back of the truck. Stepping to the back of the bed, he unhitched the tailgate and let it drop open on its side chains. "If I'm riding in the back," he announced to no one in particular, "I'm doing it in proper redneck fashion." He sat on the tailgate and let his legs dangle.

Darbie raked her fingers through her hair and smiled. "That will certainly make it easier for me to push you out," she teased, crawling to the back of the truck and sitting next to him.

"Get this machine moving," Porter called to Alma.

"Hey, I think *I* want to ride in the back," Alma objected, grinning.

"Somebody's got to drive," Darbie returned, "and I'd like it to be the guy who's the most mature and levelheaded. That means you're the man for the job."

Alma put the truck in gear, revved the engine, and made a quick, wild U-turn in the street, almost jarring Porter and Darbie from their perch on the tailgate.

"You won't have to push me out." Porter laughed, grabbing the side of the truck to steady himself. "Alma's going to dump us both on the road before we get out of town."

Alma drove out of town with Darbie and Porter laughing, joking, and waving crazily to passing motorists. As Alma turned the truck up the winding road out of the valley, Darbie suddenly called out in a panic, banging on the side of the truck with her fist, "Hey, stop the truck! Stop the truck!"

Startled, Alma quickly pulled off the side of the road onto the shoulder and slid to a stop in the gravel. Climbing from the truck, he went back to where Darbie was sitting next to Porter. Both men stared worriedly at her, wondering what was causing her sudden stroke of panic.

Calmly she smiled, shrugged, and spoke to Porter and Alma as though she were explaining something complex to two young, inquiring boys. "We can't just run off to the mountains like this," she declared, motioning to the empty truck bed with a wild sweep of her outstretched hand.

"Like what?" Porter asked, his brow furrowed as he glanced quizzically toward Alma, hoping that he might have a clue as to the reason for Darbie's strange outburst.

"Are you blind?" she returned, feigning great patience. "Do you see any hot dogs, potato chips, drinks, or watermelon?" She shook her head. "Can you give me one good reason why we should charge off to the mountains on a beautiful afternoon like this and not go prepared to have a picnic?" She hopped off the tailgate. "If we're not going to have a wiener roast," she declared, beginning to walk down the road, "then I'm going back to town." She waved Porter and Alma away. "You two go do what you want, but if you don't know what to do with this kind of a day in the mountains, then you'll just have to go on without me."

Porter and Alma looked at each other, their heads cocked to one side. Finally, Porter shook his head and called after Darbie, "We know what to do with this kind of day. We just weren't sure if you knew. We were testing you. You passed the test. Now we can drive back to town and pick up the stuff for the picnic."

Darbie stopped and turned around with her hands on her hips. "I know you're lying. You're just saying that. You didn't really think of the wiener roast."

"We always have a wiener roast when we take the truck for a drive." Alma spoke up, joining the wild joke. "Ever since I was just a kid, we'd have wiener roasts in the truck. Well, not *in* the truck," he quickly corrected himself, "but we took the truck so we could have the wiener roasts." He held up his hand as though taking a solemn oath. "Honest. This truck has taken me to more wiener roasts than I can even count." He waved Darbie away as he started back to the cab. "You can walk back to town if you want, but Dad and I are driving back to the store to pick up the stuff for our wiener roast. If you're brave enough to come along, we'll show you how to have a wiener roast Huggins-style."

Alma climbed back into the truck and Darbie, suddenly laughing at the elaborate joke she had started, scrambled back to the truck and jumped onto the tailgate next to Porter just before Alma put the truck into gear and made another quick U-turn as he headed back to town.

The three of them stopped at the grocery store and bought franks, buns, chips, drinks, marshmallows, and a ripe watermelon, and loaded them in the back of the truck. "Hey, I'm pretty sure it's my turn to ride in the back," Alma announced enviously as Porter and Darbie resumed their perch on the tailgate. "I always liked riding on the tailgate."

Porter shook his head. "It's your truck. You have to drive. Besides, you're a kid, and kids have to be buckled up inside." He shrugged. "Those are the rules."

"Who came up with those rules?" Alma protested.

"I'm the dad," Porter deadpanned, "and you're the kid. I get to make the rules." He jabbed a thumb over his shoulder toward the cab. "Hop in, Alma. You're driving. I don't want you bouncing out of the back of the truck. It's safer up front."

"But it's not funner."

"We're talking safety here, not fun."

Alma glanced toward Darbie for support, but she just shook her head and held up her hands. "I can't argue with your dad."

"Chicken," Alma grumbled, fighting back a grin as he went to the cab and climbed behind the wheel.

* * *

Alpine was a forty-minute drive from Eagar. A tiny town of two or three hundred people, it was nestled in the clutches of pine- and aspen-covered hills, sitting at about eight thousand feet, where the air was clean and cool. Alma drove through Alpine, passed the Luna Lake Reservoir on the east side, and then took a dirt road off into the trees. When he came to a small stream that trickled down the mountain and under the road, he pulled off under a stand of white-trunk aspens with a few tall ponderosa pines mixed in for variety.

By the time they reached this spot, the sun was dropping rapidly to the west and, although the air was still pleasant and on the warm side, there was the slightest hint of cool in the approaching evening.

"I say we get a fire started before the sun goes down," Porter suggested.

Within a few minutes, Alma had a fire going, Porter had gone looking for wiener sticks, and Darbie had set the food out on the tailgate of the truck. By the time the sun dropped behind the green western hills, the three of them had eaten and were huddled around the fire sitting on two gray rocks and a stump while they roasted marshmallows, having a competition to see who could get the most golden-brown marshmallow without it bursting into flames. By then the evening air was turning cool, and none of them had thought to bring sweaters or jackets, so the crackling fire felt good.

"I'm not crazy about hot dogs unless they're roasted over a campfire," Darbie remarked as she gradually turned her marshmallow over the glowing coals. "In fact, I suspect the last time I had a hot dog was at a cookout somewhere." She smiled and shivered at the same time.

"It's been a few years for me too," Porter remarked, glancing across the diminishing flames at Alma, who glanced up and caught his eye before turning his gaze back to the fire.

"And when was that?" Darbie inquired innocently.

Porter fidgeted and glanced at Alma, who silently studied the fire. "Back in Panguitch. It was a little like this. Not so many trees, and we were next to a river—if you can call the Sevier a river instead of an overgrown ditch."

Darbie glanced in the direction of the little stream trickling twenty feet from their campfire. They could hear the gentle splashing, but they couldn't actually see the stream in the dark. "Well, I don't think I'd call that a river either, but it does add a nice touch to this spot."

"Once Alma and I even caught a fish in the river with our bare hands."

Darbie shook her head. "I doubt there are any fish in our little stream."

"And one time Dad got dunked in the river," Alma remarked, a wry smile on his face. "I don't remember why, but I'm guessing he deserved it."

"I'm positive he deserved it." Darbie smiled and hugged herself, rocking back and forth on the stump she was sitting on. Nodding toward Alma, she added, "And I suspect Alma and I could toss you in this creek just for old times' sake."

Alma looked up and grinned. "That sounds like a plan."

Porter held up his hands and shook his head. "I can live just fine with the old memory. I don't have to relive anything tonight."

Darbie glanced at Alma. "I don't think we were asking him if he wanted to volunteer. I say we just toss him in."

Porter pushed himself to his feet. "And I say it's getting late and we need to get back down the mountain."

Their simple ride in the truck, which originally wasn't supposed to take more than thirty minutes, had stretched into several hours. They ended up driving down the mountain in the dark, and it was almost eleven when they finally pulled up in front of Darbie's place.

Darbie jabbed Porter in the ribs with her elbow. "Thanks for inviting me," she said tiredly. "And the old truck made it just fine." She laughed and continued. "When I first saw this truck, I wasn't sure it would make it down the street, let alone up the mountain."

"You weren't the only one who had doubts," Porter came back. "Alma here was pretty confident that he could patch it up and get it going, but I wasn't so sure. Of course, I did stand around and mumble a few words of encouragement from time to time, and I think that probably made a huge difference."

"I don't remember very many words of encouragement," Alma replied, his cheeks burning a bright blush in the dark as Porter and Darbie praised him.

"Oh, I encouraged you to take it to the dump, didn't I?"

They all laughed as Porter opened the door and let Darbie out of the truck. Without being invited, he walked her up the walk to the front door.

"Thanks again," she said as Porter pulled open the screen door for her. She playfully held out her hand to shake his and added with a teasing glint in her eyes, "The picnic was a very neighborly thing to do. We'll have to do it again sometime."

"Alma and I do try to be good neighbors," Porter answered, taking her hand and shaking it but holding it beyond a mere handshake. They studied each other in the dim glow of the yellow porch light. "Thanks for coming," Porter stammered. "It wouldn't have been the same without you."

"Porter Huggins, you've changed," Darbie said softly.

Porter released her hand and stared down at his feet.

"It's a good change," she added, then she turned and slipped into the house, closing the door behind her.

Alma and Porter drove home in silence, but when Alma parked the truck on the cement slab and shut off the engine, he stared straight ahead and commented softly, "Tonight brought back a lot of memories."

Porter cleared his throat and shifted anxiously in his seat. "I'm sorry about your mom," he said just above a whisper. "I know that just feeling sorry doesn't change anything, but I am sorry. Things should have been a lot different. *I* could have made them different." He hesitated. "I wish I could go back and change so many things."

"Yeah," Alma said simply.

Porter swallowed hard. "Everybody likes a happy ending," he commented hoarsely and shook his head. "I don't know that there will ever be a really happy ending to my life story. I'm afraid there will always be something missing. I'm sorry about that, for both of us."

Alma nodded his head but didn't say any more.

* * *

Two evenings later, Alma was tinkering under the hood of the truck while it was parked on the street in front of the house—not that there was anything that needed fixing, but he liked being around the truck, knowing that it was his, that it actually worked as well as it did. Darbie and Porter were sitting in lawn chairs on the front lawn. Darbie had stopped by with a half dozen tomatoes from her garden, and Porter had invited her to stay for a few minutes to visit.

While they were sitting there, a stranger in his early fifties drove up in a bright red Yukon and stepped out. Spotting Alma by the truck, he wandered over to him. They visited for a few minutes while looking the truck over. Finally, Alma closed the hood, and he and the man strolled over to where Porter and Darbie lounged on the lawn.

"This is Mr. Eckard," Alma explained, dusting his hands off and pushing them into his front pockets.

"Paul Eckard," the man added, extending a hand to Porter, who shook it.

"Mr. Eckard wants to buy the truck," Alma explained seriously.

"I've driven by here all summer," Mr. Eckard offered in explanation. "I spotted that old truck right after you brought it here. I've watched it change. The first truck I ever had was a '71 Ford, navy blue. I bought it used, but it was a great truck—until my best friend took it out to get a load of wood and rolled it coming down a winding mountain road. Totaled it." He shook his head and then smiled appreciatively toward Alma's truck and added, "But it wasn't as nice as that one your son's got there. I'd like to buy his."

Porter chuckled and turned to Alma. "And what did you tell him?" he asked, already anticipating Alma's flat refusal.

"He's offering five thousand for it," Alma stated without revealing anything by his tone or expression.

"Did you tell him to write you out a check?" Porter joked.

Alma remained solemn. "It's worth more than five thousand to me," Alma spoke to Mr. Eckard.

"You've fixed it up real nice," Mr. Eckard admitted, glancing in the direction of the truck.

"It runs really well," Alma pointed out.

Mr. Eckard pondered a moment. "Six thousand."

"It's not just any old truck," Alma remarked.

"It's got sentimental value," Mr. Eckard guessed.

Alma nodded.

"That's understandable. I guess that's the reason it caught my eye the first day I saw it here. You've put a lot of work into it." He smiled wanly as he scratched the back of his head. "My wife will probably kill me, but . . ." He coughed and stuffed his hands into his pockets, still eyeing the truck. "I did tell her that I was going to own that truck." He chewed on his lower lip while his eyes narrowed as he studied the truck intently. "I'll go seven thousand, but that's about my limit. Even sentimentality has a ceiling price."

Alma hesitated and glanced at Porter. Porter continued to smile knowingly. "I don't know that it's worth seven thousand dollars," Alma admitted. "It's an old truck. It might mean that much to me, but not to somebody else. You might have owned a truck *like* that one, but you didn't own that particular truck," Alma said, pointing at his truck.

"Seventy-five hundred."

Alma seemed to catch his breath without answering immediately. He looked away from Porter and stared at the truck.

Sensing a weakening of resolve, Porter pushed up from his chair. "The truck really isn't for sale," he declared, a bit irritated that Mr. Eckard was pressuring Alma.

Mr. Eckard didn't relent, though. "I really shouldn't, but I'll go eight thousand. I'll have a check over here first thing in the morning. You can cash it and make sure I'm good for the money before I pick the truck up."

Alma continued to stare at the truck without responding.

Porter fidgeted, no longer smiling, no longer confident in Alma's response. "The truck's not for sale. It's got sentimental value."

"It's got a little sentimental value for me too," Mr. Eckard came back with a grin. "I'm willing to pay for the sentimental value." He shook his head. "Of course, I'll have to keep the details secret from my wife."

"Are you willing to pay ten thousand dollars?" Alma asked him suddenly.

Porter and Paul Eckard both flashed Alma a surprised glance and then turned to each other. Mr. Eckard looked away. He was suddenly solemn, the smile gone from his face. "Is that an offer?" he questioned slowly. "A firm offer? Not just a bluff?"

"Nobody's going to pay ten thousand for it," Alma said. "When I brought it down here, I couldn't have gotten five hundred for it."

"Probably not, but it's a different truck now. You've put a lot of work into it." Mr. Eckard walked out to the truck and looked it over again. He opened the door and sat in the front seat, gripping the steering wheel.

Porter, Alma, and Darbie watched him without saying anything to each other. "Why don't you just tell him it's not for sale?" Porter finally hissed. "You're wasting his time and yours."

"He's never going to pay ten thousand for it," Alma replied indifferently. "I might as well be asking for twenty thousand. Or fifty."

A moment later Mr. Eckard returned. "Ten thousand dollars is a chunk of change for an old truck," he remarked, his gaze still riveted to the truck. "My wife would shoot me if I paid that much for it." He rubbed his nose with the back of his fist and then tugged on his chin with his thumb and forefinger, still deep in thought. "You didn't answer my question, though," he proceeded slowly. "Is ten thousand a firm offer? I mean, if I pulled out my checkbook and wrote a check for ten thousand dollars, could I take the truck?"

Alma glanced between the truck and Mr. Eckard, an intriguing smile playing almost imperceptibly at the corners of his mouth. Porter observed him silently, his eyes narrowing just a little. It was almost as though he were holding his breath. "I'll take ten thousand for it," Alma answered with finality.

"Done!" Mr. Eckard exploded with a triumphant grin. "The wife will kill me, but I'll still have the truck."

"You're not selling the truck," Porter burst out, confronting his son. "We just fixed it up."

Alma grinned, shrugged, and responded under his breath as Mr. Eckard walked back toward the truck, "He's offering me ten thousand dollars. I'll never get ten thousand dollars for it. That's a steal."

"But you don't want to sell it."

"But it's ten thousand dollars. I'll more than get my money out of it."

For a moment, Porter's eyes widened and his jaw dropped. His mouth moved, but no words came. He wet his lips and shook his head furiously. "I didn't ever think the truck was about money. I thought the truck was about . . ." He gulped, dazed. "Well, about the truck. I offered to buy you a truck, a new one." He jabbed a finger out at the truck. "A better one than that. You refused. You wanted *that* truck. So who cares about the money? What difference does it make if he offers you fifteen thousand? You've always wanted *that* truck."

"But Mr. Eckard has the money. I've had my fun working on the truck. Now I get ten thousand bucks thrown into the bargain. You can't beat that."

Porter gaped at his son, shock registering in his eyes and face. He turned to Darbie, who'd remained silent through the bargaining process. "He can't just sell the truck," he said to her as though she were some objective arbiter who would be forced to make the final, binding decision.

"I thought the truck was his. Can't he do what he wants with it?" she inquired, trying to sound impartial.

"Sure it's his," Porter sputtered, shaking his head and beginning to pace. "But he's always wanted the truck. He can't just give it away to the first stranger that comes along."

"I'm not exactly just giving it away. He's offering me ten thousand dollars."

"Do you know how much you've put into that truck?" Porter demanded.

"Not ten thousand dollars."

"Alma, I'm not talking about money here. Think of the work, the time, the dreams, the memories. That's what the truck is. It's not about money. It's never been about money. It's about a whole lot of other things, things that one lousy, fat check can't ever give you. You can't sell the truck, Alma."

"I already accepted his offer."

"Retract it. There's nothing signed."

"But I want to sell it."

"I won't let you!" Porter burst out in frustration, shaking his head. "Forget it!"

"But it's his truck," Darbie pointed out gently.

"Maybe," Porter snapped, "but that doesn't mean—"

"He should be able to sell it whenever and to whomever he wants," Darbie cut him off calmly. "That's all part of ownership. How can it be his if he can't do what he wants with it?"

"Because it's not just his. It's mine too!" Porter argued. "He's not the only one who worked on it. I sweat plenty over that thing myself."

"But I didn't ask you to do any of that," Alma countered calmly. He shook his head. "You just wanted to do that."

"I put money into it too."

"But I didn't ask you to. Is that what you're worried about, the paint job and the seat covers and the—"

"No, I'm not worried about that stuff. I don't give a hang about the money, but I figure that truck's a little mine too. Maybe a whole lot mine. I don't want you selling it."

"But it's still Alma's decision," Darbie reasoned evenly.

"Then *I'll* buy it," Porter snapped. "I'll buy it right now. And I'll beat his stinkin' offer. I'll pay ten thousand, one hundred dollars." He turned toward Mr. Eckard. "The truck's not for sale," he called out. "I just beat your offer." He turned back to Alma and Darbie. "It's done. The truck stays. It's mine."

For a moment, Porter fumed silently, glowering at Darbie and Alma as Mr. Eckard approached from behind. Porter quickly turned to him. "I'm sorry you wasted your time here," he explained testily, "but the truck isn't for sale. For any price. My son should have told you that to begin with."

Mr. Eckard chuckled. "I'm glad to hear that, because my wife really would have killed me if I'd bought that truck for ten thousand dollars." Turning to Alma and nodding at Porter, he added, "I think he does kind of like your truck." He waved at Darbie. "I'll see you around, Darbie. Nice to have met you, Alma." Turning to Porter, he held out his hand. "I'm glad to see you're so attached to that old truck." Without further explanation, he walked to his Yukon.

"What was that all about?" Porter asked, confused and perplexed. He glanced back and forth between Darbie and Alma, who were both smirking. "What's going on here?" he demanded, finally sensing a conspiracy.

"I was never going to sell the truck," Alma explained quietly as Mr. Eckard drove away. "I just wanted to know if *you* would." He jabbed a thumb at Darbie. "It was kind of her idea. She figured you were pretty attached to the old Ford. I wasn't so sure, but she claimed she could prove it."

"Wait a minute," Darbie protested, holding up her hands. "I didn't put anybody up to this. I just said Paul Eckard would do a good job as an interested buyer."

"This was a setup?" Porter asked, incredulous.

Darbie and Alma burst out laughing. "Actually," Alma replied, "it was a little bit of payback for tricking me when you made me think the truck had been stolen." He nodded and shrugged. "And I also wanted to know if the truck meant anything to you or if it was just another pile of junk." He continued to laugh. "Paul Eckard used to sell cars down in Phoenix. He said he could deal and keep a straight face. He did a pretty good job, don't you think?"

"So you all played me for a sucker?"

Alma smiled and shook his head. "Darbie and I just had to know what you were feeling."

"You satisfied?" Porter grumbled, trying to hide the smile that was threatening.

Alma glanced in Darbie's direction, and they both nodded and laughed.

17

Porter opened his front door and was greeted by Darbie, who was standing in her jogging clothes with a smile on her face. "Hello," he said haltingly, surprised to see her there. He looked her up and down. "Alma's not here." He smiled. "So I hope you're not here to recruit me as a jogging partner. Like I've told you, I don't jog."

"No, I was just out for an evening walk. Alma and I jogged this morning." Darbie turned and made a sweeping gesture toward the street. "I was passing by and thought maybe you'd be brave enough to walk with me. Nothing strenuous. You can even bring your oxygen bottle and portable IV. I certainly don't want to put any of our senior citizens in danger." She smiled impishly and folded her arms while Porter considered her offer.

"I guess I'm good for a walk," he answered cautiously. "A slow one. No reason to break out in a sweat this late in the day. And I think I can manage it without my oxygen bottle—as long as I can lean on you if I get tired."

She raised an eyebrow. "I suppose that all depends on how you lean. You are just my neighbor, you know."

Porter held up his hands and shook his head. "You can trust me . . . neighbor."

A few minutes later, the two of them were walking side by side down the road. Porter sensed that Darbie had something on her mind, so he remained quiet until she decided to speak.

"I stopped by the school this afternoon," she finally commented after they'd walked a hundred yards or so. "Alma's still not registered."

Porter studied Darbie out of the corner of his eye before responding. "School doesn't start for a few weeks, does it?" he questioned slowly. "Is there a deadline?"

"Not really," she answered, her cheeks coloring as she glanced down at her feet. "I was just wondering about him." She took a quick breath. "Is he staying here?"

"Where else would he go?" Porter asked defensively.

Darbie stopped walking. She hesitated for a moment and then faced Porter. "Maybe it's none of my business," she burst out suddenly. "I was just thinking." She shook her head, turned, and started walking again.

"It probably isn't any of your business," Porter agreed with a smile, catching up to her, his tone softening, "but I'd like to hear what you're thinking."

Darbie continued walking but shook her head.

"There's a burr under your collar," Porter pressed good-naturedly. "Tell me about it."

Darbie stopped again, but this time she didn't face Porter. "I was just wondering if Alma is moving back to Panguitch."

"What put that idea in your head?"

She faced Porter and then looked away. "Can I be honest with you? Really honest? You can always tell me to mind my own business," she added quickly.

"It's probably too late for that," Porter returned with a guarded smile. "You've probably already crossed that line." He cleared his throat. "Go ahead, shoot. I'm listening."

She swallowed before pushing on. "I just don't think Alma sees Eagar as his home."

"It wasn't home to me a year ago," Porter argued. "Living here makes it home."

She nodded. "I know that," she answered softly. "I like Eagar. But I chose to move here."

"And Alma didn't, is that what you're saying?" Porter inquired suspiciously. "Did he tell you he didn't want to be here?"

Darbie shook her head. "Not in so many words. It's nothing he's said. Especially not lately." She hesitated. "You know that he and I talk a lot." She smiled coyly. "We don't just jog. And he stops by just to talk, more often than you probably know. He's opened up to me. I feel like I know him." She shook her head as though she weren't sure anything she was saying made sense. "I mean, he seems happy here right now." She paused again. "I think it's just something I feel. Call it woman's intuition." She put her hands on her hips, gazed about, and smiled reflectively. "I wish I'd known him in Panguitch. You know, with friends he's grown up with, surrounded by things and places he's familiar with. Don't get me wrong. I sincerely believe that Alma wants to make a go of it here. He wants to make things right between you and him. He's come a long way since that first day you brought him here. But Eagar's still not home."

"And what are you suggesting?" Porter asked. There was a cautious edge to his tone.

Darbie shook her head. "I've probably said more than I should have."

Porter chuckled. "But you did say something. Now don't just leave me hanging, wondering what else is on your mind. And you do have something else on your mind. You're busting to tell me, too. You're not being terribly subtle. I know this whole thing isn't about taking a neighborly evening walk."

Darbie heaved a quick sigh. "Have you considered letting him go back?"

"To Panguitch?"

Darbie nodded anxiously.

Porter smiled and slowly shook his head. "I've spent a whole summer trying to make this his home." Porter looked away and studied a shiny black crow perched on a fence post thirty feet away. "I've tried to be a real live, breathing dad, not just a vague memory. Believe me, I've tried my darnedest to make up for lost time. And believe it or not, I've made progress. Things are so much better now than they were when I first showed up in Panguitch at the start of the summer. Why would I throw that away and have us both go back to the way things were before?"

"What makes you think that things would go back to the way they were before? And what makes you think you would be throwing anything away? You'd be giving him something."

"I've already given him something—a new home, a dad who's actually in his life."

"But can't you see, Porter? You forced him here."

"Darbie, he's my son," Porter countered, annoyed. "I brought him here." He pointed down the street to no one in particular. "Do you think any of the parents around here ask their kids if they really want to be in Eagar?" He shook his head.

"That's different. This is their home."

"No, it's home because their parents said it was home, either before or after they were born. They didn't call a family council and say, 'Where do you want to live this year?' The parents made that decision."

"His heart's in Panguitch, Porter."

"And his dad's in Eagar. What do we do, buy a home in Flagstaff so we can meet halfway?"

"Porter, I'm not trying to butt in." She heaved a sigh and shook her head. "That's not exactly true. I guess I am butting in. It's not any of my business, not really. But I like Alma. I can't help it. I want to help him. He didn't ask for my help. He didn't put me up to any of this. He doesn't know I'm talking to you. If he did, he'd probably feel like I was butting into his business too. I want what's best for him—what's best for both of you."

"What's best for him—best for both of us—is that we stay together. We're a family. You're suggesting that we break that family up again. Look, Darbie, I've made a whole lot of mistakes in my life. Some of them I'll never correct. Not really. I can get over them, but I can't change the consequences that come my way. But there's a lot between Alma and me that I can change. I abandoned Alma and his mom. It's taken me a long time to realize and admit that. I used to gloss it over by rationalizing that things just weren't the same between Allyson and me, and that since we were incompatible, it was all right for both of us to just split, to go different ways. That's what I told myself to make things right." He pointed to his head and then added, "To make things *seem* right up here." He clenched his fist and pressed it against his chest. "And in here." He shook his head. "But it was no good. That was always a cheap, lousy argument that I manipulated to make myself look better. The fact is I abandoned them. I turned my back on both of them. And there wasn't a good reason."

His voice caught, and he pressed his lips together, fighting back a sudden wave of emotion. "I'd give anything to be able to go back to Allyson and tell her I'm sorry. Anything. I'd do anything. I'd crawl, I'd grovel, I'd beg." A mist passed across his eyes. "I can't ever change things with Allyson. That's a story that's always going to have a sad ending. But I can change things with Alma. I think I've made a huge start on that this summer. We're starting to be a family again—not a family like we could have been with Allyson, but under the circumstances, this is the best I can do. And you're suggesting I turn Alma loose and send him back for someone else to raise?" He was incredulous at the thought. "I can't do that."

Tears shimmered in Darbie's eyes, and she touched them lightly with the tips of her fingers. Swallowing, she shook her head. "I'm not suggesting . . ." she choked. She cleared her throat and took in a breath of air. "I'm not suggesting," she continued, her voice more steady now, "that you and Alma split up. You need to stay together."

"That's why Alma's going to go to school here."

"You need to stay together," Darbie repeated. "But," she added quickly, as though she had to get the words out of her mouth before she changed her mind, "maybe you need to be together in Panguitch, not here." As soon as the words were out of her mouth, she seemed to brace herself for Porter's denial.

For a long moment, Porter studied her, trying to understand what she had just told him. Slowly, he inhaled, and then, puffing out his cheeks, he exhaled. "You're trying to get rid of both of us," he said, attempting a joke. "All right, I'll stop bothering you. But you're the one who stopped by today," he added, wagging a finger under her nose.

She smiled sadly and shook her head, pressing her lips together while she stared at the ground. "If you want to know the truth, Porter, I'd miss you. Both of you. At the first of the summer, I really didn't think I'd ever say that to you."

"What you're really saying is that you'd miss Alma."

She shook her head. "Alma's a great kid." She swallowed. "But his heart's in Panguitch. That's where he needs to be. Maybe you need to be there with him."

Porter rubbed the back of his neck while he shook his head and smiled. "I can never go back to Panguitch. Absolutely no way." He glanced up at her. "I don't know if they've ever had a lynching in Panguitch, but even if they haven't, I'm pretty sure they'd be happy to arrange one for me. I married the best girl in town, and everybody thought she was marrying down—way down. Then I left her," he said hoarsely. His short confession pained him all over again. "Let's just say that no one in Panguitch has me on his Christmas card list. Most of them are waiting anxiously to read my name in the obituaries."

"You're too dramatic. Wouldn't you consider going there for Alma?"

"What kid wants to be with a dad who's the biggest jerk in town?"

Darbie shrugged and kept walking, but Porter knew he hadn't convinced her of anything. "I wish I could go back," he muttered imploringly. "I really wish things were different." He shook his head. "They're not."

"Porter, he's like a bird in a cage. He sings. He seems happy. He puts on a good front. But if you open the door of the cage, if you give him a choice, he might fly away and never return. On the other hand, once you give him a choice, he might leave the cage but still hang around. But then it's his choice. He's free. You need to open the cage door and give Alma his choice. He might fly away or he might stay, but I'm convinced that once you give him the choice and once he's made his decision, he's going to love and respect you even more, wherever he is."

"Darbie, he's not a bird in a cage. He's my son. I can't afford to lose him, not now. Not ever again."

"Believe me, Porter, you won't be losing him. You don't want him wondering his whole life how things might have been different in Panguitch. Maybe he'll be perfectly happy here. Maybe Eagar is the very best thing that could happen to Alma. But let him be the one to choose it. Let him be the one to say, 'I'm here because I choose to be here.'"

"You think it's so bad here with me?"

She pondered a moment. "No," she answered quietly. "Porter, I know you're afraid to lose him." She pressed her lips together. "But I believe the only way you'll ever keep him is to let him go."

Long after Darbie walked home, Porter sat on the front steps considering her pointed observations. At first he resolutely refused to entertain the option of letting Alma return to Panguitch, but after arguing and debating with himself until darkness settled around him, he grudgingly admitted that Darbie's intuition might be valid.

* * *

The following afternoon, Alma washed and waxed the truck on the front lawn. As he was finishing, Porter ambled from the house and joined him. "You should have let me wash and wax it," Porter remarked. "You're the nuts-and-bolts guy. I'm Mr. Clean."

Alma wadded up the cloth he'd been using and tossed it into an empty mop bucket. "When I first brought it here," he commented, wiping his brow with the back of his arm and wetting his lips, "I didn't ever worry about washing it." He shook his head. "Waxing it wasn't even on my radar. Now I think of putting a little fence around it with a sign saying 'Keep your greasy hands off the merchandise.'"

Porter laughed. "Any place in particular where you'd like to take it now?"

Alma got a dreamy look as he considered the question. A grin spread across his face. "You really mean anyplace?"

Porter nodded.

"I'd like to drive it down Main Street in Panguitch." He laughed. "And I'd like to take Teddie Dodds on her first date. She turned sixteen the first of July, so I'm probably too late for her first date." He reached out and rubbed at a tiny dull spot on the paint with the bottom of his T-shirt. He shook his head and smiled. "Even though she promised to wait for me, she's probably already had that first big date, so it wouldn't be the same." He laughed out loud. "But I'd like to see her face. She'd faint if she saw the truck now."

"Do you think the truck would make it to Panguitch?"

"Sure," Alma returned confidently. "This is a mean machine."

Porter stepped over and ran his fingers along the fender, silently debating. "Why don't you see if Teddie Dodds is still waiting for that first date?" he asked quietly. "Take her in the truck." He smiled plaintively. "Drive it down Main Street. Show it off."

Alma studied his dad quizzically, trying to decide if he was joking. "Could I?"

"It's your truck," Porter answered with a weak smile. "But," he quickly added in a playful tone, "if she's already had that first date . . ."

Alma hesitated, still unsure of how serious his dad was.

"Go on," Porter ordered, smiling. "Call her. Now."

Alma laughed. "She's probably already forgotten about me," he said over his shoulder just before he disappeared into the house.

While Alma was away, Porter picked up the rag and polished the truck's hood to kill time. When Alma reappeared fifteen minutes later, he dropped down on the front steps, quiet and a bit subdued.

"What'd she say?" Porter asked, straightening up, still holding the rag in his hand.

Alma stared solemnly at his dad. "Benny Hatch asked her out a week before her birthday—for the day after her birthday," he announced. "Ron Talbot and Tyler Hunt asked her after that." A grin tugged at the corners of his mouth and finally exploded into a laugh. "But she turned them all down. She knew I'd brought the truck here to work on it, so she told Benny and Ron and Tyler that she was saving her first date for me in the truck. How does this Friday sound?"

"What do you have planned for your big date?"

"I'll take her for a ride up the mountain, show her what the truck can do. We'll have dinner at the café. Maybe we'll catch a ball game over at the park. There's usually one going on this time of year. Of course, we'll have to drive up and down Main Street a dozen times or so." He laughed. "We won't be doing anything really special, but we'll be doing it in the truck!"

Porter smiled ruefully. "Did you tell her what you've done to the truck?"

Alma shook his head. "I want to surprise her. Can you leave before Friday?"

Porter hesitated, then shook his head. "This is your big date, not mine."

"You mean you'll let me drive there alone?"

"Once you get off I-40, all you've got to do is get on Highway 89, and it takes you right to Panguitch. You can't get lost. Besides, that old truck probably knows the way without you even steering."

Alma studied his dad to see if he was joking. "And you won't come?"

"I'm still a marked man in Panguitch. They've got wanted posters with my picture on 'em all up and down Main Street. Walter and Toni will look after you."

Wild excitement bubbled inside Alma as he looked from Porter to the truck. "How long can I stay?"

"How long do you want to?"

Alma grinned, his eyes bright and sparkling. "How does forever sound?"

"Forever's a long time." Porter stepped back from the truck and studied it from the front to the rear bumper. "You don't like it here in Eagar?"

"Eagar's okay," Alma returned gently. "But Panguitch is home." He felt guilty making that confession. "It's nothing personal, Dad. Panguitch is just where I grew up."

"You're free to go, Alma," Porter offered quietly.

There was a long pause. Gradually, the smile drooped from Alma's mouth and his excitement evaporated. "You don't want me here with you?" he asked uncertainly.

"I want you to have what you want." Porter turned and faced his son. "But I don't want you to ever think, even for one second, that I'm giving you up. I walked out on you a long time ago; then, at the beginning of the summer, I showed up and forced you to come back here with me. I was wrong both times. I don't want you to ever feel like I'm forcing you to stay here." He smiled. "I'd love to have you here, Alma. But you've got to decide where you want to be. I think you'd like living here. It's not Panguitch." He shrugged. "But Panguitch might not be Panguitch anymore. At least not the way you remember it."

Alma laughed. "You think Panguitch has changed that much over the summer?"

Porter shook his head. "Panguitch is probably the same."

Alma became serious. "You think I've changed?"

"We all change, Alma."

Alma nodded. "You've changed too. Maybe you'd find that Panguitch isn't such a bad place anymore."

Porter smiled ruefully. "I don't think I'll take that chance."

"Are you saying . . . I can go to school there?"

"I'm saying . . ." Porter coughed. "You're free, Alma." He forced himself to grin against the sadness welling within him. "You've got the truck. The truck can take you anywhere. You just have to point it in the right direction."

Alma stepped over to the truck and touched it as if for the first time, as if it were a living, breathing thing. "I'm going back to Panguitch, big guy."

"There is one thing," Porter called out.

Alma turned to him in anticipation.

"Of course, your going back depends some on Walter. After all, he might have been really glad to see you leave. If you call him up and tell him you're coming back, he might figure that he's getting dumped on. Who in his right mind wants an ornery teenager hanging around? He just got rid of you, and now you're going back."

"Walter will take me back," Alma insisted confidently.

Porter took in a slow breath. "He probably will," he murmured softly.

* * *

That evening as Alma finished waxing the truck, Porter sat in the living room with a book in his lap, but he wasn't reading it. He heard a soft tap on the front door. Setting the book aside, he answered the door in his bare feet. Darbie was standing there. For a moment, they stared at each other.

"Are you going to let me come in?" she finally asked.

He seemed to stir from a trance. "Sure, come on in," he said, jumping back and opening the door wider. "Do you want something to drink? I've got lemonade in the fridge. It's ice cold."

"Lemonade sounds good."

The two sat quietly in the living room sipping tall glasses of lemonade. Darbie finally broke the silence. "Alma told me," she said simply. "When?"

Porter nodded and sipped his drink, keeping his eyes focused on the wall across from him. "Probably the day after tomorrow."

"Are you sure you should?"

Porter grasped the damp glass in both hands and smiled plaintively. "That's a strange question coming from you. Since you're the one who talked me into it."

She nodded. "I'll miss him." She laughed. "He was positively bubbling when I showed up this evening and he told me the news. I love to see him so excited. But I just hate to see him go. I'd like to go with him and watch him drive Teddie Dodds up and down Main Street in his fancy old truck."

"Maybe you can. Alma might be in the market for a stepmom." He shrugged, smiling ruefully. "If you're interested."

Darbie shook her head. "No thanks. But," she added after a short pause, "if someone was looking for a stepson, she couldn't find a better one than Alma. But being a stepmom has its own set of complications."

Porter smiled knowingly. "Too many other relationships to deal with?"

"Too many complications," she returned, refusing to elaborate. She took a long drink from her glass.

Porter watched her for a moment and then stared down at his half-empty glass. There had been a time when he'd been content to stay alone in his house without worrying about anybody else. In fact, there had been a time when he'd enjoyed that self-imposed solitude. At first it had been an adjustment having Alma around, even though Alma was independent and far from being a burden. But Porter knew instinctively that his house would be a lonely place when Alma left. He felt a lump in his throat and tried to swallow it away, but it stuck.

Finishing her lemonade and setting the empty glass on the coffee table, Darbie got up from the sofa and announced, "I'd better go. I just wanted you to know that I am glad you're letting Alma go back to Panguitch." She reflected momentarily and then added, "You won't really lose him, Porter. He'll be more yours this way. He's come to love you. He didn't feel that when he first came. I could tell then. I can tell now."

Shortly after Darbie left, Alma poked his head in the front door, announced he was going for a short ride, and invited Porter. Porter declined. As soon as Alma was gone, Porter went into his office, picked up the phone, and dialed a long-distance number.

"Hello, Calvin?" Porter burst out, sounding more jovial than he really felt.

"Port?" Calvin stammered on the other end. "You're the last person I was expecting. How are things going down in Arizona?"

The two of them exchanged a few pleasantries and did a little bragging that quickly evolved into good-natured teasing. Then Porter announced bluntly, "I was just calling to let you know that Alma's going back to Panguitch in a couple of days. I thought you'd like to know." Porter cleared his throat and then added, "That is, if Walter will put up with him. I haven't called him yet."

There was a pause on the other end of the line. "Things didn't work out?"

Now the pause was on Porter's end of the line. "Things worked out fine," Porter said. "We experienced a little turbulence to start with, but once we got used to being together, we had some pretty smooth sailing." He hesitated and then went on. "I'm letting him go. He'll drive the truck to Panguitch Thursday."

"He got it working?"

"*We* got it working," Porter corrected him with a proud grin. "Actually, Alma got it working, and I spruced it up a bit. You'll be impressed. It looks pretty hot now. You'll want to buy it off him."

"Well, it's good I talked you into taking it back with you."

"It was a regular pain at first, but I got over it. I'm kind of proud of that old truck now. I'm almost tempted to make Alma leave it here. I considered telling him he could go back to Panguitch as long as he left the truck with me." He laughed. "But I think he'd fight me for it—and win—so I figure the easiest thing is to cut my losses and let him take it."

For another moment, Calvin was silent on the other end of the line. "So why's he coming back to Panguitch?" he finally ventured cautiously.

"I finally realized that I couldn't force him to stay here forever. I definitely couldn't keep his heart here. So I cut him loose."

"I see."

Porter hesitated. "You'll take care of things on that end, won't you? I guess I don't even have to ask."

"Yeah, we'll keep the truck running," Calvin replied knowingly.

"It's not the truck I'm worried about, Calvin."

"I know, Port. I'll watch out for your boy," Calvin promised.

"I know Walter and Toni will look out for him, but . . ." Porter hesitated, reluctant to express his fears. "But," he pressed on, "if you could be a little creative and put in a good word for me every now and then, I'd appreciate it. I'd just as soon he didn't forget me."

"Why don't you come back to Panguitch? You don't have to stay in Eagar. You could run your sales stuff from here. It might be a little rough on you for a while, but folks around here tend to be forgiving if you show them a good reason."

"And how do I do that?"

"You'd have to figure that one out on your own. But I'm guessing that winning Alma over is a good start."

Porter pondered a long time. "It probably won't happen, Calvin," he responded hoarsely. Chuckling humorlessly, he went on. "It wouldn't be all that good for Panguitch's reputation. You know, I'd show up one day and the town of Panguitch would reinstate public stonings, hangings, and floggings all at once. What town wants that reputation?" He cleared his throat. "Maybe Panguitch does," he said, answering his own rhetorical question. "Provided I was the one that got stoned, flogged, and hanged." He heaved a sigh. "No, Calvin, I think I'll stay right here in Eagar."

Calvin laughed. "Well, if you change your mind, I'll try to find you a place to stay. And don't worry about Alma, Port. I'll keep him in line. And I'll help him keep the truck running."

18

"Do you think Darbie will mind going in the truck?" Alma questioned as they drove up the street to Darbie's house. "I mean, this isn't a picnic, and the two of you won't be riding in the back."

"You're the one who asked her," Porter pointed out. "And we can go back and get the Mercedes if you want. We don't have to take the truck."

"I'm okay with the truck, but I told her that this was kind of a nice affair. She's never eaten at Molly Butler. She sounded impressed when I told her about it. She said she wouldn't wear her boots and overalls, so I'm guessing she'll dress up." He laughed.

Porter looked around and ran his hand over the new seat covers and the dashboard. "This old truck isn't all that bad now. Besides, Darbie's not the kind to stick her nose up at a truck."

Both men strolled up the walk to Darbie's front door to escort her to the truck, but before they reached her steps, she opened the door and met them with a wide smile, wearing a pair of black dress pants, a white silk blouse, and white dress sandals. "I was hoping you'd bring the truck," she greeted them as she closed the door and stepped between them, looping her arms through theirs and starting down the walk. "I would have been disappointed had you pulled up in Porter's old Mercedes." She shook her head. "Next to the truck, the Mercedes doesn't have any personality."

As they approached the truck, Porter asked, "What's your preference, middle or shotgun? Or do you want to drive?"

Darbie cocked her head to one side in a pose of feigned solemn thought, her forefinger laid against the side of her chin. "Why can't I ride in the back? What's the sense of having a truck if you don't ride in the back?"

"If you're brave enough, I'll let you ride in the back," Porter responded. "I might even ride back there with you." He looked her up and down. "It doesn't look like you dressed for it, but if you're in the mood for a good truck ride . . ."

"Maybe on the way home." She laughed and let Porter help her into the truck, where she sat between him and Alma.

There was a special ease among the three of them as they drove out of town to Molly Butler, which was in Greer, a tiny town twenty miles from Eagar up in the mountains, just a few miles from Sunrise Ski Resort. Molly Butler was the oldest operating restaurant in Arizona, having been established even before Arizona was a state. Though it was rustic in appearance, it was also a very reputable eating establishment. The three of them joked and teased each other as they made the drive up the mountain to Greer, and then headed down the single street that passed through the town and made their way to the famous Molly Butler Restaurant.

"I've never been to Molly Butler," Darbie announced as they pulled into the gravel lot and parked the truck. "I've heard lots about it, but I always figured it was out of my league, a bit too fancy for me."

Porter laughed. "That depends on your idea of fancy. If you don't wear boots and jeans, they won't even let you in," he joked. "But the food's good."

The three of them were relaxed and in a playful mood as the hostess escorted them to their table. "What's the first thing you'll do when you get back to Panguitch?" Darbie asked Alma after they had ordered and the waitress had brought them their salads. "What's the most exciting thing a person can do in Panguitch?"

Alma blushed as he stabbed his fork into his salad. "Oh, there's nothing that exciting in Panguitch. It's a lot like Eagar, just not so big."

"So why don't you stay in Eagar?" Porter questioned lightly, but there was a touch of sadness in his tone.

"Yeah," Darbie joined in playfully, "that's a long ways to go if you're getting the same thing that's here. And I'll bet they don't have a single English teacher as nice as the one you're leaving behind in Eagar."

Alma laughed, and his cheeks burned red. "That's for sure." He took another bite of salad, chewed, swallowed, and then added, "It's not that there's any one big thing in Panguitch that grabs you." He became a bit solemn. "It's just that it's home. There's nothing that great about the place."

"And here I thought Panguitch was a bit of heaven on earth," Darbie teased. "You disillusion me."

Alma chuckled without looking at her. "I definitely don't want you driving through there someday and thinking . . ." He grinned sheepishly. "Well, thinking there's something amazing there, and then you find out that it's just a pretty ordinary little hick town in the middle of nowhere."

"You still haven't told me the first thing you want to do."

Alma glanced across the table at his dad. His cheeks colored again as he forked some more salad and pushed it into his mouth.

Porter cleared his throat ostentatiously and spoke. "There's a certain girl in Panguitch—Teddie Dodds—who turned sixteen a few weeks back, and she's faithfully waiting for Alma to sweep her off her feet and take her on her first big date. Provided, that is, he takes her in his truck."

"Now that's exciting," Darbie said sincerely, raising her eyebrows and nodding her head approvingly. "Does this Teddie Dodds know you're on your way?"

"He called ahead to make sure she was still faithful to her vow," Porter answered for Alma. "He didn't want to make the trip and discover her madly in love with one of his old buddies—although he did find out that some of them had asked her out behind his back. But Teddie claims she's driven them off, just waiting for Alma to show up in his new, improved set of wheels. Personally, I think she's more interested in Alma's truck than she is in him." He laughed.

Alma picked at his salad. "That's going to be kind of a surprise for her. She remembers the truck when it was a piece of junk. She doesn't know it's been fixed up. That will be a shock for her."

"And where are you taking Teddie Dodds on her first big date?"

Alma's blush deepened, and he ducked his head. "Just dinner. The big excitement will be just showing her the truck and taking her for a ride."

"You see," Porter explained, cutting in and enjoying seeing his son's discomfort, "Teddie, like the rest of us, didn't ever think that Alma could fix up the truck."

"So will she be impressed?" Darbie inquired.

"She'd better be. Or I'll go looking for a different girl."

"There are a few Eagar girls who are already impressed and would love to take a ride in your truck," Darbie teased.

"Yeah," Porter joined in, "why do you have to charge off to Panguitch? Stay here and impress the girls. Is this Teddie better-looking than that Brandi girl?"

"Oh, please!" Darbie groaned. "Teddie might not be as pretty, but she's probably not as conniving either. Don't measure Teddie Dodds by Brandi's standards. If he's looking for a nice girl in Eagar, I can find him someone better than Brandi."

They all laughed.

"Don't you think you'll miss all of us great people here?" Darbie quizzed him, winking across the table at Porter, who smirked.

Alma poked at his salad. "Actually, I'm going to miss a lot of things about here. I've been thinking about that a lot," he added quietly. "I'll miss you." He cleared his throat. "And Dad," he added huskily. He brightened, looking up and grinning. "I really was looking forward to taking English from you. But you're probably a regular hard case when it comes to your English class, aren't you?"

"You have to work for what you get," Darbie admitted. "I don't give anything away, if that's what you mean."

"Maybe I'll take you through correspondence. I know Panguitch doesn't have an English teacher as good as you."

Darbie shook her head. "Correspondence is no good. Too much gets lost in the mail. It's being there that's the real secret. If you're going to take my class, you have to do it in the flesh." She laughed. "So if you feel you're being deprived of a genuine education in Panguitch, you come back to Eagar, and I'll give you your money's worth." She touched her mouth with her napkin. "I know the Round Valley football team is going to be disappointed. They were counting on you to make the season for them. This could have been your big year here. And theirs."

Alma smiled forlornly. "You'll make me have second thoughts."

"Why are you going back?" Darbie playfully posed the question as though she were completely baffled. "When you have it so good here with us, why leave?"

Alma smiled wanly. "I guess I've just always figured that going back was the thing I wanted to do."

They finished their dinner but stayed at the table visiting, wanting to prolong the moment, knowing this would be their last evening together. "We've got to go on one last ride in the truck," Darbie finally said, pushing back from the table and standing up. "If you were leaving the truck here, it would be different. It wouldn't be quite so hard to see you go, but since you're taking it with you, you'd better give Porter and me one more good ride."

"I know," Alma said, standing up, "we'll take Beaver Pond Road. You two can sit on the tailgate, and we'll make the loop up over the mountain."

"In the dark?" Darbie questioned skeptically.

"There's a full moon out," Alma countered. "We might even see some deer or elk this time of night."

"I'm not sure Darbie wants to sit on the tailgate of the truck while you race over the mountain," Porter pointed out.

"I can tell Porter's chicken," Darbie contradicted him. "I'll ride on the tailgate. If Porter wants to ride up front, maybe you can ride in back with me."

"I'll ride on the tailgate with you," Porter came back quickly.

They drove out to Beaver Pond Road, and then Darbie and Porter piled out of the truck and sat on the tailgate, one on either side of the truck. "I've never known a girl who was so excited to ride on the tailgate of a truck with a guy!" Porter teased Darbie as Alma started down the road. "You sure you're not nervous?"

"Not as long as you stay on your side of the truck," she warned with a smile. "But if you cross over to my side, I'll have to call Alma to intervene."

"And here I was starting to worry about you. You were the one pushing for this ride. I thought you might have some ulterior motives."

"You're safe with me, Mr. Huggins," she returned pleasantly.

They made the whole loop in about forty minutes, spotting a half dozen deer and twice that many elk. They also saw a raccoon, two skunks, and a lone coyote darting across the road.

When they returned to Darbie's place, she and Porter hopped off the tailgate, and Alma came around to the back of the truck to tell Darbie good-bye. "Thanks for everything," he said softly, holding out his hand.

She took his hand and shook it firmly but held onto it. "Are you sure I can't talk you into taking my English class?" she asked as she finally stepped back.

Alma grinned. "I'll be back." He glanced over at his dad. "If he'll let me come for a visit."

"You don't even have to ask," Porter responded, studying his son.

"I already pulled strings. You're in my class if you're here at the start of school," Darbie assured him. She dropped his hand, took him by the shoulders, and pulled him in for a tight, squeezing hug. "Since you won't be my student, I guess I can hug you. I'd have to be a little more circumspect if you were going to be in my class."

Alma returned her hug, and then they both stepped back while he stared at the ground, not sure what else to do.

"Honk just before you leave," she instructed, "and if I'm not still in bed, I'll race down there and tell you good-bye," she said with a smile. Turning, she strolled up her walk and disappeared into the house.

"What will happen between you and Darbie?" Alma asked quietly as he and Porter pulled into their driveway and he killed the engine. "I mean, after I leave?" He chuckled and shook his head. "Of course, you don't have to tell me anything. I mean, I'm not trying to pry into your personal life. It's not like I'm your dad or anything." He grinned broadly and shrugged. "So you can forget I even asked the question." He paused a moment and then quietly added. "I am a little curious, though."

"Is this some kind of an interview?" Porter joked. "Because if it is, the wrong guy's asking the questions. I'm supposed to be asking you all this stuff." He glanced over at Alma, who gripped the steering wheel and stared into the darkness, nodding his head slightly. "But just to satisfy your burning curiosity . . ." He hesitated and then went on. "I really don't have any plans. Nothing that I've worked out."

"I like Darbie," Alma commented seriously. "She's . . ." He searched for the right word. "Genuine," he finally said. "She's a lot of other things, but she's definitely genuine. She's so much like Mom. Mom always listened to me the way Darbie does."

Porter pondered a moment, pressing his lips together and running his hand along the truck's dashboard. "There's quite an age difference between Darbie and me."

"Ten years." Alma pulled the key from the ignition. "I've done the math. But there was that much age difference before I showed up, and you were dating her. At least that's what you seemed to be doing. Telling me there's an age difference doesn't answer my question."

"Darbie deserves a really sharp guy. Someone who doesn't have a past."

"Have you ever considered politics as a career? Politicians don't answer hard questions either. They just throw up smoke screens and learn to dodge."

Porter heaved a sigh. "Look, Alma, I don't want to make any more mistakes in my life. And I don't want to mess up another person's life."

"Dad," Alma groaned, "what's so hard about saying that yes, you're going to keep dating Darbie, or no, you're not going to date her anymore?"

"Because maybe I don't know, and a lot has to do with her. She's not interested anymore. Not in a serious way. She already told me that."

"That was at the beginning of the summer. Things have changed."

Porter shifted uneasily in his seat and cleared his throat. "Do you suppose we could talk about something else?" he returned in exasperation.

Alma laughed and shook his head. "So you won't give me a straight answer? I know you don't like taking advice from your own kid, especially when it comes to your dating life, but if I were going to place a bet, I'd bet that Darbie likes you. Probably more now than at the beginning of the summer."

"I suppose she told you that," Porter stated doubtfully.

"No. But I think she's dropped enough hints for you that *you* ought to know." Alma hesitated and pursed his lips. "Of course, there's the distinct possibility that she's a little like you. She might not be willing to admit to you or me or anybody else what she's feeling. Not in so many words. But she stopped being 'just a good neighbor' a while back."

"And what makes you such an expert?" Porter demanded. "How many dates did you say you've had in your life? Maybe five, if you count the times you walked out to the school bus with a girl?"

Alma grinned and rubbed the back of his neck. "Actually, I haven't had what I'd classify as a real date. I'm saving that for Teddie Dodds this Friday. Remember?"

"But that doesn't stop you from handing out all of this romantic counseling."

Alma glanced over at his father. "This is really a touchy subject with you, isn't it? I mean, you're already breaking out in a sweat, and I still haven't asked you any of the *hard* questions."

"All right, Mr. Expert who's never had a date in his whole entire life, what do you think I should do?"

"Follow your head and your heart."

"Now who's talking like a politician? For your information," Porter said, holding up a forefinger, "the head usually contradicts the heart. The head and the heart send different messages. You have to know which one is the right message. Take it from someone who's experienced his own share of confusion over the years."

Alma shook his head. "I think your head and your heart are telling you the same thing about Darbie."

"Look, Alma, what if things got serious?" He quickly held up his hands. "I'm not saying they are. I'm just speculating."

"Worse things could happen."

"Would you care?"

"I'll be in Panguitch, and I wouldn't be the one getting serious."

"Look who's being evasive now."

"This doesn't have anything to do with me."

"You said you didn't want a stepmother."

Alma smiled and shrugged. "I'm not crazy about having a stepmom." He thought some more. "I might make an exception for Darbie."

"She doesn't want any stepkids."

A teasing smile tugged at the corners of Alma's mouth. "She might make an exception for a guy like me."

Porter laughed and opened the truck door. "No shortage of humility in you," he said playfully as he stepped out.

"Before I leave, do you want me to ask her out for you?" Alma teased, climbing out of the truck.

"You've been asking her out all summer," Porter said over his shoulder. He shook his head. "I'll take care of my own dates. Just because you're a grease monkey doesn't mean you know anything about women. I sure don't need you running a dating service for me."

19

Porter set the duffel bag into the bed of the truck and stepped back. "Well, is that everything?" he asked, putting his hands on his hips and surveying the truck without looking at his son. He forced a smile and attempted a joke. "Will it make it, or shall I call Walter and have him bring his trailer?"

"If it doesn't make it, it's your fault," Alma returned playfully.

Porter shook his head. "My job was all looks. And you'll have to admit the old bomb looks pretty good. It *looks* like it will make it, but I don't know what kind of work you did under the hood. That's your area of expertise. If this baby blows up between Eagar and Panguitch, you have only yourself to blame."

"I didn't figure the truck would ever look like this," Alma remarked in amazement.

Porter grinned. "That's because you weren't counting on my help." He cleared his throat anxiously. "Are you going to stay awake? You were up pretty late last night. I didn't think you had that much to pack."

"I guess I was doing more thinking than packing," Alma answered huskily. "Don't worry. I've got a big bag of sunflower seeds, so I should be able to keep my eyes open."

The two men stood side by side next to the truck, fidgeting nervously, neither one knowing exactly what to say to the other. "You give me a call when you get there," Porter ordered, more to eat up the silence than to give instructions, because Alma had already promised a dozen times that he would call. "Of course, I won't expect anything until the middle of next week, because there's no telling how long it will take this pile of junk to drive that far."

"I'm figuring on seven or eight hours, tops. If you don't get my call by late this afternoon, you'd better hop in the Mercedes and come looking for me." Alma kicked at the gravel underfoot and chewed on his lower lip. "I'm glad I came, Dad," he said quietly, without looking at his father. "I know I was a bit of a pain for the first little while, but . . ."

"I'm glad you gave me a chance, son. I needed that." Porter swallowed as he contemplated his next words. "I haven't told you this, but I figure . . . Well, I just want you to know that . . ." He shook his head. "Alma, thanks for helping me get to know your mom better." Tears welled in his eyes. "I've loved talking to you about your mom. I feel like I know her now, the way I should have known her all along."

Alma slowly nodded and sucked in a deep breath while he touched at a tear in his own eye. For almost a minute, neither one of them spoke. Finally, Alma remarked lightheartedly, "You sure you don't want to come with me? There's room."

"Don't tempt me."

"I could probably even get you a date. Millie Hancock is single. Her husband died last year. She's probably ready to start dating again."

"Millie Hancock has to be in her sixties," Porter returned dryly.

"She likes younger men. She's probably pulling social security now. Marry her for her money." Alma guffawed. "Like I said, there's plenty of room in the truck."

Porter chuckled humorlessly. "There may be room in the truck. I doubt there's room in Panguitch, though." He shook his head and held out his hand. "Well, you'd better hit the road, or it will be late afternoon and you'll still be in Eagar."

Alma nodded. "Tell Darbie good-bye for me." He grinned. "I'd stop by on my way out of town, but she's probably still in bed."

"I'll tell her," Porter answered quietly. "She's going to miss you. She'll have to find another jogging partner."

"You better hurry and get in shape before someone else fills the position." Alma took his dad's hand and shook it firmly, warmly, while both men looked into each other's eyes. After a moment, he dropped Porter's hand, took a step forward, and threw his arms around him. Porter returned the warm embrace, and they stood there hugging each other tightly. Tears welled up in both of their eyes. When they finally separated, they didn't look at each other.

"Now you remember, Alma," Porter said hoarsely as he fought with his emotions, "this place is always home." He pointed back to the house. "That door's always open for you. I don't care if I'm home or out of town, the door will always be open. The porch light will always be on, night or day."

Alma glanced back at the house, and even though the sun was up, he noticed that the porch light was on. He guessed that Porter had turned it on as he came outside lugging the duffel bag.

"You show up, son, and you walk in. Don't worry about knocking or ringing the bell. This is your home. It'll always be your home. Panguitch is just a place you're visiting. You come back whenever you can."

Alma nodded and hugged his dad again. "Thanks, Dad," he whispered. Tears shimmered in his eyes and were beginning to creep down his left cheek. "I'll be back. I promise. And don't be afraid to drive over to Panguitch. You better come after dark, though," he kidded, ducking his head.

Those were his last words before he stepped quickly to the truck, pulled open the door, and slid onto the seat. He turned the key, and the engine grumbled to life. Glancing at his father, who stood with his hands pushed into his pockets, he put the truck in gear, waved once, and then drove away.

Porter stood in the front yard and watched the truck pull onto the street and move away. He remained there long after the truck disappeared over a hill a couple miles down School Bus Road. He continued to stare at the place where he had last seen it, and he strained to hear the sound of the truck's engine until it faded into nothing and was swallowed up in the ocean of sounds all around. Even then, Porter stood unmoving, feeling an explosion of emotion inside him that seemed to constrict his chest, making it difficult to breathe.

Finally, Porter ducked his head and closed his eyes. He didn't want to return to the house, knowing that once he stepped inside he would sense how truly empty it was now. He found it strange that he had lived in this house for over a year and had never focused on the fact that he was alone. Now, however, even before returning to that same house, he knew that one step inside would powerfully confirm what he only surmised standing in the yard. He chose to remain in the yard, even though there was really nothing for him to do there. And he had work to do in the house. There was a computer sale begging for his attention, but he had no desire to even worry about business right then.

Porter ambled over to the concrete slab where the shed had once stood. He recalled how he had dreaded bringing the truck home at the beginning of the summer, how he had resisted the idea of working on it or having anything else to do with it. Now, more than anything, he wished that the truck was back in its familiar spot and that both he and Alma were up to their elbows in grease.

Dropping down on his haunches and resting his forearms on his knees, Porter tried to remember the days and evenings that he and Alma had worked here. He recalled their talks. He again felt the shame and the pain as he had opened up to his son and tried to explain and, at first, justify his past. He wished now that he had done a better job of helping Alma understand how he, Porter, had changed.

"So you got him off?"

Porter jumped slightly, pushed himself to his feet, and turned around. Darbie stood a few feet away. Her hair was wet, and she wasn't wearing makeup. She was dressed in faded blue jeans and a black-and-gold Round Valley Elks T-shirt. "I'd planned to sleep in this morning," she remarked, smiling shyly. "I figured that would be the easiest way to keep my mind off Alma leaving. I hate those kind of good-byes." She shook her head. "But I woke up early and couldn't get back to sleep. I hurried into the shower, but . . ." She breathed deeply and shook her head. "I thought that maybe he'd . . ." She laughed. "I guess I was just hoping that he'd stop and say good-bye." She folded her arms. "I know he told me good-bye last night and all, but I was still hoping. I'm sure he had a ton of things on his mind."

"He wanted me to tell you again," Porter offered gently. "He said so right before he left."

She shook her head and pressed the tips of her fingers to her mouth. "I'm going to miss him," she said just above a whisper. "I really got close to that kid."

"He kind of grows on you, doesn't he?"

"He certainly does. And I thought I was immune from that sort of thing."

"That's his mother's doing. She made him like that."

"She must have been some mom."

"You would have liked her. A lot."

"That's what Alma always told me. He'd get that big grin on his face and that wild sparkle in his eye and say, 'You and Mom should have known each other. You'd have been best friends.' I think we would have been."

"I can see that," he mused. "You know, the longer Alma was here, the more he and I talked about Allyson." He smiled ruefully. "This will sound strange, but I fell in love with her all over again. I realized what a chump I'd been, what a blind fool. I love her, Darbie. I have to live with a ton of regrets, but I still love her."

Darbie reached out and gently touched Porter's arm. "I believe I can understand that. And I think that's one of the things I appreciate about you, that you were able to fall in love with her again. I'm glad you told me how you feel. That means a lot to me."

Porter took in a quick breath of air. "Could I interest you in an omelet? Alma showed me how to throw one together. I've only done it a couple of times, and he was there to coach me, but I wrote everything down."

Darbie glanced down at her wrist, but her watch was missing. "I'm hungry enough to eat an omelet—if you can make one as good as Alma's."

Porter shook a finger at her. "If you accept the invitation, you go with whatever I give you. I make no guarantees."

They both laughed and started for the house. As they walked, Darbie reached down and took Porter's hand. As soon as Porter opened the front door, he was glad that Darbie was with him so he wouldn't have to face the empty house by himself. Having Darbie there shaved the edge from the bitter loneliness. He led her into the kitchen and pulled out a kitchen chair. "Wait for me here. I'll get the recipe from my office."

"I hope he gave you detailed instructions. I want a really good omelet."

Before going to his room, Porter noticed that the door to the stairs leading down to Alma's room was ajar. He started to close it, but on impulse he went down the stairs. Alma's bedroom door was open. Since Alma's arrival, Porter had never been in his room. Alma had always kept his door closed, and Porter had never intruded, never crossed that threshold of privacy. He started to pull the door closed and then reconsidered. Right then, more than anything, he wanted to step into the room that had been his son's all summer. It was as though he wanted to drink up any lingering influence Alma might have left behind.

He pushed the door open. A suitcase stood at the foot of the bed. Stepping in, he hefted it and discovered that it was full. That's when he spotted the tool chest next to the dresser and a couple of shirts and a pair of slacks still hanging in the closet. Pulling open one of the dresser drawers, he discovered a few pairs of underwear and socks.

Turning, he stepped from the room and hurried up the stairs to the kitchen. "He left some of his things," Porter announced worriedly. "He must have gotten in too big of a hurry."

"Maybe it's stuff he doesn't want," Darbie suggested.

Porter shook his head, trying to make sense of everything. "He left his toolbox."

Darbie shrugged. "Maybe he's giving you a reason to drive to Panguitch." She smiled. "I can imagine Alma thinking up something like that. He's got a devious streak in him. You'll get a call tonight and he'll say, 'Hey, Dad, I left a few things behind. Do you think you could run them over to me?'" She breathed deeply. "And before you know it," she added quietly, "you'll be on the road to Panguitch. And I'll be in Eagar all by myself."

Porter shook his head. "I don't think he realized he was leaving without that stuff. His suitcase is packed. The tool chest is right there where he could pick it up. He wouldn't leave the tool chest. Maybe the clothes, but not the tool chest." He glanced at his watch. "I wonder if I could catch him."

"Yeah. If you were speeding the whole way, you might catch him about the time he pulled into Panguitch."

Porter nodded. "Maybe," he muttered, but he found himself wanting to go, wanting to see Alma once more, even if it was just to hand him his suitcase and toolbox.

"Hey, what about that omelet?"

Porter got the recipe from his office, and a few minutes later the two of them were working on breakfast.

"It looks as good as Alma's," Darbie observed appraisingly as they sat down together.

For the next couple of minutes they were both silent as they ate.

"Alma actually managed to turn you into a chef," Darbie remarked, wiping her mouth on a paper napkin. Porter blushed slightly. She studied him for a moment and smiled. "You're different, Porter."

He looked up and realized she had been studying him. "Different how?" he questioned.

"Different." She shrugged. "Different . . . in a good way." She reached across the table and put her left hand on his. She left it there for a moment and then gently squeezed his hand before pulling hers back and dropping it in her lap.

He smiled wanly. "Well, that's definitely specific."

She laughed, set her fork on the edge of her plate, put her elbows on the table, and rested her chin in her cupped hands. "There was a time when I couldn't see you as a dad. You were just an old bachelor." She watched his reaction of surprise and laughed musically.

"And so now I've graduated from old bachelor to old dad, is that it?"

"Something like that."

"So that's the reason you were willing to have breakfast with me. You felt safe with this old father figure."

She shook her head. "Actually, I've been thinking that any guy who could have a son as good as Alma couldn't be too bad." She laughed out loud and picked up her fork, looking down at her food instead of at Porter.

"I already told you that Alma's mom gets the credit for that."

"But I see a lot of you in Alma too."

"It's probably more that some of Alma has rubbed off on me rather than the other way around," he retorted self-deprecatingly.

They returned to their eating, taking their time to chew their omelets slowly. "What now?" Darbie finally asked.

Porter looked up and stared across the table at her. He considered her question for a moment and then answered jokingly, "I guess it's back to being an old bachelor. That's one thing I'm good at."

Darbie shook her head. "I disagree," she said seriously. "You make a lousy bachelor. You make a much better dad."

Porter poked at what remained of his omelet. "There was a time, right after Alma arrived, when I longed for my carefree bachelor days. It's kind of tough getting back into the dad thing, especially when you're face-to-face with a teenager who isn't supposed to be a stranger but is."

Darbie shook her head while she chewed. "You had it easy. Alma isn't your typical teenager. Some teenagers would make you crave bachelorhood." She smiled. "Alma isn't one of them. I was looking forward to having him in English," she added quietly, almost as an afterthought. "And I'll miss our morning jogs and the times he would just drop by and visit."

"You have yourself to blame for all that," Porter commented plaintively, not really accusing her but gently reminding her of her own encouragement for him to let Alma go.

She nodded, and as she did there was the distant rumble of a truck in the morning air, a rumble that reminded them both of a truck that had left that morning and was now miles away, headed for Panguitch. But the longer they listened to the rumble of that approaching truck, the more familiar it sounded. When the sound slowed and a vehicle pulled into Porter's driveway, they stared across the table at each other and, without speaking, pushed back their chairs and ran for the door.

Bursting through the front door, they stared, perplexed, at the truck parked in the driveway with the engine running. Alma pushed open the door and stepped out with a huge grin on his face.

"You must have remembered you left half your things," Porter remarked, surprised that he was so glad to see his son again, even though it had been less than two hours since Alma had pulled away that morning. He wanted to bounce down the steps, throw his arms around his son, and hold him again, but he fought back the urge, not wanting to embarrass Alma in front of Darbie. At the same time, he experienced a pang of sorrow, realizing that the few things remaining in Alma's room would soon be gone. He hadn't realized until that moment that he had subconsciously derived a certain satisfaction in knowing that there was still something of Alma remaining. Now even that would be gone.

Porter smiled. "I wondered how long it would take you to figure out you'd left your things behind. I was thinking I was going to have to make that trip to Panguitch after all. What would you do without your tool chest?"

Alma grinned sheepishly. "As I was pulling out of Eagar, I knew I was leaving something behind." He shrugged and pushed his hands into his pockets and fidgeted on the front lawn, first looking down at the grass, then back at the truck, and finally up at Porter and Darbie. "But I kept driving because I didn't know what else to do. Then it finally hit me. I had to come back, and I figured it would be easier to come back after fifty or sixty miles instead of after four hundred." The grin disappeared from his face. "I didn't come back for the tool chest. I left that on purpose. And the other stuff too." He swallowed hard and looked directly at Porter. "I came back for you, Dad."

Anticipating a protest, Alma quickly held up his hands and shook his head. "I know you'll have a hundred reasons why you can't go, so I don't even want to hear them. And I know how stubborn you are. I figure I got my hard-headed stubbornness from you." He jabbed a thumb over his shoulder in the direction of the truck. "I made up my mind between here and the freeway that I wasn't taking the truck back to Panguitch alone. It's our truck now. You helped me get it to where it is. The one thing I figured out this morning between here and the freeway is that it's just not the same driving it alone. We both need to go back." He smiled warmly. "And show it off. And I promise that you won't have to go on a date with Millie Hancock." He grinned teasingly. "Unless you really want to."

A pained look of worry pinched Porter's features. Darbie's gaze went between him and Alma. A mist had settled in her eyes, but she didn't say anything.

"It was my truck when I came," Alma explained gently. He slowly shook his head. "But not anymore. It's *our* truck now. That's what I finally figured out as I was leaving town. I realized that I was excited to return to Panguitch, but not alone. I realized that I didn't even want to go if I had to go alone. I know Panguitch isn't your home like it's been mine. Maybe it's not even mine anymore. Maybe now it's just a place I want to visit."

"But, Alma," Porter stammered, "Panguitch is . . ." He gulped awkwardly. "I don't know. I just can't . . ."

"I'm coming back here, Dad," Alma said softly, gently. "That's why I left my other stuff here. I decided that for sure last night and this morning. I wasn't ready to tell you, though. I guess I've been sort of moving that way ever since you told me I could leave. I don't know that I really figured everything out until I was packing last night and loading up the truck this morning. I still want to go to Panguitch for a visit. But not for good. I'm kind of looking forward to being a Round Valley Elk." He grinned sheepishly. "Especially if Darbie can pull some strings and get me in her English class." His cheeks glowed a bright red. "I guess I'll have to learn to call you *Miss Montgomery.* That'll probably be the hardest part. I'd still like to be your jogging partner."

Tears shimmered in Darbie's eyes. "All the strings have been pulled. I've already got you signed up. And I'll still need a jogging partner." She pressed her lips together and swallowed down her emotions. "I think I was having a harder time watching you go than Porter was, because I was afraid I'd . . ." Her voice broke, and she pressed her fingers to her mouth. "I was afraid I'd never see you again," she finished just above a whisper. Unexpectedly, she stepped forward and threw her arms around Alma's neck and squeezed him tightly. "Welcome back," she whispered in his ear. "Welcome home."

"I can't just barge in on Walter and Toni," Porter protested weakly, his resolve against going crumbling rapidly.

"We don't have to. We'll stay at the Blue Pine Motel. How long will it take you to get your things together?" Alma pressed Porter.

Porter's mouth began to move, but no words came out. He looked over at Darbie, who smiled back at him and nodded her head.

"You've got to do it," she persuaded gently. "You know you want to. Besides, who could possibly pass up the chance to stay in the Blue Pine Motel for a few days?" She looked around her. "I'll watch your place here." She laughed and wagged a finger at him. "But stay away from this Millie woman, whoever she is."

"Yeah, that will be a chore," Porter muttered, ducking his head and chuckling to himself. "It'll take me a few minutes," he told Alma, still overwhelmed. "I haven't even showered and shaved."

"I need to fill the truck up with gas again," Alma said, backing up toward the truck. "I'll do that while you're getting ready."

"I guess I'm going to Panguitch," Porter remarked weakly to Darbie as Alma climbed into the truck and started backing from the driveway.

Darbie reached out and took his hand and squeezed it affectionately. "I'll miss you—both of you—so hurry back." Without warning, she pushed up on her toes, leaned forward, and kissed him gently on the mouth. "I'll be waiting for you."

The kiss caught Porter off guard. He caught his breath and then he blurted out, "Come with us. I'll get you your own room at the Blue Pine. Or somewhere else in town if you prefer. Maybe Millie Hancock's got a spare bedroom. I'll let you choose."

She shook her head and smiled. "Maybe another time. When things are different." She dropped his hand. "You'd better get packed. Alma will be back before you know it, and he won't want to be standing around waiting for you."

Porter started back for the house but paused on the front step. Slowly he turned and glanced toward the street where the truck was driving away. He watched it disappear; then he slipped into his empty house with a thrill of excitement, anxiously anticipating his return to Panguitch with his son, driving the truck.

About the Author

Alma J. Yates was born in Brigham City, Utah, and raised on a small farm just outside of town. He served an LDS mission in Mexico and then attended college at BYU, where he graduated with a degree in English. He taught high school English for several years in Snowflake, Arizona, where he began writing seriously. It was while he was teaching English that he published his first novel. Eventually he became a school administrator, but he continued to pursue his writing dreams, publishing many short stories and articles and several novels. Several years ago his sons acquired an old, beat-up, '71 Ford truck from their grandfather. As they were fixing up the truck, Alma realized that there was a story in the old truck. Shortly after that, he began writing *Finding Dad.*